Out of Silence

ANNIE TRY

To Gill
Happy reading
Annie

instant
ap•stle

First published in Great Britain in 2017

Instant Apostle
The Barn
1 Watford House Lane
Watford
Herts
WD17 1BJ

British Library Cataloguing-in-Publication Data

A catalogue record for this book is available from the British Library.

This book and all other Instant Apostle books are available from Instant Apostle:
Website: www.instantapostle.com
E-mail: info@instantapostle.com

ISBN 978-1-909728-66-0

Printed in Great Britain

Dedication

For all those who strive to stay professional when their own world is crumbling.

1

Consequences are strange, aren't they? Would I have met the boy if I hadn't set the alarm? Last time there was an urgent psychology case from immigration and I didn't show up, it was redirected to the service at Tower Hamlets.

The jarring ring had jolted me out of thick, troubled sleep. With one still heavy arm, I lunged half-sighted at the clock, sending it spinning across the floor. The soulless 'tring.. ng.. ng' carried on defiantly, only slowing as it battered its twanging head against the dusty skirting board between the packing cases.

It had halted my dream. For a while there, we had been whole, a complete family. Ella, Jamie and I. But we were being sucked away from each other – I was struggling to reach my son – but he was receding, pulling away, fading – always out of my reach – dissolving into blue, then orange, light.

I rolled myself into the pillows and as the trilling wore itself out, I tried to hang on to part of my night-time image. Just a glimpse of Jamie – please – the essence of Jamie again. It was gone – only in these rushing, frustrating nightmares could I ever remember my son moving, running, hugging me, shouting 'Daddy'. Would I ever understand why he had been taken from me?

I pulled myself out of bed and walked barefoot to the kitchen, stepping over the piles of dirty clothes. My head felt thick – I wanted coffee. I rinsed a mug under the tap and put the kettle on. I tried to remember why I had set the alarm. It was Monday but, well, it was a long time since I'd been early or even on time for work. There must be some other reason.

It wasn't until I had gulped down the steaming black instant that it came back to me. The head of department was off sick, so I would have to run the allocation meeting. At least I remembered it, last time I'd missed it altogether and with flu having overcome the art therapist and occupational therapist that left only the trainee and newly qualified counsellor. They had selected two clients each for themselves and left the other six for this month. It would be a long meeting. Which poor confused wretches were being referred to our service now, eh?

I made another coffee and took a couple of paracetamol. I tried to tell myself I could eat breakfast, but one smell of the milk carton and a futile hunt for bread confirmed that resolve as a bad idea. I took my mug back into the bedroom and set about trying to find a shirt that didn't smell too dirty to wear to work.

One lukewarm shower, a quick brush of the hair and beard while pulling on Friday's clothes and I was rushing for the train. Just in time, I pushed into the carriage, trying to find enough room for myself and my old leather briefcase. I always feel uncomfortable in confined spaces – I'm not fat, but nor am I thin, and my 6 foot 3 inch height makes me aware of the way I tower above the small ladies who have the misfortune of travelling in the carriage with me. The Tube is no better – I had to wait to go down onto the Victoria line and then travel jam-packed with my face pressed against the doors.

But somehow I arrived in work nearly on time, desperate for yet another black coffee. My head was pounding and my mouth foul. I hated feeling like this in the morning, but my difficulties sleeping meant that I ended up watching night-time rubbish on TV with a Scotch or two for several hours each night. It was a crazy, useless routine that I hadn't the energy or the will to change. Today it seemed quite a struggle to climb stone stairs to the first floor and push on the heavy doors into the Psychology Department.

As I made my way down the echoing bare-tiled corridor towards the room where we were meeting, I sighed, and stifled a yawn.

Anita, our art therapist, caught up with me.

'Got that Monday morning feeling then, Mike?' she asked. Always wearing a slightly puzzled look, she was now managing to look concerned and quizzical at the same time. I smiled, replying with a shrug, thinking I'd better not confess to a Monday, Tuesday, Wednesday through to Sunday feeling.

She was hurrying to keep up with me, so I slowed to her pace.

'Did you have a good weekend?' she asked.

'Yes, thank you. Quite quiet – fairly uneventful. Relaxing.' I fleetingly remembered weekends before Jamie's death, the years around the millennium. They were full of Saturday outings, and beautiful Sundays as Ella gently bullied me to go to our very lively church. Those were good weekends.

'Ah well, back to the grindstone!' Anita laughed, as if she was relishing the challenge of a new week. I smiled with her and wondered if she realised that in fact I now hated weekends. I started off positively looking forward to not coming into work and then the blank space of empty hours, with no one to talk to, seeped into the core of my being.

But work was no better these days. I wasn't looking forward to this meeting. The usual games would be played by everyone, each avoiding being persuaded to take another case to stretch each of our already bulging caseloads. As therapists we all knew how to do it, flattering each other that this was someone's specialty or teasing at the details of a case until we decided he or she was better seen elsewhere. We all had our own apportioned waiting lists with our own priorities within it and we all knew we would never catch up. Every time we discharged one – cured or abandoned for lack of cure – we would pick up another needing even more frequent appointments. I was fed up with it; I'd been doing it for far too long. Another eighteen years till my previously planned retirement age, but I'd never make five years unless something changed. The way I felt on this particular Monday, I wasn't sure I would make five weeks.

I pushed open the door for Anita to go in before me. The meeting was in the family room of the old hospital, which now housed the Blackminster Mental Health Team. The whole place still had the lingering stale odour of an old inpatient ward and the family room was no exception with its ramshackle collection of old stained armchairs competing for space with three mug-ringed coffee tables, a flip chart frame with no paper, two large wilting plants which were obviously nobody's responsibility to water, and a huge plastic hedgehog which opened up to reveal a home, complete with furniture, for a doll family of five. It was a donation from a parent who had noticed there were hardly any toys in the family room and it had proved to be quite a talking point at staff meetings. I don't think any children ever played with it.

I was passed the stack of files for new referrals. I took the top one off the pile. I turned to the occupational therapist.

'Jane, this one is just for you. It's a forty-year-old with obsessive-compulsive disorder – she'll need lots of visits and a carefully shaped programme. I'm sure you can do it.'

'I'm very busy, you know, Mike. It's a bit of a departure for me. I'm fine with straightforward moderate anxiety, but this seems a little, er, complicated.' She crossed her arms and I promised to support her and help her with a plan. I don't know why she believed me, but she eventually took the file. She even agreed to take two more clients 'for assessment only, then someone else may need to see them' – one was a girl with suspected anorexia and the other a lady with extreme anxiety. Jane neatly wrote her name on the front sheet of each file, and then ignored the rest of us as she began writing and attaching notes for secretaries. I knew she would keep her own records immaculately and always be able to track the files with their perfectly planned assessments and interventions.

Next were two separate referrals for young men, both with clinical depression.

'I'll take those – they'll need cognitive therapy,' said Georgina, my trainee. She had almost finished her module on depression. Now all she needed was a chance to try out her skills.

'Are you sure you want them both?' was my only feeble attempt at dissuading someone with very little experience from getting overwhelmed.

'Yes, I'll be fine. You will make sure I know what I'm doing!'

I doubted it, but handed her the files.

Anita, with a little thoughtful frown, gathered two more cases to go into a women's group she was about to set up, and we all decided the suicidal seventy-two-year old was best seen by geriatric psychiatry. I suggested two further cases could be assessed by the new counsellor, Leslie, who immediately panicked because she had no spaces. By the time we'd all described our waiting lists to her and the way we managed to live with them, she reluctantly picked up the files.

I turned my attention to the last referral, which was addressed to me personally. This didn't mean much – I quite often passed files on to someone else. But it looked interesting, so I glanced at it while Jane made us all coffee.

'What have you got there?' asked Anita.

'This one's from the MO at the immigration service. One of you might be really interested to take it.'

I started to read out the letter dated 3rd October 2006.

Dear Dr Lewis

*Thank you for seeing this young lad, age and real name
unknown. He was the subject of much media interest a
few months ago, when he was refused entry to any
country after being found as a stowaway in the boiler
room of the Spanish cruise ship, Margarita. His ethnic
features would indicate that he is of African origin.
However, he has not spoken to anyone since he was first
discovered, starved and dehydrated, ten months ago, so
this cannot be confirmed. He has made no response to any
of the questions asked of him in a total of twenty-one
African languages.*

'How many?' asked Georgina. 'Aren't there hundreds
of African languages and dialects? Twenty-one doesn't
sound many.'

There followed a discussion about languages. It carried
on until I remembered I was in charge.

'Are you ready for me to read the rest?'

I continued:

*Johnny was admitted to this country on 21st July this
year, and is now the subject of a court order. This
requires him to have a full psychological evaluation.
Depending on the results of the examination, he may
need further therapy to render him fit to return to court
to ascertain his immigration status and consider whether
deportation is appropriate.*

'Then where would he go?' asked Anita.

I shrugged and continued reading:

Our medical team report that he is still underweight but otherwise physically well. He has a ten-inch long scar on the inside of his right arm consistent with a deep wound from a sharp instrument. The team have ruled out any physiological cause for his lack of speech. His hearing is also in perfect order. The Spanish crew reported that he had begun to understand some Spanish during his enforced stay on the liner. He was very quiet and no one on the ship can remember him speaking.

Johnny now has a social worker, Shirley Hills, who will accompany him to his appointments with you. She reports that over the two weeks she has known him he has begun to understand her more, especially if she accompanies her commands with some hand signals.

We would be grateful for your early report.

Yours sincerely…

I finished reading and looked around at the rest of the team. Anita spoke first.

'It's Johnny Two, the Silent Boat Boy.'

She was remembering the headlines – snippets of information were emerging from other people's recollections, too. Jane leaned forward.

'Wasn't he found squeezed into some tiny lock-up in the engine room?'

'Yes, that's what I read. They reckon he'd been without food for at least fifteen days. The doctor they interviewed said he probably survived without proper water because he licked the condensation forming on pipes.'

'He was feverish and hallucinating – pretty near to death when they found him,' added Georgina. She solemnly took a swig of water from the bottle of Highland Spring she always carried with her.

'Nice-looking lad from the picture in the paper,' mused Anita.

'Um, really fit, I thought,' added Georgina.

'Fit?'

Amid the laughter, I found out from my trainee that 'fit' in this context meant 'handsome'. I was getting out of touch. I had somehow missed this entire news story. I usually watched TV, but keeping up to date had seemed so unimportant lately that I'd sit there flipping through the channels until I found something less harrowing than the news. I had given up reading a newspaper long ago, probably when it had stopped being delivered because I never got round to paying the bill. Ella had been the one in our marriage who had been organised enough to nudge me if something needed paying.

As the laughter and good-natured teasing died down, I cast my eyes back over the letter. Everyone was looking at me expectantly waiting...

'This lad, Mike, he'll have to be yours because the judge has ordered a psychological evaluation,' said Anita.

She was right of course. With my boss on sick leave and the only other clinical psychologist enjoying the woes and wonders of new motherhood, I had to give in. I shrugged.

'OK, mine he is, then – and that concludes the allocation of this week's victims.' I tried not to sigh as I gathered up my papers and left the room.

I could hear Anita's heels on the tiled corridor as she tried to catch me up. I turned and watched her as she came towards me. She is not a tall woman, but she always has poise, even when she is hurrying. There was something different about her today, but I was not sure what – hair, maybe. Perhaps she'd recently had it cut into that short bob? I couldn't remember what it usually looked like. I'm not good at these details.

'You all right, Mike? You seem a bit – well, I don't know – preoccupied; down, maybe.'

Strange how we never used the word 'depressed' when talking about each other. I faked a laugh.

'Anita, this is not down. I've been there, and believe me, this is not down. More of a bit of a dip.'

'Well, if you want to talk about it...' she turned away; probably satisfied that she didn't have yet another depressed person to sort out. Who'd work here, eh? Not exactly jolly, even the members of staff were cracking up.

She walked towards the stairs to go down to the art room. I turned into my room. Among the chaos of my desk was perched a neat tray of files for today's clinic. I glanced at my watch – already fifteen minutes late starting.

The first name on the list of appointments was Mrs Barnes – an excessively tidy woman. Too tidy, actually, and a compulsive hand-washer as well. The room was a shambles. I'd left it in a mess the Friday before, meaning to sort it out before this clinic. I picked up the three dirty mugs and hid them with some other forgotten ones in the bottom drawer of my large wooden desk. I'd salvaged the desk when we moved here, spotting it abandoned on a visit and labelling it with the number of this room. It is incredibly heavy but I hate those new MDF ones the NHS invests in these days. My two easy chairs are tatty, but in better condition than those in the family room, probably because I never see families in here. Otherwise there is a similar air of neglect. The coffee table has evidence of misuse and the books always manage to fall over and migrate to the end of the shelves over my desk.

I gathered up the papers piled on the two chairs and put them into a more orderly pile on my desk. Then I swept my arm over the coffee table to get rid of a few stray biscuit crumbs and odd paper clips. It looked a bit better. I wandered out into the waiting area. The department secretary spotted me from reception.

'Your patient cancelled, Mike. Didn't you see the message in the book?'

'She never cancels! Did you ask her why?'

'Emergency dental appointment. She thought she would manage until next week's appointment. It's all written in the book!'

When I looked, I saw there were four other messages in the book as well, but I hardly registered them. I went back to my room.

With an unexpected gap, I felt suddenly free. I ignored the pile of admin and all those unsorted papers, made myself another good strong cup of black coffee, put 'engaged' on my door and looked at the boat boy's file. The hospital sticker on the file had 'John Two' with the address of the hostel where several asylum seekers had been housed pending the outcome of their residency applications. The space for date of birth said '>null<'. Probably the first time that bit of information had been so completely unknown to our medical records department. Even abandoned babies had an estimated age. The rest of the file was disappointing in its lack of information – apart from the earlier gossip all I knew was that he was a selective mute – someone who for some reason would not or could not talk. Intriguing. It raised so many questions. If only I had the energy to think of them.

2

During the course of the day, in gaps in between my clients, I found myself thinking about the boat boy and turning back to his file. The scar down his arm seemed to indicate that he was probably the victim of an attack, so may have been traumatised even before he hid in such a tiny space in the liner.

I found that working with other people seemed secondary; an interruption to what I should really be doing. Towards the end of the afternoon I asked the departmental secretary to reorganise the next week's patients to make a gap for Johnny. Then I thought I could do with more background before I saw him. There was very little about the social worker in the letter, only her name and the suggestion that she was getting through to him with sign language. I went to the office.

'Patricia, I have the name of a social worker here and I don't know where she works – can you find me a phone number?'

Patricia hardly looked at me.

'Add it to the pile.'

'It would really help if I could have it straightaway. Please.'

Patricia looked up at me and shook her head. I suppose it is a bit odd when someone who is usually so inactive suddenly does something as proactive as trying to find a phone number. I told her the name and it only took her a matter of seconds to come up with the number. I returned to my room.

I hesitated before dialling. It was more usual for me to let a referral hang about until the very length of the delay in starting on it made it a priority. But this case was different. When I phoned Shirley Hills' number the voice that answered with her name sounded rushed and breathless.

I explained I was taking Johnny Two's case.

'That's jolly good, Dr Lewis. I need help with that boy straightaway. I'm at my wit's end with him, you know. I've tried everything I can think of to get him to talk and he *refuses* to answer back. He just looks at me with his strange dark eyes and it gives me the creeps.'

'It can be difficult when people don't talk, I agree. But it's very likely he might not be "refusing" to talk to you – maybe he is not able to talk.'

I heard a sharp intake of breath and her manner became more curt as she answered, 'I don't believe that for an instant. He's stringing us along. You must have read the MO's letter. Nothing wrong with him.'

I felt myself bristling. I dislike dealing with assertive social workers. I tried pleading for the boat boy again.

'Some traumatised people can't talk at all, you know, Ms Hills. It's not a matter of choice for them. If he seems creepy to you, perhaps it's only because he is wary and he needs to watch you closely to see what happens next. It must be very confusing for him, I should think.'

I wasn't surprised by the tone of her reply.

'Well, he should be over his problems by now. He's lucky to be here, that's what I think. He's in a hostel with six other immigrants, with everything paid for; he should be all right.'

While she was saying this, Patricia knocked on the door and passed me some A4 sheets. I took them from her and realised she had downloaded newspaper articles about Johnny Two. I tried to concentrate on what Shirley Hills had just said.

'He learned to understand a little Spanish, didn't he? Who speaks Spanish in the hostel?'

'Well, no one. But he'll have to learn some English now.'

I was becoming distracted by the newspaper headlines in front of me. 'STOW BOY SILENT', 'JOHNNY GO HOME', 'AND STOWAWAY'S ASYLUM STATUS UNCERTAIN'.

'Has anyone explained that to him, Ms Hills? He might not know. He may think he will be put with some Spanish-speakers any day now. Or with his own kinsmen. It must be very puzzling for him.'

She was not going to give him any sympathy, though. I spent a little longer trying to draw out some empathy.

'From the information I've been given, Ms Hills, I'm going with the hypothesis that something absolutely dreadful happened to this young man and it is so bad that he is unable to speak about it.'

'Why do you think that, Dr Lewis? He could just be after an easy ride. I hope he doesn't fool you. A lot of them want to come to this country to live off benefits, you know.'

'What about the scar down his arm, Ms Hills, and the fact that he was prepared to stay hidden so long on the *Margarita*? What do you make of that?'

'Well, I don't know, do I? It's your job to find out. All I know is he is sullen and surly and hasn't spoken a word. It's really rude to clam up like that.'

Poor kid, fancy being landed with Ms Hills. I found myself wondering how some people become social workers. She certainly wasn't one of the bright, efficient, modern breed. They were usually well aware of psychological nuances. But here she was working with traumatised youngsters seeking asylum, yet her understanding of trauma appeared to be non-existent.

'I shall look forward to meeting him anyway, Ms Hill, and yourself, of course.'

I gave her instructions to find my office and, being as polite as I could, I rang off.

The articles Patricia had found added colour but little substance to the story of the boy. I noted that he had sores where he had been rubbing against metal tools when the boat moved. There was a photo of him, lean and thin, looking frightened. This couldn't have been the picture that Georgina had seen. He looked anything but 'fit' in either sense of the word.

The phone call had not been much help either. Shirley Hills had given me very little useful information about Johnny Two. In fact, the information remembered by the rest of the team from the news reports had probably been more helpful – if it were accurate.

So I was still left with the problem of how to communicate with Johnny when he came to his appointment. I thought back to other clients with speech difficulties. I had worked with a deaf chap, but his wife had come with him and she knew how to sign. Signing – perhaps that was a way forward. The medical officer's letter suggested Ms Hills had some success with that. I glanced around my office. Somewhere I had a guide to a fairly simple signing language, Makaton. I knew no Spanish and was not confident I could learn even a few basics by next week. If he were a selective mute, he wouldn't talk back even in Spanish with a translator, so using simple sign language might be the easiest way to reach this lad. I'd have to teach him as I went along, of course. Maybe Ms Hills would help – not very sure on that one. I hadn't used Makaton for years, but perhaps I could brush up on it enough to help him communicate. But I still had no idea how I was going to sort out what was wrong with him, and as for writing a report, how would I gather enough information to be able to do that?

I hunted through all the papers I had in my office. I knew I had something about mutism, but half my stuff was at the flat. I made a few notes which turned into a long series of unanswered questions and were not very helpful. I made myself another black coffee. By now it was after six and everyone else had gone home, but as usual returning to my empty flat had no appeal. I was hungry, so I went to the little kitchen off the staff room to raid the coffee scheme biscuit tin. It occurred to me that I must remember to give the secretaries money towards coffee; I couldn't remember when I last did.

The department corridors were empty and echoey, suggestive of the building's former role. It reminded me of my training days, when my tutor decided I should volunteer for a night shift. I could remember beds in the darkened rooms and the dimmed light in reception where the ward sister sat most of the night, while the auxiliaries ran around quietening troubled patients. But now there was a marked absence of crying and strange calling, interspersed with snoring. Just me, putting off going home. Just silence.

Eventually, at about eight o'clock, I decided I'd sat about not doing very much for long enough and had better make my way back to Sydenham. Fish and chips again for supper. At least it wouldn't add more to the great pile of washing up.

A few hours later, back in the flat, with the takeaway meal washed down with a beer, I felt a little refreshed. The TV was on, as usual, but as I flicked round the channels I couldn't be bothered to choose what to watch. I had given up pressing the controls when I recognised some quiz show, but today I couldn't conjure up enough interest to even make a vague guess at any answers. For once, I switched off.

I stared across at the row of packing cases. I considered whether to go through them. I knew it would be a hazardous task, not only because all those years ago I had packed in haste and there were kitchen knives and broken glasses among books and papers. No, the things I really feared were the constant reminders of Ella and Jamie. I poured myself a large Scotch and as its warmth began to reach me I felt emboldened enough to look. I hauled the first one over by the sofa.

I made a pact with myself not to open anything that was not obviously work-related. Thus blinkered, I quickly scanned through two boxes and was working through the third, when I found some neatly labelled papers. I remembered that the ordered nature of these was the result of a holiday girl's work experience. She had been about to take up a university place for a psychology degree and had already decided she wanted to train as a clinical psychologist. Finding tasks for an eighteen-year-old had proved difficult, but the secretaries had suggested she 'sort me out', so she had ended up organising all my papers with the proviso that she could read any she found interesting. I could remember that summer; she appeared whenever I didn't have a client in my room, plonking herself on the floor, quickly forming piles of journal articles around her. Then she'd start reading – serious reading, totally immersed, and I would end up stepping over her long brown legs each time I needed to leave or enter my office. In the end, we'd had to agree that in the mornings she arranged the papers into files and in the afternoon she was free to read them somewhere else. So here was a whole section of a lever arch file labelled 'Mutism'. Bingo.

Unfortunately, the whole section turned out to be three long papers on the same case, which had obviously taken my interest at some time. I skimmed through the separate write-ups, all from different academic approaches, but it was such a straightforward case of a six-year-old who had been in a house fire and then not spoken for four months, that it bore no relation to this lad from a foreign country with so many unknowns. No clues there, then, for the definitive approach. It was years since I had worked with someone with mutism, but there was nothing I could do. I would have to make it up as I went along.

At least I still had one possible tool. I poured myself another Scotch, cleared a space on the sofa, and opened the Makaton guide.

3

On the day of the appointment, I regretted setting it up so soon. I felt I needed more time to prepare – even though I wasn't sure how. I placed the file on my desk and read the referral letter again. I opened the Makaton booklet at the page with the most commonly needed signs. I had revised a few, but I knew I was far from fluent. I should have left the appointment until after a multidisciplinary supervision meeting, when at least I could have had the benefit of other people's ideas.

I glanced at my watch as I entered the department. Five minutes to go before they were due to arrive at 9.30. I hurried into my room feeling rather unsure of myself and dreading their arrival. I gathered papers together, stacking them in a neat-ish pile on top of the grey metal filing cabinet, hiding the dead plant. I brushed old sandwich crumbs off the low chairs and ran my arm over the coffee table. The sleeve of my tweed jacket was now covered with grey dust. I sighed as I brushed it off.

It was now not long after 9.30. I eased the door open a little to try to see into the waiting area. A short, plump, middle-aged woman with bright baggy clothes, lots of beads and chunky shoes, reading an out-of-date copy of *Hello* magazine was sitting in one of the larger wooden-armed chairs. A young man, gangly and awkward, stood quietly by her, clenching and unclenching his fists, his head bowed. I estimated he must be about nineteen and what I could see of his high cheekbones and tightly curled hair reminded me of a Nigerian friend I had at college. I took a breath, ran my hand over my beard to try to flatten it a bit, and walked out into the waiting area. Before I could speak, Ms Hills stood up and in a fluttery, slightly breathless voice, introduced the young man to me.

'You must be Dr Lewis. This is Johnny. He's the one from the boat.'

I turned to the boy, trying to meet his gaze.

'I'm very pleased to meet you, Johnny. Won't you both come in?'

The boy raised his eyes from his study of the carpet to look at the social worker. She pointed at the door I had just walked through. He stood there, waiting and watching her. She frowned and bustled past him, her manner halting my usual welcoming chat. Johnny followed her and closed the door.

The three of us stood among the clutter of furniture in my untidy room, observing each other warily. Ms Hill's musty perfume surrounded us. Johnny's forehead looked wet and the fast rise and fall of his chest betrayed his nervousness.

I spoke. 'Johnny, would you like to sit down?' I indicated the chairs.

Again he looked at Ms Hills.

'He doesn't understand you, you know,' she said, raising and dropping her eyebrows as if she had told me a hundred times.

'I know that, but he does need to hear the spoken word.'

She made a disapproving cluck and folded her arms. I stood by the chair and tried again.

'Please take a seat, Johnny.'

Extending one chubby ring-covered hand, Ms Hills pushed him towards me and refolded her arms, watching him. Johnny stood where he was pushed. He glanced at her and bowed his head. Ms Hills tutted loudly and went to push him again.

'No, leave him, he's fine. Perhaps you'd like to wait outside while I work with him?'

I opened the door and with a roll of her eyes Ms Hills left the room, but before I even started to talk to Johnny he backed away from me, nearly falling over the low table and then moving crabwise towards the door. His large brown eyes stared, his bony hands shook and he took huge gulping, noisy breaths. I called Ms Hills back in and suggested she sat quietly in the corner. She pursed her lips with a smile and I am sure she would have swaggered across the room if she hadn't had to squeeze herself through the gap in the armchairs to sit on the upright chair furthest from my desk.

Johnny's breathing quietened a little with her in the room. I signed for him to sit down, in the easy chair closest to Ms Hills. I noticed her edge a little further from him. It was going to be difficult dealing with the dynamics between boy and social worker while assessing him at the same time.

I flicked through the sparse file to try to gain time to think. On the surface it looked as if I had got nowhere, but maybe even our inauspicious start showed we were now making a little progress towards beginning to understand each other. After all, Johnny had communicated his fear. How was I going to make him feel safe in my room?

Instead of sitting in the other comfy chair near him, I took myself to the opposite side of my desk, so that it was clear I would do him no harm. Johnny was now slowing his breath, but his hands were fisting and stretching again, so I wondered if he used this movement to steady himself. His dark shiny skin stretched over his high forehead and with his jaw tightly clenched I was aware that he was on alert, sprung, ready to flee. As he slowed his rapid breathing, he wrapped his thin arms round his body, perhaps in an effort to control his trembling. He seemed to be making himself ready for whatever came next. I used my rudimentary knowledge of Makaton sign language as I spoke to him.

'Hello, Johnny, my job is to find out what is the matter. I have to discover... I have to get to know all about you, including how intelligent... how clever you are.'

Probably the sign for 'clever' was the same for 'intelligent' anyway, I couldn't remember as I had stroked my forehead and raised my thumb while I spoke.

'He won't understand you,' said Ms Hills. I didn't need her to tell me that again – his blank expression showed me. I tried a slightly different approach.

'I will help you,' I said, showing 'help' with my hands. He looked for a moment as if he might understand – 'with your mind,' I added, pointing to my head. He darted an anxious look towards Ms Hills, who simply clamped her lips together. I felt even more that this was going to be impossible.

I found myself committing the therapist's cardinal sin of talking about a client in his presence as if he were not there.

'Is he always like this, Ms Hills, or does he sometimes smile?'

Ms Hills twisted round her index finger some strands of greying untidy hair that had escaped from her gaudy ponytail band and frowned a little as she replied, 'He smiled sometimes at first in the detention centre. One of the Spanish sailors kept coming to see him, you know, from the cruise ship he'd been hiding on. I was told he smiled when the sailor came.'

I nodded, pleased to hear that someone had taken an interest in him. Ms Hill continued, 'But he doesn't like me – I haven't seen him smile once since he's been at the hostel.'

She leaned towards me, her long beads falling against the coffee table. Almost whispering, she added, 'I don't think he likes the other people in that hostel either, you know. He probably has a "personality problem".'

She made it sound like some terrible disease. I made a kind of 'uh ha' noise and she carried on, 'He's sort of excessively tidy, and they are a bit messy. He's had new clothes and things too – and he's getting some decent English food. You'd expect him to be a bit happier or at least grateful.'

Ah, this was more like it. I looked up from the file where I had scribbled 'depressed affect?' and 'obsessive-compulsive?', and cleared my throat, ready to make some remark about him maybe feeling low, but Ms Hills raised her hand to stop me.

'I tried asking him why he was so ungrateful but, you know, I don't think he understands. Anyway, I don't try talking to him any more, not since he made a pass at me and…'

'What? Did you say he made a pass at you?'

I thought I had misheard – I glanced at the frightened boy, his hands twisting together and his breath still laboured. He didn't look as if he could hurt anyone. He was far too anxious and unsure of himself. I looked back towards Ms Hills with her baggy trousers, big glasses and flowery top over her ample figure. She was not exactly a young boy's dream.

'We were on the Underground when it happened. He grabbed me with both arms!' She shifted her chair again and it clunked against the radiator before she continued, 'It's a good job I'm trained to deal with such things, or he would be locked up by now.'

'What did you do?' I was trying to take this at face value, but Johnny was now cowering away from her, obviously distressed by her tone.

'Well, I managed to get him more to the side of me and pulled him off the train at the next stop. But he was still clinging on. Embarrassing, it was.'

'When did he let go?'

'Not until we had gone up the escalator and out into the open again – he must have thought what happened down there didn't matter, or something.' Her voice was rising with anger. Johnny's large eyes were darting from her to me.

'How many times had he been on the Tube before?'

'I don't know, do I? It was the first, and last, time with me!'

'Perhaps he clung to you in terror?' I quietly suggested. Ms Hills coloured up.

'What do you mean –"terror"?'

'Maybe he was scared by the noise of the trains or the people? It would be quite frightening for any non-Western foreigner, wouldn't you think?'

'He's not a baby – he's a grown lad. I don't believe it was that. He made a pass at me and I just don't feel safe with him any more.'

I tried again. 'Could you imagine being on the Underground for the first time? It must be like going into a strange noisy cave. And the screech of trains – it's quite eerie if you think about it.'

'I've been on those trains since I was a small child, Dr Lewis. I don't suppose it's at all scary for him. No, I think he knew what he was doing.'

She folded her arms again and settled back in her seat, smiling slightly with clenched lips. Maybe it had been flattering for her to think she was an object of desire for a teenager. I tried not to look back at her as I wrote 'Panic reactions in new situations?' in my notes, then crossed out the question mark. He had definitely panicked in my office when I had sent Ms Hills out earlier. I scribbled a few more notes about the session so far, my writing becoming smaller and more nonsensical as I tried to think of what to do next. I surprised myself by silently praying for guidance.

I glanced up at Johnny. He was now gripping the sides of his chair, whitened knuckles on his dark hands, still watching us. Perhaps it was his child-like fear that helped me think of the thick felt-tipped pens on my shelf. They had been useful before for my very shy patients and any children who had been obliged to wait for their parents in the waiting room.

'Would you like to do some drawing, Johnny?'

His tension was getting to me – he'd been in the room for nearly twenty minutes and I hadn't even begun to gain any rapport with him. Even now, as I moved, he was holding himself tight and pulling away as if expecting me to hit him.

I found some unused paper from the muddled pile on my desk and began to draw. First I drew a stick man – I can't actually draw much else – but I added what were meant to be sports trousers like his, and short black curly hair. I wrote 'Johnny' underneath and pointed at him. He looked at the paper and gave the faintest of head movements, which may have been a nod. I then drew another figure with a beard and big nose, wrote 'Mike' by it, and pointed at myself. He seemed to be with me so far.

I folded the paper to bring the two figures closer together and drew smiles on the faces. I thought I had lost him at this point but, after a brief hesitation, I was surprised to see his thin hand stretch tentatively forward towards the paper. I passed the drawing to him and he carefully examined how I had folded it, then opening and closing it a few times – pulling the stick men apart and then pushing them together. It felt like a breakthrough, although it was probably only a young man discovering the fascination of the simplest bit of origami ever. I revised my age estimate of him downwards – maybe fourteen, no more than sixteen. I coughed, making him jump and drop the drawing. Once more he drew back in his chair, watchful and wary.

I handed him the paper again, talking gently until he took it. He folded it once more, this time watching me carefully, more cautious now. I again pointed at him and myself and the figures on the paper. Glancing at Ms Hills nervously, he came to stand by me. Perhaps he thought I meant he was coming home with me? I had given the instruction 'come close to me' and had no idea what to do next. With both of us on one side of my desk and the paper and pens in front of us, I indicated to him to sit where I'd been sitting and passed him the fresh paper and pens.

He tried to hold a red felt pen between his finger and forefinger but then gripped it in his fist as he made an attempt to copy the picture I had already done. The room was quiet apart from the sound of his rhythmic breaths and the squeak as he pressed the pen hard on the paper. His lines were wiggly but it was possible to make out the two figures he had drawn. He looked up at me and I nodded. He turned the paper and took hold of the edge, using both hands to fold it exactly as I had with the original. He examined the result, moving the paper. Then he handed it to me and I opened and closed it to bring the figures closer. He frowned, then he looked up and slowly took another sheet of paper, watching me to test my reaction – I pushed the whole pile closer to him and found more from the drawer of my desk.

Ms Hills and I were then treated to watching the exciting process of someone learning to draw with pens, or perhaps remembering a lost skill. The colours of the pens were tried in lines – then those lines became crude buildings or ladder-like shapes. He went on to try curves, spreading them all over the paper, obviously fascinated, as they took on shape and form, losing their initial wobbles. Next, a fresh piece of paper and a very careful, studied rainbow. And he smiled; tentatively at first, but becoming broader as he saw that Ms Hills and I recognised his drawing. We almost spoiled his moment by trying to teach him the English for rainbow, but Ms Hills somehow excelled herself by coming out with the Spanish for it: *'arco iris'*, and it was as if the rainbow itself was with us in the room.

I get through a lot of coloured pens, as they usually disappear out of the waiting room, but this time I was thrilled to find many sheets of paper, a plastic wallet to keep them in and a fresh pack of thirty felt pens for Johnny to take back to the hostel.

4

I was back in my office after lunch, looking at the photocopy of Johnny's rainbow picture, when a blustery Ms Hills phoned. The rainbow moment we had experienced in Johnny's appointment seemed to have been overtaken by some thundery clouds. I could hear her anxiety and anger through the tightness of t's and spitting of s's.

'Whatever are you doing with him? He doesn't need to learn to draw, you know. He needs assessing. You're meant to do a psychological evaluation with tests, aren't you?'

I responded as calmly as I could.

'I cannot assess him until we find a means of communication. He doesn't seem to understand any English so I can't ask him general knowledge questions, discover his mood state or even give him instructions for a non-verbal assessment at this stage.'

'Aren't you doing a report, then?'

'Yes, I will, but I need to establish some form of communication first.'

Ms Hills cleared her throat. I could imagine her pulling herself up to her full five foot two. 'That's all well and good, Dr Lewis, but where does that leave me? What do I say to the court? We only have three weeks and then I am meant to go back with some answers. I thought this would only take a couple of sessions.'

I managed to hide my feelings of panic when I replied, 'Three weeks? Why wasn't I told? That's far too soon to be able to add anything useful to a decision about his future. If anyone had asked me, I would have suggested six months at the very least. Even that might not be enough. I can't be expected to work miracles – he's not speaking, we haven't been able to identify what he understands.' I caught my voice rising. I slowed my speech down and carried on, speaking very clearly, 'I might be able to give you some answers once he has begun to communicate. Learning to draw may well be the only way he will be able to do this in a short time span. Many traumatised people who become mute do not speak for years. It's obvious that he is very scared.'

'Or he's a good actor. I still think he's conning us all. Can't you psychoanalyse him, or something?'

I sighed inwardly at the simplicity of her thinking. What did she think psychoanalysis was? Some kind of magical mind-reading, perhaps.

'He will need to communicate for that, Ms Hills. And the few words of Spanish he picked up on the liner won't be enough, even with an interpreter. I may involve the art therapist, Anita Goodwin, at some stage, but even then it wouldn't be valid if we imposed our interpretation onto his drawings when he comes from a completely different culture.'

Despite Ms Hills' misgivings, before we had finished the telephone conversation I had persuaded her that she should return to court and push for at least six months to enable me to undertake a psychological evaluation. Having a plan seemed to make her less anxious and rather less hostile, which was a relief. The last thing I needed was an antagonistic social worker. But even if I did manage to gain her full cooperation, would six months be enough? Would I know anything by then? I wasn't sure I had it in me to unravel this one. I rang Anita.

'Hello, Mike, what's up?'

I filled her in quickly on my progress with the boat boy. Telling her about it seemed to somehow make it sound like a fairly authentic approach. Once I started talking about the drawing, she began to make excited noises. I could imagine her leaning forward over her desk, one elegant hand waving about to illustrate her words.

'What did he draw first – straight lines? Yes, that figures. Then circles and ladder shapes? Do you realise he followed exactly the same stages as young children do when they're learning to draw?'

'I hadn't thought of that. It was all very deliberate and careful.'

'Well, under-fives would develop skills over several months, of course, but it's incredible that someone in his teens, say, should follow the same course when he's new to it.'

'Do you think he was new to drawing, then? It was fascinating to watch him, but I'm a long way from helping him communicate. What I need to find out from you is whether there is some suitable drawing assessment which he could do.'

'Are you trying to pass the buck, Mike, or do you really want to know?'

The thought came to me that she was interested enough to take him on if I asked her. That would save me a load of hard work. Very tempting, but then the court had requested a psychological assessment. I laughed.

'No, no, he's definitely my case. But I could do with your advice now and again.'

'Well, I'm perfectly willing to help out where I can. It sounds like a really interesting case. Not sure I'd be very much use, though. His drawing skills are very basic and we don't even know what culture he is from, so interpretation would be difficult.'

I was pleased then that I had mentioned culture to the social worker, which led me to tell Anita all about Ms Hills. Anita was great – she had lots of ideas to help Ms Hills feel more empowered and therefore more competent. I had been too busy judging Ms Hills to notice that she had her own needs.

We finished our conversation and I glanced up at the wall clock. I was astounded to find I had been on the phone for forty minutes. We should have both gone home, but Anita always had time for people and as for me – well, what had I got to go 'home' to? I suppose I could search through my packing cases again in the hope that there was something else useful in any of them.

It seemed to be an exceptionally exhausting train journey home from Victoria to Sydenham. I diverted my route from the station to pick up a doner kebab from Grecko's in Sydenham High Street. The flat was cold, so I switched on the fan heater and sat in my coat in the lounge while I ate the takeaway. I surveyed the boxes around me. I could not remember the contents of any of them. They were labelled with the room destination – 'Lounge', 'Bedroom', 'Kitch'. I suppose I had imagined unpacking them when I arrived, not nearly five years later. I finished eating, squashed the wrappings into the overfull pedal bin in the kitchen, and returned to the lounge to open a box at random.

The box I selected revealed many items I had not looked at for a long time. The photo album from when I was a teenager was easy to cope with. I even laughed as I reminisced over the photos of a slightly overweight, middle-class, well-turned out young man with a girl on each arm. I remembered those girls – both of them professed to be totally in love with me, at the same time, but as soon as I chose between them and asked one of them out, Patsy, I think, they both abandoned me and focused on my best friend, David. I couldn't remember many names as I looked through the album. It was all parties and outings – with a few lads and girls sitting looking cold on the beach or trying to look as if they were having fun sitting on a nondescript bench in a long-forgotten park. But Patsy and her friend were featured often, reminding me of how I'd felt special and fought over, for a while.

I noticed a small hard-backed poetry book among a pile of *National Geographic*s. I tossed the magazines to one side – they could go for recycling now I'd forgotten why I kept them. I remembered this book all right; it was full of love poems. Inside the gold-leafed cover was her inscription: 'To my darling Mike, yours always, Ella.' Ella – the one I'd reckoned to live my life with, the mother of my child.

'Always' had turned out to be ten years, three months and fourteen days. I still missed her so much that the ache of her absence was sometimes a physical pain. We'd had some good times when we were first together – we'd hated being apart, and every word of love had sounded unique, eternal. Thinking about it made me smile.

Maybe it would have been 'always' if we hadn't been through such hell. It pulled us together at first, while Jamie fought for his life, while we counted off the weeks of chemo and focused on every movement, interpreting it as a sign of recovery. But all our prayers and yearnings didn't halt leukaemia's destruction.

I sat on the floor by the boxes, locked in the memories I had tried so hard to suppress. I realised that I was moaning, voicing their names, over and over: 'Jamie, my Jamie. Ella, my darling Ella.'

'What happened to us, Ella?' I thought, as I flicked slowly through the book of love poems. I knew, of course. We both grieved separately. I was locked into sorrow and she couldn't reach me. She needed me. That's why she turned to someone else.

If only Jamie had lived.

I rummaged around in the box, until I found what I knew I needed. A photo of a smiling child on his sixth birthday, wearing a pirate outfit, complete with patch over one eye. A birthday cake with 'Many Happy Returns' on an icing ship. His last birthday. I dusted the photo frame and glass on my sleeve and propped the photo against my pile of books on the coffee table.

'From now on Jamie, your place is in this room,' I said.

Strangely, I felt OK. Sad, but together.

It was only later that I realised I had found the book and thought about Ella, and Jamie, without having to hide in a couple of bottles of whisky. I'm not sure I even woke up for my usual small-hours tipple that night.

Something seemed to be giving me a new sense of purpose at work. I found ways of tidying up cases that had been around for years, mostly by making long-overdue referrals to other people who could take a fresh approach. But for one chronically anxious lady, Mrs Bayton, who I usually saw weekly, I was really pleased with my intervention. It was drawing with Johnny that started it. I half-remembered a similar drawing with folds in it, in a book on therapeutic activities. I found the book on my office shelf, *Creative Therapy: Activities with Children and Adolescents*. I hadn't opened it for several years. Among other things there were activities for working with anxiety. Although she was way past the intended age group, I chose a task I thought Mrs Bayton might appreciate.

As usual, Mrs B was sitting sighing in the waiting room twenty minutes before the appointment time. She was pulling at the sleeves of her grey jacket. My voice startled her.

'I'm ready if you are, Mrs Bayton. We're going to do some drawing today.'

'Oh dear, Dr Lewis. I can't draw to save my life. I was never any good at art. I'm sure I will make a dreadful mess of it. You won't be at all pleased with my efforts. I really don't think I can do drawing, the thought of it panics me awfully.'

43

She was breathing fast and looking flushed as she gathered up her brown leather handbag and stood up, dropping her gloves as she did so.

'It will be fine, no artistic talent required.' I waited for her, and then showed her into my room.

It took a few more minutes to calm her down, then I asked if she were ready. She gave a quick nod. I drew a spiral, turning the paper as I wrote in the way her thoughts spun into anxiety and panic. She had given me the perfect example with her response to the idea of drawing. In the outside of the spiral I wrote 'Stress-free' and on the inside 'Total panic'. Then we did it all again with hypothetical positive thoughts coming from the middle to the outside.

'That's me, Dr Lewis. I spiral down all the time. If I practise maybe I'll be able to spiral up again, too!' I looked again at my drawings – yes, they could look as if they spiralled down or up. Mrs B drew pages of spiralling positive thoughts. I was amazed at her energy and enthusiasm as she gained insight into her cognitions. As usual, I ended the session by asking her when she would like her next appointment.

'I'll need some time, Dr Lewis, to try all this out. It's so exciting, I can't wait to practise my new way of thinking.'

As I showed Mrs B out of my room I spotted Anita in the waiting area. She was reaching up to put a poster up on the noticeboard. Her brown wavy hair was flopping over her face and, with her hands full, she flipped her head back to move her fringe away from her eyes.

I smiled expansively. 'Hi, Anita. How are you today?'

She turned towards me with one thumb still pressing on a reluctant drawing pin.

'I'm fine, Mike. I'm glad I've seen you today – I wanted to ask you if you would like to borrow a fairly basic book on art therapy, to maybe help you with Johnny?'

'Good idea. I'm not sure how much I can take in before next session – I'm seeing him on Tuesday.'

'Well, I haven't got it here, but I could drop it into your flat, tonight, if you like. My friend lives in Talbot Road and I'm popping round there later.'

The thought of anyone seeing the way I lived totally eclipsed the fact that Anita was suggesting she should come to my place.

'No, don't put yourself out – tomorrow will be fine, thank you.'

I turned back into my office, suddenly feeling quite foolish. But she had a friend round the corner from me – must be a boyfriend – she was just trying to help. I wasn't sure how she knew where I lived, though.

When I got home that night, it was still light. I stood in the large bay window and watched the traffic, glass of red wine in my hand. Just thinking. I used to do that quite a lot as I looked at the busy-ness of the street. Sometimes there were children or people with dogs in the little park opposite. It all happened out there, making me feel separate, remote. If I saw a family with a small child, I usually became a bit morose. But today I found myself thinking about Anita visiting her friend. What if she had turned up unexpectedly? Would I have let her in? I turned and viewed the flat as if through her eyes. It was more of a dump than a flat. I'd left a half-finished whisky somewhere, I could smell it. And maybe a dirty plate or wrappings? There was certainly the rancid odour of old takeaways.

I started pushing all the boxes into the never-used dining room. This was a small, dark room that had old lady's wallpaper on it, complete with brighter patches where someone else's pictures had protected the paper. Moving the boxes left space to arrange the little furniture I had in the sunnier sitting room, with its bay windows, I unpacked some bright orange cushions for the battered brown leather sofa and pulled in a multicoloured cotton rug I'd had covered in piles of clothes in the bedroom. The rug did a good job of hiding some of the bare boards, which really needed re-sanding and varnishing. I surveyed my work and noticed the dust on the windowsills, floor and even across the back of the sofa. It still looked rather bare, too. No coffee table. I tipped the contents of one of the half-empty tea chests into the next and tried it out on its side with a cloth over it. I'd picked up this bright red cloth in a market in Portugal one holiday – I had been impressed when the stallholder told me that all the little bulls in the pattern on the cloth were made by tying and dying it. Ella disliked my find and it never went with any of our colour schemes, so it still looked quite fresh and new. I wasn't quite sure it went with the orange cushions but at least it gave me a respectable surface. No neat little mat-things for coffee cups, though. I might need those to keep that bit of material clean.

I took myself to the superstore down at Bell Green, and bought two huge leafy houseplants. I bought some fresh food too, along with a few cleaning fluids and polish. I couldn't remember if I had ever invested in serious cleaning stuff – although I had been known to buy some washing powder and washing-up liquid, on occasion.

By the end of the evening I had at least one clean room. I sat down on the sofa, and then remembered one of the items I had tipped out of the box now serving as a coffee table. It was an art book – bought on a visit to the Tate Modern with Ella. Instead of switching on the television, I fetched it, and then settled down to try to work out whether there was anything there that might give me an idea about how to work with Johnny.

5

The following week I was in my office preparing for the Monday meeting. I was early, with plenty of time to think through my course of action with the boat boy case. I'd forgotten all about my trainee, Georgina. She hurried into my office after the briefest of knocks and before I had even called out 'Come in'. Her expressive eyebrows were drawn tightly together and she looked pale and tired.

'How are you, Georgina? Everything going all right?'

She stared at me for a moment. 'I need to speak to you urgently, Dr Lewis. I now have six clients and I don't know what I am doing with any of them.'

Even as I said, 'You only have to ask,' I realised I'd forgotten our supervision session last week. I think I'd given her some supervision the week before – but maybe not. She was fairly restrained, considering.

'I thought we had supervision last Tuesday, but you had a client all morning and I was booked up myself in the afternoon.'

'I'm sorry, Georgina. It was Johnny Two.'

Georgina looked unimpressed. I continued, 'Let's talk about your most difficult client now.'

Her most difficult one was one of the young men that she had been allocated last week.

'I rang him after the meeting,' she told me. 'He wanted an appointment immediately, so I offered him one for next Tuesday. That's tomorrow.'

'That's good.'

'Not good enough for him. He has rung sixteen times since then, trying to talk to me.'

She paused, her face watching mine for a reaction. I shrugged.

'Well, that is a lot – was he trying to change the appointment?'

'No. He is insisting on talking to me to confirm the appointment we have already made. The secretaries have been brilliant at protecting me, but I have still spoken to him three times. There's something strange about him. I am really worried about taking this case.'

I usually go with an experienced clinician's instinct, but Georgina was just a trainee. I began to think she was more nervous than she had originally appeared. But to be sure, I went into supervisor mode: 'Right, Georgina, let's look at this more closely. What's his history, where did the referral come from, and why?'

She pulled the second file out from the pile she was holding. It was very full, with a battered cover.

'This is an old file on him, Mike. He was seen here by a psychiatric nurse and previously in Kent somewhere, by two psychologists.'

She started to read out details from the psychiatric nurse's report, made two years ago. Everyone who'd seen him had passed him on because of his 'dependency'. He had a criminal record for harassment of not one, but three 'girlfriends'. One of these girls had never been out with him or shown any interest in him.

'Why did I give this chap to you?' I asked.

'Well, I wanted to see anyone depressed so that I could do cognitive therapy with them. The old file wasn't with the referral. One of the secretaries, Rachel, remembered his name and found me the previous notes – he'd been given a new hospital number for some reason.'

I took the new, thin file to look at the referral from the GP. It was an unremarkable request for therapy. Georgina was right; we couldn't have seen trouble coming from that. Another time when someone in the NHS had bungled things nicely and not matched their name to their previous notes.

'Have you met him yet, Georgina?'

'No, but there was someone loitering outside yesterday who followed me to the Tube station. I lost him there.'

'Are you sure you were followed?'

'Ninety per cent, although I'd been a bit rattled by the sort of things he was saying and by then I'd read the notes, so I was a little scared.'

I could hear the sound of chat and laughter outside my door and realised that people were beginning to arrive for the allocation meeting. I suggested to Georgina that we skipped the meeting and sorted this out instead. How could I be so stupid? I'd given my trainee a stalker to deal with.

I stuck my head out of my room and spotted Anita coming down the corridor. I quickly explained to her that I had to sort out a crisis with my trainee and, with a little querying raise of her eyebrows, she smiled and patted my arm.

'That's all right, Mike – I'll organise this lot in there and you can give Georgina some supervision. From what I hear she is having a spot of bother.'

Why did everyone know things were going wrong before I did? I half-heartedly told Georgina off for not coming straight to me last week, but while doing so I realised that most of last week I had my 'Do not disturb' sign on the door. I don't think I'd read many of my messages either.

Georgina is usually very composed. One of those trainees who make you feel like you know nothing because she arrives for supervision on time, well-prepared, with all her reading done for each client, a hypothesis about what is going on and a whole formulation about what is keeping the problem going, the client's abilities to overcome it, the lot. But not today. Today she was a frightened woman. Her hands shook as she started to talk about this chap – Gerald – and the things he had already said to her. He had said she had a smooth, silky, sensual voice. She'd told him it was inappropriate to talk to her like that, and he had laughed. Next time he called, when she had said, 'Umm, I'll have to find out,' he had told her he loved hesitant women, because he was a masterful man. He had rung three times to give the message that he was looking forward to meeting her and to say that he was sure she would be able to make him feel much happier. Relating this to me, Georgina was struggling to keep back the tears.

'I ought to know how to cope with all this, Mike, but I don't know how to handle it.'

I thought, 'Nor do I,' but I knew one thing for certain. This was definitely not the client for a trainee, especially an attractive female in her first year, however competent she seemed.

'Well, the first thing you do is find a rape alarm, in case he has worked out who you are.' She took a sharp intake of breath and I tried to reassure her. 'I don't suppose he has, but we can't be too careful. And you can hand over those files to me, because this is one young man I hope you will never meet. I will arrange his appointments with me, on your college days, so that you don't even see him in the waiting room.'

Georgina reached for a tissue from the box on my coffee table and blew her nose loudly. She looked up at me and let out a long breath – probably a sigh of relief. She tossed the two files onto the coffee table, their contents spilling all over the floor. By the time we'd picked up all the bits of paper and more or less reassembled them, she was smiling again. She hardly needed supervision for the rest of her clients – out came her near-perfect plans and formulations.

After we had worked through her remaining clients, it was too late to join the meeting, so we made a coffee and, for the sake of her education, I started telling her about Johnny Two.

'What's your formulation, then, Mike?'

Trust a trainee to expect you to do things properly.

'Not quite reached that point, yet, Georgina. I'm still trying to gather information. I'm looking at post-traumatic stress, of course, which may be the sole cause for his panic, or he may have an underlying anxiety. I'm meant to report on his cognitive abilities as well, but I'm a bit short of standardised assessments for someone who doesn't speak.'

'You could use the cubes out of the WISC without language.'

I'd forgotten she'd worked with children as a psychology assistant. The Weschler intelligence scales were a standardised assessment tool. All the cubes test would tell me would be whether he was cognitively able to copy complex patterns, but it was something.

'That might be a good idea, Georgina, although I'm not sure how I'd score it without knowing his age.'

'Would you like me to borrow the WISC from college, so that you can look at it and see if it's any good? I don't suppose there's one here.'

She was right – as an adult outpatient facility we didn't have children's assessments.

Georgina gathered up our used coffee mugs and left the room. After she left I tried to remember what else was in the WISC. I could vaguely remember a test copying squiggles and shapes. If no one knew Johnny's age there were probably a few children's things I could use, then give a range of likely ability scores. It would be better than nothing.

Soon after Georgina left, Anita appeared as if she'd been waiting for a moment to catch me. There had not been too many referrals, and she had pleaded the heaviness of Johnny's case on my behalf, so I actually had none to add to my list. Just as well now I had taken over Georgina's Gerald.

Anita mostly wanted to talk about Johnny.

'I feel bad,' she said. 'You asked for my help and I immediately accused you of wanting to pass the case over. I'm sorry. If I can be of any help, I will. Would you like me to offer a few sessions of art therapy and see what happens there?'

I was pleased to have anyone's help on this one. I explained my own thoughts about Johnny and I put forward Georgina's idea, which opened up some new possibilities. Meanwhile, I would still work with him to overcome his trauma even if that didn't lead to an immediate return of his voice.

Anita enthusiastically described what she could do using art, and how it was really accessible to people of all ages and with all sorts of problems.

'I know Johnny's a bit different, but it might be possible to reach him with a combination of my art and your psychology.'

'We will have to think outside the box, Anita. Traditional trauma-focused psychology won't suit this case.'

Anita smiled, and lifted her hands. 'We'll get there, Mike, you wait and see!' She looked at her watch. 'I must dash, I have a client at 11.00.'

After she'd left the room, taking all her enthusiasm with her, I began to question myself and my abilities. Not for the first time. Was psychology 90 per cent bluff? I wondered. I had a theory that none of the greats, Freud, Watson, Klein, Beck, had ever known what they were doing but had stumbled on something that had worked over and again for a few clients. We ordinary clinicians tried to do things scientifically, even calling ourselves 'scientist-practitioners', but I had a sneaky feeling that we still did the same thing. The only difference was we tried to hide it more.

My greatest concern was that I might stumble along with other people's good ideas and still not have the skills to find all the answers the court needed. That would remain to be seen. I'd have to come up with something soon.

6

I was on my way to get myself a coffee at lunchtime when the phone rang. I went back into the office to answer it. I recognised Anita's voice.

'I have a gap this afternoon, at around three. Would that be a good time for a joint appointment with Johnny, if he is booked to see you then?'

I immediately felt a bit out of my depth. But then reasoned that I was out of my depth anyway, with only a plethora of ideas for the appointment and no actual plan.

'How will we work it out, then? Would it be best for me to have part of the session with him and then bring him down to you?'

'I've thought about what I could do, but I will need your guidance as we go along. I can introduce Johnny to various art materials and, beginning with the theme of the rainbow, we could try to link a few things to his experience.'

'How can we do that?'

'I can start with the boat arriving – I saw the story in the newspaper so I may be able to draw something he could recognise. Then we can see where that takes us. He might be able to add something in of his own.'

'But Anita, you'll be doing all my work,' I protested.

'No way, Mike. I'll be the instrument, if you like, because I'm the one who can use art in therapy. But I'll need your guidance, and you will need to try to help me focus on the right things. I'm rather more used to saying to people, "Imagine your life as a path and draw yourself as you walk through your experiences." Somehow, I don't think he would understand that.'

I agreed to give it a go although I still had some misgivings.

The appointment was at 3pm, and sure enough, there they were in the waiting area on time. I took Johnny and his social worker into my room and explained the plan to Ms Hills, signing in Makaton as I did so, in case Johnny could understand. There was nothing but a shrug and, 'If you think so, doctor,' from Ms Hills. She didn't look as defensive today. She was tired, maybe.

I took them down to the art room. Johnny was walking really close to Ms Hills, despite my nods and smiles of encouragement. We reached the art room, where Anita was wiping down the table in the centre. She walked forward smiling, taking Johnny's hand and shaking it in both her own.

'You must be Johnny. I'm Anita,' she said. 'We are going to draw and have lots of fun this afternoon. Come and see what I have set out for you.'

I don't think Johnny understood a word, except perhaps his given name. But I could see him relax – Anita's warm personality appeared to cross all culture and language barriers. He followed her over to the table with scarcely a glance towards Ms Hills or round the room with its numerous hanging pictures and other kinds of art. Paper, brushes, bottles of paint, pastels, crayons and other art materials crowded the surfaces round the sides of the room.

Ms Hills sat on a chair near the wall and I walked to the table where Anita had laid out many art materials. She had some felt-tipped pens but these were very definitely placed to one side as if some inferior art medium. She had tucked her hair behind her ears and rolled up her sleeves. She was donning a painting shirt as she spoke to Johnny, covering her turquoise blouse and black trousers. She then offered him an identical painting shirt. He took it from her uncertainly and she indicated to put it on. It was covered with someone else's old paint, even though it had obviously been through the wash. Johnny was very unsure until Anita produced one for me. Feeling rather silly, especially knowing that I was unlikely to do any painting, I put it on. Johnny did the same.

Anita passed him a brush.

'See if you can hold your brush like this, Johnny.' His long brown fingers adjusted their hold and he moved the dry brush across the paper, watching Anita's movements.

'Now, this is how you use the paints. First, dampen your brush, then a little bit of colour on there – no, that's a bit too much, wipe your brush on the side of the paint pot like this.' He was a quick learner and was soon using measured amounts of paint. They worked together making doodles and shapes on the same piece of paper, with Anita keeping up a steady patter about the colours. It didn't take many minutes for Johnny to attempt a rainbow on his side of the paper. Anita showed me, then saying *arco iris* – a rainbow'– she pegged up the paper to dry. I had only mentioned in passing that Shirley Hills had known the Spanish for 'rainbow', but she had remembered in case of need.

A fresh piece of paper and a slightly different approach from Anita, next. She took some charcoal and deftly drew the *SS Margarita*. As it became apparent what she was doing, Johnny became quite excited. He looked round for Ms Hills. I called her over.

'He wants to show you Anita's drawing – she's drawn the *Margarita*.'

Ms Hills did that movement again – looking up in the air as if I were a totally exasperating child.

'If we can all manage to respond to any efforts he makes to communicate, we may help him to keep it going,' I told her. 'We have to be patient, but I expect we'll get there in the end.'

'I hope so, Dr Lewis. But I still don't understand all this drawing business. It's just using up the time you need to find out about him for your report.'

I remembered what Anita had said before about involving the social worker.

'I'll move your chair over here, Ms Hills. You can really help by smiling to encourage him, then I'll phone you later and tell you what I've learned about him from the session.'

She grumbled something under her breath but settled closer where she could at least hear us and partly see what was going on. Johnny was watching Anita's sketch as she filled in details, eventually drawing him coming down the steps onto dry land. She offered him the charcoal.

The first thing he did was black in her outline of him. Then he drew a big oval with a loop from it by the figure's hand.

'That's his bag,' said Ms Hills. 'He had a sort of canvas thing with a string handle.'

'Do you know what was in it?' asked Anita. But she didn't. She had only seen the bag empty, later, when he had used it to carry his second tracksuit and T-shirts and pair of pyjamas, transferring them from the detention centre to the hostel.

Anita made a sketch of the bag open, and passed the drawing to him. Johnny was very quick on the uptake and began to draw items in the bag. Unfortunately, he couldn't draw well enough for us to know what he was doing. He kept rubbing over his drawings, trying to change them. The picture became a blur of smudged charcoal, and Johnny's pink palms looked filthy. Anita passed him a tissue, showing him how to clean off his hands. She then drew the open bag again, using the despised felt-tipped pens, and passed them to him to try again.

There wasn't much in the bag. One item appeared to be sort of gourd-shaped, with a stopper at the narrow end. Probably he had water in it at one stage. There seemed to be a knife – and we soon knew it was one because I noticed a palette knife on the windowsill. I pointed to the knife in the drawing and the palette knife until he smiled. I nodded wildly and remembered to say, 'Yes, yes.' We couldn't identify the third item. It may have been a necklace or a belt, but whatever it was, Johnny drew it and then became withdrawn, losing eye contact with us and looking at his hands. He shook slightly.

'I think we've lost him, Anita. Maybe we need to take things really slowly. Help him now to have some fun – perhaps draw a picture of one of us, or that plant on the windowsill. Anything, really to reorientate him into the here and now.'

At first Johnny looked away, despite Anita's really good lightning sketch of Ms Hills. He had tears running down his face – a fact which I mimed to Anita. She crouched by him, uttering soothing words, and passed him a tissue, indicating the need to wipe his face. She plonked her sketchbook on his lap. He finished wiping his eyes, then picked up the picture, turning to show it to Ms Hills. Luckily, it wasn't too much of a caricature, but had captured the essence of Ms Hills in some indefinable way. Ms Hills took the picture from him, a small smile curling from the edge of her lips.

'That's really good, Mrs Goodwin. You could earn your living doing this.'

Anita and I exchanged glances over her head and decided not to point out to Ms Hills that in fact Anita did earn her living through her art. She began to help Johnny draw a person – showing him the level of eyes on a face, shading for high cheekbones like Johnny's own. They looked together into a mirror which she had taken out of a cupboard. I watched her smiling, him serious, drawing her finger across her own cheekbone before pointing to his. She was totally immersed in teaching him and she had very neatly helped move Johnny out of that past experience back to the present.

Johnny left with the pile of pictures, after Anita had photocopied them 'just in case'. I wasn't too sure what we had that would be useful for the report, but I stayed in the art room as she cleared up, and quickly made notes about Johnny's reaction to each bit of the session and detailed observations regarding the bag's contents and the mysterious object. What was the significance of that? I looked at the photocopy of Johnny's drawing again.

Anita interrupted my thoughts.

'You know, Mike, I think we should take Johnny to an art gallery. He'll have more of an idea about how to express himself through art if he widens his experience. I know he could look at books, but it's not the same as seeing full-size pictures displayed. What do you think?'

'Do you think Ms Hills will let us? She'll have to come as well. I can't really see the value of it myself, but if you're sure it would be helpful, I can talk to her.'

'I'm sure, Mike. I'm not sure why I'm sure, but he seems to have some sort of natural understanding of art. Even if it doesn't give us more information about him, it will help him to trust us a bit better.'

So, a little later on, I was on the phone to Ms Hills. I remembered I had promised to contact her with some feedback from the session, anyway. She wasn't in the office when I rang, but I was given her home number. When I rang this it was immediately answered, but I couldn't hear a word she was saying. Dog barking was all I could hear and it sounded like a huge animal.

'Quiet, Butch, quiet. Good boy, that's better.' The barking was now a dull growl. 'Who is it, please?'

'It's me, Mike Lewis.'

Ms Hills went into long explanations about her dog that was a guard dog and always barked for the phone and anyone who passed the house. I hoped she wasn't on a busy road.

I told her a few things I had discovered from the session. There wasn't a lot, apart from the link between the mysterious object and Johnny's withdrawal, so I had to spin it out, explaining what I could put in the report about his willingness to cooperate and his general level of ability in learning a new skill. She seemed happy enough with my explanations, though. Then came the hard bit.

'I've discussed the situation fully with Anita Goodwin. We think it may be beneficial to take him to an art gallery and help him to understand how expressions can be conveyed through art. This would also have the benefit of building up further trust with ourselves, to help him feel relaxed enough to begin to communicate.'

I wasn't prepared for her response.

'Are you two an item, then?'

'No way. I mean, no, of course not. This is a professional link to get the best out of our client. I can assure you...'

'I'm sorry, Dr Lewis. I didn't mean to offend you. I don't know what made me say that. It's just that you've gone from talking about how you are working with Johnny to how you are working together with Johnny. It sounded sort of established and *personal*. Which day were you thinking of?'

It took a while to settle on a day early in the following week. Ms Hills could only manage an hour and a half at the most, but we decided that would have to do.

When I put the phone down, I started to think about my reaction to her suggestion that Anita and I were personally involved. A huge longing for Ella overwhelmed me. I left a note for Anita in the office giving the time of the gallery visit, and pushed off back to the flat, ready for a glass of red wine.

Was it really looking as if Anita and I were a couple?

7

Ms Hills was late. I stood on the steps of the Tate Modern with Anita, chatting about work matters, for about twenty minutes in the drizzle, before we spotted Johnny. He walked towards us with his head held high, all the time glancing around him as he negotiated his way through the crowds. Then he saw me as he drew near to the steps. He smiled and began to hurry, which resulted in Ms Hills looking vexed and breathless by the time they reached the bottom of the steps. Johnny waited by her, nodding and smiling, while Ms Hills regained her breath. He had with him a translucent carrier bag through which could be seen a spiral-bound sketchbook and his pack of felt-tip pens.

'I suspect he thinks he has come to draw pictures,' said Anita.

'It won't matter if he does,' I answered. 'There are usually a few art students here.'

'Yes, but with felt pens?'

'I'm sure you'll provide him with pencils and oil pastels – don't you always carry them with you?'

'How do you know that?'

'Oh, just a hunch.'

I didn't think I'd better tell her about the day when I was quietly working in my room when, from the other side of my door, I heard a clattering sound followed by an annoyed voice muttering, 'Oh, fiddlesticks!' I'd never heard Anita swear, then, before or since. I opened the door to see a whiteboard leaned against the opposite wall and Anita kneeling on the floor gathering up the contents of her shoulder bag. She didn't see me, so I was about to offer to help her when I realised that among the many pencils, boxes of pastels and artist's drawing pens strewn up the corridor were quite a few items of a feminine, personal nature, which had burst out from their box. I had quietly closed the door.

I turned my attention to Shirley Hills and Johnny. Ms Hills looked very flushed and there were small beads of sweat showing on her forehead. She was pushing her escaping hair back into her bright ponytail band as she spoke.

'Do you need me?' she said. 'I don't think he'll run off. He knows you now. It's a bit irregular, of course, but I've got a real crisis with one of my others and if this is going to take an hour and a *half*...' Her emphasis on the half-hour spoke volumes for her opinion regarding this visit. I felt relieved – it would definitely be easier without her.

'Sure, we'll manage. You'll need to give me your mobile number in case there's a problem. As long as Johnny is happy to be left with us that will be fine.'

Anita was even more opportunistic than I was. 'Look, if you need more time, we've both set a morning aside for this, so how about we meet back here at one, say? If that's all right with you, Mike?'

I agreed, adopting what I hoped was a kind, accommodating expression. Thanking us, Ms Hills hastily scribbled down the number on the back of a crumpled receipt, before rushing back down the steps.

Somehow, we hadn't tried to explain to Johnny, so he started to follow her. We raced after them and the three of us tried to explain to him in words, signs and Ms Hills' suddenly produced Spanish that he was to stay with us. Some of the relaxed pleasure that was apparent when he first arrived had evaporated now, as he glanced anxiously from one to the other of us, but eventually he understood and came back up the steps with us into the Tate.

I'm not sure he'd ever been into a building like this before. He stood in the foyer and looked. Maybe he needed time for his eyes to adjust from the brightness outside to the dim light in the foyer. I stayed with him while Anita bought tickets.

'Johnny, we're ready to go now, to look at the pictures.' He turned to me, looking confused. Anita opened the catalogue she had bought and talked gently to him as if she knew he would understand every word. He didn't, but her calm attitude as she pointed to the galleries and indicated which pictures were there, seemed to soothe him. She took his hand as she guided him into the Impressionists' gallery. I was not sure Ms Hills would have approved, but it did the trick. I trailed along behind them as Johnny received an individualised tour. We were in a special exhibition highlighting works of Turner, Monet and Whistler. Apparently Turner came first, and to some extent influenced the others. Even if Johnny didn't understand, I learned a lot, as Anita pointed out rainbows, and named colours and effects. Johnny's reaction was interesting – his hands were echoing the shapes of the elements of the picture. Clouds, steam, spires, water. It made me realise how stilted sign languages like Makaton were, when I watched his sinewy brown-backed fingers carve symbols of beauty and form in the air.

I felt like a spare part as I wondered along behind them. We'd been here more than an hour and I was beginning to find it tiring, all this culture in one gallery. When Ella and I went to exhibitions, we had always flitted from one picture to another – never noticing the detail that Anita was now trying to explain to Johnny. Those two, Anita with her knowledgeable, calming commentary and he, with his expressive hands, were bonded in a union of art appreciation. At my third suggestion of a coffee break, we all went down in the lift to the basement café. Only when the doors had closed in the lift did I remember that Johnny might not have experienced lift journeys before, but Anita was ready and took his hand again when his eyes began to dart quickly around.

It was good to feel I had a part to play, albeit small, after Anita's hijacking of my client. I organised drinks for all of us – even establishing that Johnny wanted water – a sign he freely gave me which looked like embellished Makaton but was exactly like the shape he was making when looking at the water on Monet's 'The Thames below Westminster, 1871'. Perched at a chrome and glass table on a spindly shiny chair, he looked uncomfortable and very out of place. We attracted several glances from people who queued for drinks or squeezed up to adjacent tables, cramped into the small space around us. I tried to imagine what it was like to be Johnny – stared at, backed away from, not matching, not belonging, not able to communicate. He was far from relaxed now, his hand clenched round the bottle of spring water so tightly that it had begun to buckle. Anita had ordered a Danish pastry which she had cut up, and was now offering a piece to Johnny, off her plate. Like holding his hand earlier, I was not quite sure that sharing food was something she should do, but Johnny ate some, having refused anything earlier – or perhaps not having understood that I was prepared to buy food for him.

Here was Anita, an art therapist, communicating very efficiently with a very difficult client. Surely I, a qualified clinical psychologist with a string of degrees, should have managed better? Yet here I was, floundering along way behind her. Maybe it was time to pass him over to her and watch her sessions of art therapy work their highly effective magic. At least until she'd broken him down... I pulled my thoughts up sharply – 'broken him down'? What sort of therapist had I become? No one does that to people. No, what I meant was, stopped him being frozen, opened him up. That sounded like a surgeon, got through to him – no, that's a bully – released him, better, but what were we releasing him from?

'Mike, come on. Time for more pictures.'

'Oh, have you finished?' I followed them as we made our way between the tables, then used the stairs to go back to the gallery.

'I want to stop off on the way, Mike. I always like to look at "The Scream", if you don't mind.'

'That's a strange picture to like,' I remarked.

'It's incredible, so much colour.'

'I thought it was black and white.'

'You're thinking of the woodcut, which is usually what you see on book covers. Come and see the painting. There's something about the use of the lines, the thickness of the paint, that produces a Gestalt so that we see it as a deep scream from the very core of the subject's being. It's a bit advanced for Johnny, yet, but it won't hurt him to see it.'

We turned left into the nearest gallery. Anita knew where she was going and hurried past rich portrayals of fantastic scenes, millions of pounds-worth of art totally ignored as she worked her way towards her macabre favourite. We kept up with her the best we could, Johnny looking frantic and me looking embarrassed, I should imagine; I certainly felt it!

She had stopped at the end of the gallery and was looking with a sort of reverence at the narrow painting. Johnny caught up with her and stopped by her, staring at 'The Scream'. Silently he stood there, shaking a little. His eyes welled up and with the back of his clenched hand he brushed tears off his cheeks. Anita turned, and seeing him by her side, she moved to let him closer to the picture, turning her attention to him. His tears were running unchecked now and his nose was dribbling. I stepped forward with a tissue, but Anita put up her hand to stop me. We watched as he cried, ignoring the curiosity of those around us. All that could be heard in that long gallery were Johnny's sobs which carried on unabated. Then there was a huge noise that rose from deep within him – a scream from his past as he beat his chest. The scream carried on rising among the emotions of the masters spilled onto the canvases which surrounded us. It filled the gallery with fear and foreboding as Johnny's voice swelled.

Anita put her arms around him, and he subsided into sobs and one croaky noise, over and over. Not quite a word, not quite a scream, not quite a cry. It rose and fell like his hands describing water earlier, finding the shape of his pain.

The security guards had responded to the scream and two of them now asked us to leave. I tried to remonstrate.

'He is mute, he can't speak.'

'He's making a great deal of noise, sir.'

Johnny's voice was continuing, rising and falling, almost melodic but eerily mournful.

'We'd better leave, Mike, everyone's upset by him.'

I looked round. Anita was right. Faces around us were drawn, tight, disturbed. One elderly lady was sobbing into her lacy handkerchief and a group of children were crowded close to their teacher.

'Come on,' I said. 'Let's go.'

8

Once outside, on the steps, Anita and I looked at each other, unsure what to do next. Johnny was still crying with those huge gaspy noises. Anita kept her arm round him and we descended the steps together. We sat down on a slightly damp, cold stone bench on the embankment and, without a plan, without a word to each other, we waited.

The wailing sobs began to subside. Johnny seemed to be trying to say something – but the words would not come. It took a huge effort for him to begin to shape his mouth round the involuntary noises he was making. I found myself saying, 'Don't try to speak. It's OK. You can tell us later.' I signed the same message, putting my finger to my lips. I wasn't at all sure whether I should be telling a mute person not to speak, but the pain of his endeavour showed me instinctively that this was not the moment. The noise itself had been a breakthrough, his silence had been broken.

Johnny seemed to understand and the sobs continued to slow. He began to get himself more in control. Anita offered him a tissue, which he accepted, wiping the whole of his face, removing the shiny, wet rivulets.

'You know, Mike, we need to get him to somewhere familiar, or at least where he'll feel safer. We can't wait out here for Shirley Hills to come and fetch him.'

It had begun to spit with rain and was cold, even for March. Johnny had his usual tracksuit over a thin T-shirt; he was not dressed properly for this weather.

'We'd better phone Ms Hills and tell her we'll meet her in the department,' I said. I stood up to go through my pockets for my mobile, but Anita smiled and shook her head slowly.

'Haven't you got your mobile, Mike? Here, use mine.'

The phone she passed me was small, and complicated. I managed to open it and pressed a few buttons in an experimental manner. Anita took it back from me, plucked out of my hand the scrap of paper with Ms Hills' number, and poked a few buttons on her phone.

'I'll talk to her while we walk, Mike. Johnny's freezing sitting here.'

We walked down the embankment towards the Underground. The grey river merged with the increasing drizzle. Johnny was shivering, so we went at a fair pace. Somehow Anita managed to talk to Shirley Hills at the same time.

'Shirley, Anita Goodwin here. We've left the gallery and we're on the way back to the office. Yes, I know we should have waited for you. I'll explain later. We'll either be in Mike's room or the art room. The secretaries will tell you where. No, no need to rush, we're all right. What's that? Watch out on the Tube? Yes, I'll ask Mike. OK – see you later.'

Oh yes, the Tube, where he had panicked and grabbed Ms Hills. I explained it to Anita in exactly those terms, without Ms Hills' interpretation of the event.

In actual fact, he was fine. He looked a little frightened, darting his eyes around in the now familiar manner and standing quite close to us. A little close for British convention, perhaps, but convention definitely goes out of the window once people are on London's Underground. It was fairly quiet at this time of day, but if he'd ever travelled in the rush hour I should imagine he'd be terrified. The sound of the train whooshing into the station was enough to panic him, even without the crowds who could have pressed in on him or made him frightened of losing Ms Hills. Whatever would happen to him if that occurred? He'd have no idea where he was going. He wouldn't be able to ask for directions.

'Penny for them, Mike.'

'Oh, sorry, I was trying to imagine what it would be like for Johnny when he first started to use the Underground.'

'More than scary, I should think. I've panicked when I got on the Tube in the wrong direction. I always feel a bit anxious if I'm on a different route, or it's very crowded, and I have a complete understanding of how to read maps and make room for myself using my elbows. Our Johnny doesn't have the benefit of all that – it must seem pretty crazy to him.'

'Or even like some sort of time travel,' I said. 'He goes down in the ground in one place, there's lots of pushing, shoving, whooshing noises and escalators all over the place, and then he emerges somewhere else. It's not really like seeing where you are and having an idea of distance, is it?'

'No, he'd probably do better on the buses. But it's too late now. Anyway, we're nearly here.'

We emerged into heavy rain and hurried round the corner to the office. At least it wasn't too far. Soon we were all standing dripping into the carpet in the empty waiting area by the open door to the office. Rachel looked up from her computer and spotted us.

'Three drowned rats. What are we going to do with you?'

Anita and I looked at each other, and at Johnny. We were pretty wet, but my jacket shrugs off most of it. I took it off and found my shirt was dry apart from a little round the neck. Anita had been wearing a light mac, so she was not too bad either. That left Johnny.

Johnny was standing with his arms round him, shivering.

'We'll have to find him something dry to wear,' said Anita

'I'm not sure we can, it can't be ethical to make a client change their clothes,' I said.

'Oh, stuff and nonsense. I can at least give him a dry painting shirt to wear while his top things dry off.'

She took his hand and he went with her, with one furtive, unsure glance over his shoulder at me. I grinned, waving my hands in the direction he was going.

While they were gone, I made three cups of black coffee. I couldn't remember whether Anita took milk or sugar, so I poured some milk in a glass I found in the top of the cupboard in the kitchen. Then, in the absence of a tray, I ferried it all into my office. They were being a long time. I rang down to see what was happening.

'Oh, sorry, Mike, we've started drawing.'

'Well, you might have told me. I've made coffee for you up here.'

'Oh, sorry. Yes, I should have let you know. Come and see what Johnny's done.'

I tried to tell myself it was perfectly OK for Anita to have a session with him on her own, when we were meant to be working together. I took the cups back to the kitchen, hoping Rachel wouldn't look up from the office and see me taking back the drinks I had just made. I told Rachel where I would be and went to join Johnny and Anita.

As I had half-expected, Anita and Johnny were bent over a painting together. Anita was talking and painting at the same time. She didn't stop when I came in.

'This is red, Johnny. Red. When we put it over the yellow here, we have orange. Orange. You try... that's good. Don't forget to rinse your brush in between in the water, like this; you do it... that's good. Now, you try to mix colours. Red, that's right, now blue. Do you remember blue? You do, good. That new colour is purple. Purple.'

They were working on yet another rainbow. This time with some sort of thick water-based paints – I read the label on one of the bottles of bright primary colours: 'Poster paints'.

Anita looked up. 'Sorry, Mike, be with you in a moment.'

I watched them and remembered my small son, with an easel too tall for him, on his third birthday. I had painted trees, houses, trains, Postman Pat. I'd had to tell him what they were – I'm no artist – but he'd splashed colour all over them, telling me whose house it was and chattering about anything, then asking me to do the 'black and white cat'. I smiled, pleased that I could remember. I reluctantly pulled my thoughts back and tried to concentrate on what Anita and Johnny were doing.

'Now try yellow, do you remember yellow? Good, that's right, and blue. Now experiment! Do your own.'

Anita indicated the range of colours, and pushed it all across the table towards him with a fresh sheet of paper. He appeared to understand.

Anita turned to me, and picking up a picture that was drying further along on the windowsill, she pulled me away from Johnny over into the far corner of the art room.

'He's beginning to understand a bit more, you know, Mike. He's very quick to catch on, as you've seen.'

'I was rather expecting you to reappear upstairs.'

'Sorry, I found him a painting shirt to put on instead of his tracksuit jacket, but he took it into the corner and took off his T-shirt as well. Then he put the jacket and T-shirt on the radiator and came and sat down. I tried to tell him we should go back upstairs, but all he did was pick up the brushes and look at me. He certainly made it clear what he wanted to do.'

I shrugged and felt rather awkward. Anita carried on, 'What we're doing now is a debriefing task, to calm him down. He became rather distressed. Do you want to see what he painted first?'

My interest overcame my irritation, and I looked. His painting was a crude depiction of a boy with a black face. The mouth was open in a huge oval. Somehow, he had captured the look of 'The Scream'. It was amazing how he had managed to make something so different look like such a familiar picture. Anita leaned forward and said quietly, 'Look at the background.'

There was a big splodge up near the corner and a small felt-pen drawing. Anita explained the splodge had definitely been his first attempt at the drawing – she had pointed to his pens when he became frustrated with his efforts with the brush. The object looked like a table, or block of wood, with someone lying on it. There was something else, too, over the table.

'Is it someone lying on a bed?' I asked.

'I don't think so,' replied Anita. 'He made a chopping sign when he drew that over the top. I think it's an axe.'

I drew away from the picture.

'I think our Johnny's witnessed a murder,' I said.

9

I was late for the office. Not my fault, for a change. There'd been a hold-up on the train from Sydenham. By the time I'd reached the department, I expected Shirley Hills to have been sitting impatiently with Johnny, but as I walked past the waiting area it was empty, apart from the usual stale smell of smoke left over from the days when smoking was allowed in the old hospital. Wretched woman, she expected me to come up with a complete report in too short a time and then missed an appointment. Actually, that didn't make any sense. Something wasn't right. I decided to give them a few minutes more and then ring to see why they weren't there.

I bypassed the waiting area and went to put the kettle on in the staff kitchen. While the kettle boiled I read the staff notices. There wasn't much to read, just an out-of-date list of courses and a few jokes put up there by someone trying to cheer us up, the secretaries, I guessed. There was a poem which started 'Eye love two you's my spellchequer'. It started me musing about how we all see the world differently and yet think there's a right way to do things. I could read that poem perfectly well but it was crazily incorrect.

I felt like a change so I took some milk from the fridge for my coffee, not sure whose, and went into my room. The phone was ringing; it was Rachel from the secretaries' office.

'Mike, I've got a call for you – Shirley Hills, she's been trying to reach you for the past hour.'

'Put her through, Rachel, perhaps she'll explain why she hasn't brought Johnny today.'

There was a slight pause on the line during which I pushed a few papers around to try to uncover a pen in case of need.

'Ah, Shirley, I expected to see you today.'

'I've been trying to contact you, Dr Lewis, but you weren't there when I rang. I can't think what time you start in the morning, I'm usually in by 8.15 myself, so I was surprised I couldn't get hold of you, especially as I know you had a 9.30 appointment today.'

I saw no reason to explain myself, but I still mumbled something about flexi-hours before asking her why she hadn't come.

'I am well aware you were expecting to see Johnny today. I'm afraid we won't be at his appointment. Something terrible has happened. He's had an accident outside his lodgings.'

I felt anxiety welling up in me. Was he dead? I steeled myself to ask the question, 'How badly is he hurt?'

'Well, it's not good – he's still unconscious.'

Alive, then. I slowed my breathing down and tried to sort out my thinking.

'What happened?'

'Well, I don't know, really. I expect he decided to go for a walk or something. I have no idea why he left the lodgings. He might have been going out with one of the other residents, you know.'

'Yes, but, how did he actually get hurt?'

'Oh, didn't I say. I thought I did. He was run over – some hit-and-run driver going too fast round those back lanes, I think.'

'And when was the accident?'

'Last night. I had a call from the warden about 9.45, that's what I call flexi-hours, when they can call you up at any old time and expect you to jump up from what you're doing and rush in. I was really tired last night, it was the last thing I needed to have to hurry up to the hospital all because someone was too careless to look before he stepped off the pavement.'

I was bristling now, struggling to keep calm. This woman always seemed to rub me up the wrong way. I interrupted her.

'So obviously he had a head injury. Is anything else hurt?'

'Well, it's his shoulder and left side that took the worst battering, I think, but he was thrown in the air and cracked his head on the pavement.'

I'd seen it on the 'speed kills' adverts – people tossed like rag dolls and landing with a crunch.

'What hit him?'

'A white van – travelling too fast round those narrow streets, of course.'

Ms Hills started to talk about the dangers of men in white vans. I was thinking about Johnny lying motionless in a hospital bed. Even as I thought of Johnny, I struggled with the image of Jamie – the helplessness as Ella and I had sat at his bedside. Ms Hills was still talking. I tried to concentrate.

'Dr Lewis, Mike, are you still there? I can't hear you.'

'Sorry, Shirley, lost you for a moment there. Can you let me know if there's any change?'

'I'm not sure if I can stay here today, Mike. One of my other lads has to see his barrister. I'll leave your number with the sister on critical care.'

When I had put the phone down, I realised what I had done. I had become the named contact for an asylum seeker. I wasn't sure it was professional. That was the problem with this lad – it was very easy to cross boundaries and end up looking after him. Just like Anita, holding his hand and comforting him in the gallery, I had become part of his life. I found myself looking in my diary to see if I could move any patients so that I could get to the hospital ready for if or when Johnny woke up. It was going to be really difficult, and I wasn't sure it was in my job description. I decided to phone Anita.

When I told her what had happened there was silence while she took it in. Then she spoke.

'What will he think is happening when he comes round? The poor boy, as if life isn't difficult enough for him at the moment. Someone he knows should be with him. I'd have thought Shirley would make it a priority to be there.'

'Evidently not. Or perhaps she's got too many priorities. Anyway, the sister has my number to ring when he comes round.'

'I think you ought to be there, Mike, if you can. I know it's unusual, but this could be very traumatic for him.'

I had been worried she might say something like this. It made sense. But hospital! I had never liked hospitals before Jamie's illness, but now, well, even the thought of them seemed to pull up a little more of the horror of watching Jamie die. I shivered as I tried to shake off the memories. I couldn't tell Anita about all that, though. Too intimate. I'd have to go and cope with it.

It didn't take long to organise. Rachel, being the efficient secretary she was, sorted it all out for me with scarcely a raise of her well-sculpted eyebrows. She even ordered a cab to take me round to the Royal London.

'That'll be on expenses, Mike. Claim it back. I'm sure it will be fine.'

I smiled. Rachel was a law unto herself at the best of times, but with the boss off sick she seemed to rise into his position. But who else was there? Me, I supposed. I was the most senior practitioner in his absence, yet until that moment it hadn't occurred to me that I was, in effect, managing the whole show at the moment. No wonder a secretary had taken charge.

I had plenty of time to think about this more on the way to the hospital. Tantalisingly close, in Whitechapel Road itself, the traffic was at a standstill. The cab driver had been pretty good at whipping through all the back ways up to now, but we were too close for any shortcuts to be advantageous. By the time we were jammed up, my thoughts had returned to Jamie. I remembered watching him lose consciousness and gradually slip away from us. Not dramatic, not sudden, but heartbreakingly silent as he lost his tenuous grip on life. Ella drew on her belief in God – she had held Jamie's hand and talked to him about better places, no more pain, and the hope of a life to come. I felt disorientated, barren, confused. Those same feelings seemed to be creeping up on me now. I had to take hold of myself.

There didn't seem much point in sitting in a traffic jam, so I paid the fare and nipped across the bus lane to the pavement. Walking was much quicker.

It was a beautiful day – too good, perhaps, for being confined to the city. Far too good to be confined to bed.

When I reached the hospital it didn't take long to reach Level 2. I had to interrupt the three nurses on the desk, who were in mid-gossip, by the look of it. I felt pretty foolish as I explained who I was. All three turned to look at me, but it was the youngest of the three, a tall brunette who addressed me, in an Australian accent, 'Why does he need a psychologist?'

'Good question,' I thought.

'Um, well, strictly speaking, he doesn't. But he has no next-of-kin that we know of, so he'll have to rely on the professionals to explain what happened to him when he comes round – or has he come round already?'

'I don't think I will be answering any questions until I've seen your identity card.'

She looked at the slightly out-of-date photo on my card and gave me the same disinterested but judgemental look that customs always give. She was obviously satisfied it was me.

'Thank you, Dr Lewis. I'm afraid we're having to be a bit careful with Johnny Two; we've been turning reporters away. I'll show you where he is.'

As I put it back in my pocket, I wondered how much my identity card was worth at the moment. I felt sure almost any male reporter could take on that fuzzy likeness with a false red beard.

I followed the Australian nurse to a side room, where Johnny was the sole occupant. He was surrounded by the hospital paraphernalia of tubes and wires that I had become used to when Jamie was so ill. Johnny's black hands contrasted startlingly with the white sheets they rested on – he was so still that I thought I was too late. I strained to hear his breathing as I watched him – I heard nothing but noticed the slight rise and fall of his chest.

The tall nurse bustled around the room, moving a chair to the bedside, then straightening the already straight sheets and checking the monitor. She seemed reluctant to leave the room, unsure of what to do.

'If you leave me with him, that will be fine. I'll call you if I need you,' I told her.

Alone with him, I moved the chair closer to the bed. I reached out to touch his hand, then thought I'd better not. I said his name a few times; well, his given name: 'Johnny, Johnny. Hello, Johnny.' No response. Johnny's faint rising breaths and the pips from the monitor were the only noises in the room. Outside I could hear the usual street sounds and the occasional ambulance. I remembered sitting with my son, after he had died, holding his hands while my brain screeched anger at the ordinariness of life outside. But even while I had been sitting there the anger had subsided. Ella, on the other side of the bed, had begun to murmur.

'Jamie – it's over – you're safe now – you're out of pain, my darling – out of pain – you're safe – my darling...'

I had wrapped my arms around her after a while, as much to stop her constant mantra as to comfort her. We were close in that room – Jamie, Ella and I. We had fallen asleep with Jamie, then been awoken by the nurse, who gently told us it was time to leave him. We had both kissed him. I had felt strong and together as I left that room, with my arm round Ella's slightly shaking shoulders. My control had lasted a mere five days.

But here, now, what should a psychologist do in such a circumstance? What could I do but sit here and look at Johnny? Maybe he could hear me. He probably wouldn't understand if he did hear. I could talk about anything or everything.

I sat there for a few minutes, thinking and remembering. Then, in a faltering voice, I heard myself telling him about my son, Jamie.

10

'You'd have liked my son. He was a bit like you, in some ways. It's something about your determination and the fact that you've got to this country somehow. The fighting spirit.'

I looked at Johnny. The steady blink of green light from the monitor reflected off his dark skin. I shuddered. This was too familiar, too uncomfortable. I decided I had better keep talking.

'He was pretty special, my kid. Ella and I both loved him intensely right from the start. He had black hair when he was born; it was so long that the midwife joked that he'd have to be booked into a barber's straightaway. He had long dark lashes, far too extravagant for a boy! He would pull his eyes open a chink and look at us, then close them, looking satisfied. I can remember telling Ella he looked happy right from the start and her saying he'd be screaming in a minute if I didn't put him down and let him have some sleep. But as soon as I put him in the Perspex cot, she picked him up, and laid back on the mound of pillows, her hair splayed out behind her and our baby resting his head on her swollen breast as he dropped into sleep.'

Johnny hadn't moved. A white sheet was tucked in tightly across him, as if to stop him from getting away. I scarcely paused. 'I think we spoilt him. I used to rush home from work in order to be with him, and with Ella, of course. We were such a happy family. I would bath him every night and read him stories, right from when he was really tiny. He loved that bear hunt one – oh, you won't know it – one where a family hunt for a bear and become frightened and slosh through mud and snow on their way back. It was his favourite. I've still got it now, although he had grown out of it before he became ill.'

I became aware that I was shaking my head and biting at my lip. It took me a moment or two to start talking again. I pulled my thoughts back to Jamie as a baby.

'He was a perfect baby. He could be really funny. Ella and I laughed a lot together in those days. Jamie was interested in everything – pulling my father's nose and hair and, of course, my beard. Trying to reach things off the table if one of us had him on our lap at mealtimes – we'd spend the whole meal playing chess with crockery and spoons. One day he discovered he could pull the tablecloth. We didn't notice at first, but we certainly knew once the first plate crashed to the floor.

'He was so much fun when he started to walk. He would toddle with a wobble, but run nearly straight. He loved balls from the start. We have a video of him with a big bouncy ball. He toddles towards it, then gets his balance on one foot to kick it as hard as he could. It only moves a metre or so, but he goes into fits of giggles, with his chubby hands up to his mouth.'

I paused, wondering which of us now had the video. Maybe it was still in one of the boxes I hadn't unpacked, or perhaps Ella had it. I had forgotten all about it but now I wanted to watch it again. I wondered whether he would have been a footballer.

Nothing was changing with Johnny. The monitor carried on bleeping in its rhythmic monotony. I could hear voices from next door – people speaking quietly, perhaps to someone in the same state as Johnny. I couldn't make out their words. I hoped no one could hear what I was saying, but somehow I couldn't stop.

'You couldn't keep him still then – he'd be climbing on the furniture and jumping. He loved to hide and leap out at you as if you couldn't see his bottom sticking out from behind a door, or under a table.

'When he started playgroup, he was fine. He got a bit tired, but they all do, don't they? I can remember several times when he was fast asleep in the book corner when I went to collect him. He hardly woke as I carried him out to the car, but nuzzled sleepily against me and finished his nap when we arrived home. One day, when he was four, one of the playgroup leaders took me to one side when I went to collect him.

'"We've had trouble keeping Jamie awake today. It's not the first time – he is often very, very sleepy. What time does he go to bed?"

'It took only a few days from there before we were seeing the paediatrician. Then it was blood tests, and scans and a short stay in hospital to try to find out what was happening. He coped with that better than we did, really. He had his favourite toys on the ward and by the second day he would tell the nurses how to take his blood pressure or listen to his heart.

'The paediatrician who told us the diagnosis was really lovely – a softly-spoken person. There were tears in her eyes when she gave us the bad news. Nothing she could say could soften the blow.'

I paused, hearing footsteps in the corridor. I listened as they passed the door and all that was left in the silence was the gentle sound of Johnny's breathing and the regular bleep from the monitor.

'It took us several days to be able to tell anyone we knew. My father took it the hardest. He was already frail and went into a sharp decline. He died shortly after Jamie – I think the strain was too much. But in those early days, Ella's mother appeared and hugged us a lot. She did all our washing and baked more cakes than we could eat. Maybe she was all that held us together.

'Jamie started his treatment straightaway. We had to go to Great Ormond Street for that. Walking onto the oncology ward for the first time was horrendous. All those children with no hair, looking so ill. Nothing prepares you for that.

'Jamie was incredible. He did scream a few times at first when they gave him injections or inserted the canula, but mostly he accepted it. We tried to explain. I said, "You're very, very sick, Jamie. So you're going to have some really strong medicine go into your arm to kill the germs that are in your body. It will make you feel poorly for a while, but that's just the medicine fighting the germs. You'll feel better later."

'He trusted me, that was the awful thing. He believed me when I said he'd get better. He still thought that when he reacted to the chemo. He was very sick, had awful diarrhoea, and his hair fell out. Soon after his fifth birthday, I can remember him asking me, "Daddy, will the medicine going into my arm make me all better, so that I can play with my new football?" I ignored all the statistics and probabilities we had been given, and reassured him. "Yes, my son, you will get better. We will go to the park and play lots of games."

'I told him a lie. Eighteen months, yes, eighteen months the treatment took. He would be on a drip for two hours every week. It didn't hurt too much while it was happening, but afterwards he was really sick for days. He'd just begin to feel a bit better and it would be time for the next dose.

'I can't forgive myself for telling him a lie. We had to believe he would recover, Ella and I, because that's the only way we could let him go through it. I wish we'd let him die sooner, with less pain. I wish I had never lied to him.'

There had been no response from Johnny. I dropped my head in my hands. This was a mistake, talking to Johnny. I brushed the tears off my face. Some of them had begun to soak into my beard, so I gave that a quick wipe on my sleeve as well. I looked around for a tissue. It was then that I became aware that there was someone stood in the doorway. She jumped guiltily when I turned towards her. In the subdued light, I thought it was Ella.

'Are you all right, Mike?'

Anita's bubbly voice was nothing like Ella's. She hadn't come into the room, but stood, waiting.

'Ah, yes, fine, thanks. A bit of hay fever, or allergy to something, I should think.' I needed to blow my nose, but settled for a large sniff instead.

'My patient cancelled so I thought I'd keep you company.'

I tried to put on a professional face.

'Well, that's very helpful. There's been absolutely no change in Johnny. I was about to go and have a coffee,' I said.

'Good idea. I'll come with you and we could come back in twenty minutes or so to see if there's any change. I'll tell the nurse, so that she can find us if she needs to.'

Anita walked off towards the nurses' station.

I glanced at Johnny. It was true. I hadn't seen him stir, and yet he didn't seem to be lying in quite the same position. I wasn't sure, though. I touched his dark hand.

'I'll be back soon, Johnny. In about twenty minutes,' I said, more as a promise to myself than to him. I could have done with some time on my own, really, to compose myself.

It was quite a walk down long, bleak corridors to the restaurant. Anita and I talked brightly and earnestly about the need for a decent eating place at work and how much better we'd work as a team if there was one. The restaurant didn't look too special when we reached it, though. Along with a badly spelled menu stuck on a glass partition by the entrance, there was a large sign saying 'No nightclothes' and another stating 'No greens'. I smiled, noticing the smell of cabbage and wondering how many patients would recognise the reference to surgical gowns.

'Penny for them,' said Anita.

I pointed out the sign, and Anita's rippling laugh lifted the moment further. I felt back on safe ground, my feelings under cover again with Anita diverted to thinking about something else. Not for long, though. The restaurant was nearly empty and we were served immediately. As soon as we had placed our apologies for cappuccinos on a little Formica table, perching our posteriors on solid metal chairs, she switched mood again. I hate it when women do that.

'I'm sorry, Mike, I was there for a few minutes before you realised I was in the room. I heard some of the things you were saying to Johnny. I wasn't sure if I should interrupt.'

'Oh, you could have done. I was just talking about anything, really. I thought he ought to hear the spoken word.'

'I agree. But I don't think anyone at work realised how awful it must have been for you when Jamie was so ill. Of course, when he... he didn't make it, we understood how you felt to some extent then. You've done well to keep things together at work, Mike.'

She was smiling, and when she briefly touched my arm, it was all I could do to stop myself from crying again. I shrugged.

'Well, you have to cope with what life throws at you, don't you?'

Anita raised one quizzical eyebrow, as she watched me open a sugar sachet and slowly stir it into the cappuccino. I don't usually bother with sugar and I never have frothy drinks. I tried to reassure Anita.

'I am OK, you know.'

She nodded. 'Of course, but have you got anyone to talk to about all of this?'

'I'm not sure I need anyone. I keep going, somehow.'

I knew I wasn't making sense. I knew perfectly well that there are some things you need to talk about.

'OK, Mike. But if you need anyone, I'm here. Or I'm sure there are others at work who would be only too willing to help, if you would prefer. But please, don't keep it all bottled up.'

I shrugged again. What do you say to that? But I felt annoyed that my privacy had been so badly invaded.

I stood, picking up my hardly touched drink, ready to return it to the kitchen trolley.

'Come on,' I said. 'It's more than fifteen minutes now and I said we'd be back in twenty.'

11

Once back in Johnny's room, Anita and I sat silently on opposite sides of the bed. I could see no change in Johnny, but it looked as if someone had been in the room. His notes on the clipboard at the end of the bed had been moved along and his sheets seemed to be a bit more loosely tucked in.

'How's work at the moment, Mike? Are you overloaded with cases?'

I tried to answer what I saw as a totally unnecessary question. Inappropriate, too, considering Johnny was a 'case'.

'Oh, you know how it is, always busy.'

There was another silence, during which we both looked at Johnny and I cleared my throat twice, ready to say something, but somehow not saying anything. Anita tried again.

'What films do you like, Mike? Are you into spy thrillers?'

I looked at her blankly. I couldn't think of anything I had seen apart from something I'd watched with Jamie about some silly creature who hated Christmas – but it didn't seem quite the thing to be discussing with Anita.

Anyway, thinking about it started a whole new train of thought about Jamie and his Christmases.

'I can't remember when I last watched a film.'

Anita shot me a quick glance. I vaguely wondered if I had upset her, but wasn't sure what else I could have said. Anita gave up trying to talk to me and diverted her conversation to the uncomprehending, unconscious boy.

'When you're better, Johnny, it would be good if we have a go at using pastels. I expect you'd enjoy that. They can be a bit messy, though. I can remember emerging from one session with a patient and going straight into a management meeting only to be told at the end that I had a blue nose!'

I looked at her nose. It was absolutely straight – a blueprint for a plastic surgeon. Perfect. I'd never noticed it before. She glanced at me, aware of my gaze.

'What is it?' she asked.

'Oh, nothing, I was imagining the blue nose!'

That rippling laugh again. Lighting up her face and lifting the mood in the room. I thought I saw Johnny stir in response.

'Is he waking up?' I asked Anita.

She leaned close over him, listening to his shallow breathing. As she sat up straighter, she took his hand, stroking it gently.

'I don't know, Mike. I can't tell. Is he kept sedated at the moment, or are they expecting him to come round? Have they told you anything about his condition?'

We both looked at Johnny. If it wasn't for his shallow breathing and the blinking monitor, he could have been dead.

I suddenly felt rather foolish. Here I was, a psychologist on a hospital ward, and I was behaving like a visitor. I bluffed, 'There wasn't really anyone around and I didn't see his notes. I'll go and see if there's a doctor to talk to now.'

There were two nurses on the desk, having a coffee and chatting together quietly. I didn't recognise either of them, so maybe there had been a shift change. I was ignored by them for just about long enough for me to begin to get irritated. I said, 'Excuse me.' Two heads, one blonde and one brunette, were slowly turned towards me, the intruder in their space. I assumed my professional persona. Waving my badge, I told them I was Johnny's psychologist. They nodded in unison.

'I need to have some idea about prognosis,' I explained, 'which includes knowing his drug regime at present. If he's likely to remain heavily sedated for the next twenty-four hours or so, then my time is better spent elsewhere. Perhaps I could see his medical notes? Then I shall need to talk to the doctor on call.'

One of the nurses reached into the trolley behind her, drawing out a thin new buff file.

'Here are the notes, Dr Lewis. Would you like me to page Dr Lester now?'

'Thank you, that would be most helpful.'

I leaned against the counter. As I opened the file I hoped I would be able to understand the medical jargon. I needn't have worried. There was very little in the notes. There was no mention that he could not speak, although he was described as a 'juvenile asylum seeker, age unknown'. The doctors admitting him in Accident and Emergency had drawn a good diagram showing his injuries. They had identified a broken collarbone, a broken femur and a head injury. He had been to surgery to set his leg and from the brief scribbles from the surgeon, it looked as if his operation had been a success.

I couldn't see what had happened about his collarbone and was mystified about the head injury. The hand-drawn sketch let me down at this point because the arrow to the head was too vague to identify the site of the injury and the scribble denoting its whereabouts was unreadable – at least by me.

There was nothing in the notes to say he had been seen by a psychologist. I flipped back through the file to the admission details and found there were no clues as to my identity there, either. Shirley's name was in the box marked 'next of kin' with SW beside it. My name was scrawled in the father's box – 'Mike 0207 495851 other contact'. Really – it wasn't good enough. I borrowed a pen from the nurses and crossed out the word 'Father', then wrote clearly above the box, 'Professional Contact'. Then I added my own version of my relationship to Johnny. 'Dr Michael Lewis, clinical psychologist, Department of Psychology, Adult Mental Health'.

I turned to the history sheets and started an entry. Under the heading 'Clinical Psychology' I began to write a few notes about Johnny's background and reasons for being referred to me. Then I added: 'In my opinion, Johnny has undergone severe traumatic experiences and is suffering from post-traumatic stress disorder. As with all PTSD patients, he may be retraumatised by hospital procedures.'

My notes were becoming quite expansive as I wrote how he might not have enough English to be of any use, but that his understanding of some simple Spanish could be helpful in communicating with him. He was unable to respond in any language. I wasn't sure what to write next. I remembered that in the days when I worked on a children's ward I had always ended with a plan. What plan did I have? I couldn't really do any therapy with him here. Maybe the plan would be to observe and be a resource to the hospital staff if he reacted badly once he woke up?

While I was giving this some thought, the doctor walked down the corridor and joined me, leaning on the counter at the nurses' station. He looked too young and tired to know anything, with a two-day stubble and black rings round his eyes. He had shiny wavy black hair, which he kept touching as he spoke. Not effeminate, but vain.

'How can I help you, Dr Lewis?' His well-educated voice had a languorous tone.

'Perhaps you can tell me more about Johnny's injuries, and I can fill you in with the little bit of background I know.'

Dr Lester took the file from me. 'Ah yes, he's the illegal immigrant, isn't he?'

'The asylum seeker, yes. In my opinion he has fled from at least one traumatic experience.'

The doctor raised his eyes from the file, smoothing his hair back.

'Sorry, asylum seeker it is, then. Anyway, your client has had a very nasty knock on the back of his head. Cracked his head on the pavement as he landed. There was some internal bleeding which has now stopped, so we are in a bit of a waiting game over that one.'

I nodded, that made sense to me. The doctor took the notes.

'There was something else. Ah yes, his right femur needed pinning, which is done, and there's a hairline crack to his collar bone. That will settle on its own, with rest. The bruising down his arm is all surface, no other broken bones. He's lucky, really.' I asked more about the site of his head injury. It was at the base of his skull and the bleeding had been confined to that area. I desperately tried to remember what I had learned on my training about the sites of injuries.

I asked him, 'Any brain damage? What do you think his prognosis is?'

He furrowed his brows and spoke slowly. 'Well, as you probably know, every case is different. The X-ray showed the bleeding to be relatively confined, but we don't know if there was impact damage. The neurologist will see him, of course, and then he might have some neuro-psych testing.'

'You know he can't talk?'

'What do you mean, because of the language barrier?'

'No, he's mute. It's probably a reaction to his trauma. Neuro-psychological testing will be very difficult.'

We had a brief discussion about the ways of assessing whether there had been any damage. There were the physical tests, of course, with his reflexes etc. The only other way was to look at how he had reacted before and compare it with his reactions now. I briefly told him about the work Anita had been doing with him and how that could be repeated, as a rather loose assessment.

'She's here, as a matter of fact. Sitting with Johnny. Do you want to speak to her?'

Again that pulling together of his brows and a rather strange stare. What was he thinking about us? I continued, 'Although perhaps we are getting ahead of ourselves here. We shall have to have a case discussion once he is a little better and decide on the way forward. Perhaps you could emphasise our involvement to Johnny's consultant.'

Wrong wording, but too late to change it. The young doctor mumbled about the obvious need to keep communications going between all professionals who were working with Johnny, and was then saved by his bleep. He walked away from me while he was still talking and picked up the phone from the wall. He turned his back on me as I heard him say, into the phone, 'Dr Lester – you paged me?'

I picked up the discarded file and continued my notes.

'Please keep good communication between myself and Anita Goodwin, art therapist. We have both been working with Johnny. Neuro-psych assessments will be difficult because of Johnny's inability to speak so may have to rely on previous information collected by those who have been working with him pre-accident.'

I returned the file to the nurse and went to tell Anita that I was going back to the office.

12

The following few days became peppered with visits to Johnny. I organised my time to find a morning or afternoon gap when I marched purposefully onto the ward with my briefcase and diary and spent an hour with him. For each visit, I was careful to have his psychology file with me and to talk some psychology with the nurses. By day four post-accident, the lack of informative medical notes in the file was causing me to become concerned. I leaned against the counter by the nurses' station and thumbed backwards and forwards through the file to make sure I hadn't missed an X-ray, or a letter to a specialist, that might make it clear that someone was sharing my concerns.

'Is there a doctor around, who knows Johnny's case?' I asked the brunette nurse.

She turned and pointed to a young man, a little way down the corridor. He was in earnest conversation with the blonde nurse, who was leaning with her back against the wall, looking up at him. They laughed.

'Perhaps you could ask him if he is free to talk to me.' The nurse smiled.

'I'll fetch him,' she said.

The junior doctor, anonymous, badgeless, strolled towards me. He could have been anyone.

'Hi there, I'm Jed, I'm looking after Johnny. What can I do for you?'

'I'm the psychologist who was working with Johnny, pre-accident.' I tipped my badge towards him as I spoke. 'I need to know what the prognosis is now. His condition doesn't seem to have changed much in the four days since his accident.'

Jed shrugged. 'Not sure, really, but he'll be examined during today's ward round to see if there's any more response.'

'More? There has been some, then?' I tried to keep sounding professional, not too involved.

'Oh yes, that social worker – what's her name? Sherelee? She said he'd opened his eyes for a few minutes when she was with him yesterday. In the nurses' observation record, I notice they had seen the same for a few minutes in the night. I think he's on his way back to us. He does seem to be having a few fits, though – it may be the result of the head injury.'

Trust Shirley not to have told me. She involved me to the extent that all the rest of my patients were shuffled about to make space for this one, and put me on the form as his father, and yet didn't bother to tell me he had shown signs of coming round or had had fits.

I thanked Jed, who immediately walked back to the nurse, and I went to Johnny's room.

Johnny lay there, looking a little more comfortable than when I saw him the day before. He was still lying virtually flat – probably because of his damaged collarbone – but he had his arms placed differently. He looked more natural. Even as I looked at him, I could see his fingers on his right hand were stretching and relaxing a little against the stiff white sheet.

I moved the upright chair as close to the bed as possible and sat watching my client. I wondered if he could hear me today. I leaned over him and spoke carefully.

'Johnny, are you awake? It's me, Mike, your bearded psychologist, here.'

I searched his face for any sign that he heard me. His eyes were closed, his long black lashes slightly moving. His thick lips twitched a little at the corners, then his body suddenly convulsed. He settled again, totally still apart from the rise of his body as he breathed. I noticed his breathing sounded a little stronger. Some good, hopeful signs, but the fitting was a worry. For lack of anything else to do, I opened my psychology notes and wrote a brief description of his state to add to all the others. I started positively with the phrase 'Some good changes noted'. As I wrote, I wondered if I was clutching at straws and whether he would make it. These little tiny signs of life did not amount to much, the convulsions could be a sign of brain damage and I was fully aware that without the tubes and intravenous feeding he would probably have died by now. Was it possible that he had not had the right treatment? Hadn't I read somewhere that the very first injury to receive attention should be the head injury? I wondered what the huge bandage round his head was covering up. I wasn't sure whether he had received any surgery – I thought all that had happened was an X-ray. I began to make a list of items to discuss with the doctor.

When it came to it, my list was more or less forgotten. I hardly had time to stand up when the consultant marched into the room with an entourage of mostly young people, probably junior doctors or medical students. They were talking quietly to each other, while the consultant walked up to the end of the bed and peered across at Johnny. I opened my own file as I stepped back out of the way, joining the crowd.

I recognised Dr Lester, who cleared his throat and waited for the group to quieten before he gave a summary of Johnny's history and condition, with a slight nod to me as he mentioned my involvement. The consultant did not even look my way, but launched into a question and answer game about the injuries with the poor students, who were by now all standing looking interested and focused on the consultant. Through the answers they were giving, I did discover that one possible prognosis from Johnny's head injury was blindness. No one mentioned that he was beginning to regain consciousness, or that he seemed to be having fits. Everyone was turning to go. I stepped forward from the group and addressed the consultant.

'There have been signs that Johnny Two is regaining consciousness. What can we expect to see from now on?'

'It's the psychologist, Dr Lewis,' explained Dr Lester again. Then he introduced the consultant as Mr Smeedson.

The consultant smiled and extended his hand towards me. 'Ah, pleased to meet you, Lewis. Yes, yes, more positive now. There may be a good recovery, although he might need surgery depending on the extent of the damage.' He turned away. I was not ready to be dismissed.

'At what stage can you determine his need for surgery?'

'We will review the position – he will need more X-rays at some time.'

He turned away again, but I continued.

'I have observed the fitting. May I suggest that he is more fully assessed at the first opportunity?'

Mr Smeedson was not smiling when he turned round again.

'Are you employed as his advocate, Dr Lewis, or his psychologist, or even medical adviser?'

'I am employed to work with him and prepare a court report for immigration. This will include a section on his progress in this country and how he has been provided for since his arrival. I therefore need to be able to report on all aspects of his care, and it would be negligent of me not to discuss the case with you.'

'Rest assured, Dr Lewis, that your dear client is in the very best hands.'

'Thank you for that assurance, doctor. I trust we can both work together for the best outcome for this young man.'

There was a small moan, which we both heard. The two students closest to Johnny stepped even closer to him, as our collective attention was drawn to him. But again he lay quietly.

'I think your client is trying to tell us something, Dr Lewis,' said the consultant, smiling once again. I smiled back and offered a hand. The one that shook mine was firm and confident.

'I look forward to seeing those X-rays,' I said.

Mr Smeedson gave a slight nod before walking out of the room, his followers dropping into file behind him, to pass through the doorway.

In the restored quiet, I listened to the bleep of the monitor and Johnny's breathing for a moment before I sat down. My legs felt as if they would not hold me. I looked at Johnny.

'Well, boy, I did my best. Maybe I am your advocate. If so, I hope I'm up to the job.'

He lay still and quiet.

13

A few days later, I visited again after the Tuesday morning supervision with Georgina. Johnny's condition had begun to improve.

When I walked into his room, I could see immediately that Johnny was more alert, although he was still sedated. He was lying flat on his back, but as I moved the chair close his eyes turned towards me and he recognised me with a weak smile. I grinned back, delighted.

'You're looking good, Johnny.'

Johnny tried another smile and closed his eyes.

I sat down by the side of the bed and opened up the medical notes. From the clustered, short scribbled comments, I could see that the X-ray of his head revealed that some of the swelling had reduced and his fits had subsided. At the end of the entries of the junior doctors was a new entry – a beautifully scripted neat section clearly written in fountain pen. Even before I glanced at the signature, I knew it must be Mr Smeedson's entry. Following a description of Johnny's present condition, one sentence had been underlined: 'In view of patient's improvement, present indications are that risk of surgery exacerbating patient's condition mitigates against planned procedure.'

He had then listed his reasons and suggested a referral to the neuro team for rehabilitation.

So Johnny wouldn't be having surgery after all. I felt strangely relieved, even though it was not clear what damage had been done. I glanced up from the notes. Johnny's eyes were half-closed – he might have been dozing again. I wondered what he understood about where he was and what was happening to him now. Did he even remember the accident? I thought for a moment and decided he had the same right to understand what happened as anyone else would, even though it would be difficult to explain. It might even retraumatise this already fragile boy, so it would have to be done very slowly and carefully. I didn't know what he had been told already and decided to check with the nurses first.

The nurses on the station were busy – this time filling in forms – but eventually I managed to speak to the Australian brunette. She had been on duty the first time that I came. I looked for her name on her badge.

'Excuse me, Kelly. I need to talk to you about my patient, Johnny Two. Are you his named nurse?'

'Well, yes, I suppose I am.' She turned back to her form-filling.

She supposed she was? Surely the girl knew? I reckoned I'd called her 'named nurse' when she preferred to be called something else – 'key worker', perhaps.

I let her finish the line she was writing, then carried on as if I hadn't noticed her indifference.

'Has anyone tried to talk to him about the accident?'

She looked up and put down her pen. 'Oh no, I couldn't really tell him anything because he doesn't understand, does he?'

'We're not sure how much he does understand. But I wondered if you knew whether anyone had tried to talk to him about it?'

'Well, the doctors haven't. But his social worker might have tried. She was speaking in some foreign language last time she was here.'

Shirley! I felt really pleased – she'd been trying out some Spanish with him.

The nurse didn't seem terribly sure that I could use the nurses' phone to ring the social worker, but I showed my badge once more and convinced her of my credentials. When I reached her on her mobile, Shirley was out and about with one of her other clients.

'Who? Sorry, can't hear for the traffic. Who? Oh, it's you, Mike.'

I asked her about how much she had managed to communicate with Johnny and whether she had talked about the accident.

'Yes, well I did try a bit of Spanish. Made him smile, which was nice. I'm not sure he understood everything I was trying to say.'

'It was a good idea to try.'

'Yes, I should have tried it before but, you know, I never felt safe round him. But, in answer to your question, no, I didn't tell him about the accident, I wasn't sure I should. Anyway my Spanish is a bit basic.'

And mine was non-existent. I decided that once he was out of hospital, I'd organise a Spanish translator and see how much he knew and whether that would be a way of working with him. As I walked back to his room, I remembered that immigration had tried him with many languages. Surely they included Spanish? Perhaps his level of understanding was rather rudimentary, or perhaps they had not realised he could not answer back when they were looking for a response.

When I went back into his room, Johnny opened his eyes again. I tore a history sheet out of the notes and, resting on the file, I drew a van and a stick figure with tight curly hair by a building. I showed it to Johnny, watching for his reaction. That was disappointing – nothing. I put a box round it and then drew the next picture. This time the van was right near the figure that represented him and in a third picture the van was right over the prostrate cartoon figure of Johnny. I knew what I was doing now, so before showing him I completed the whole cartoon strip – with Johnny being taken on a stretcher into an ambulance and coming to the hospital, and then one with him here in the bed, first with closed eyes and then with open.

I held the series of pictures in front of Johnny. His took it from me, holding his arm high and turning the history sheet in front of him. He may have had trouble focusing on it, because he moved it backwards and forwards, turning it this way and that. For a while he held it still, appearing to be looking at my pictures in sequence. Then he dropped his arm back down on the bed and closed his eyes. I went to take the paper from him, but he held it tight – the knuckles of his fingers white against the surrounding dark skin.

I sat by him for a few minutes more, but he didn't open his eyes again. His breath began to slow and even out as he fell asleep. I glanced at my watch – I was late for an appointment. Reluctantly, I decided I must go. Leaving the notes on the nurse's station as I passed, I hurried out of the hushed hospital and back into the busy real world as I pushed through the crowds and onto the Tube to make the journey back to the office.

By the time I arrived back in the Psychology Department, I was half an hour late for Mrs Bayton's appointment. One of the secretaries had made her a cup of tea and found her some not too out-of-date magazines. As I passed through the waiting area, I invited her to follow me into my office. As she plonked herself down on one of the chairs, I realised that I still had dirty coffee cups around the room and the coffee table was covered in crumbs. Strangely, the usually fastidious Mrs B didn't seem to notice.

I was ready to apologise, but Mrs B spoke first.

'I've been spiralling up, doctor. Not quite there yet, but better!'

She produced an A4 ring binder out of a huge brown handbag, and began to show me her collection of spirals. She unclipped sheets of paper from the folder and started to spread some of them over the coffee table. I was astounded by the sheer number of them – how ever had she managed to do anything else? I started to look through them. Mrs Bayton sat back in her chair, smiling – perhaps even smirking. The spirals were good, she had written her worrying thoughts neatly along the lines of each negative one and the corresponding positive was strong and clear. I put aside two I particularly liked.

'You've done well. You have really taken this idea on board. I am enjoying reading them, especially this one.' On the page I held was the negative statement: *I feel hot and uncomfortable when I think about walking down the road to the library. I have to take my books back because they are overdue. I am frightened that the librarian will be angry because they are late.* The corresponding positive one simply stated: *I have no need to be afraid of anyone, especially not a librarian. She deals with far worst offenders than I do. I am only very rarely overdue. I can easily return my books.*

I looked up at her. 'I see you are brilliant at this approach, but has it helped in practice?'

'Definitely, I am so much more confident, but,' she then turned to the back of the file. A smaller section, neatly numbered. 'These are the ones I'm stuck on, doctor.'

We spent half an hour going through a few examples, with Mrs B muttering 'of course' and 'why ever didn't I think of that before' as we found the positive for each downward spiral. The situations were ordinary humdrum tasks that went wrong. A tablecloth she washed that didn't lose the beetroot stains, a forgotten phone call to the plumber. All the negative spirals had the same element of self-blame. I was just about to point this out to her when she noticed herself.

'I wasn't thinking straight, was I? If I remember to imagine what a good friend would say, then I can work out the positives myself. Oh, look at this one – I was really exaggerating how awful it was to forget an item on my shopping list – wasn't that what we used to call catastrophising? My friend would just say, "Don't be such a nutter, making all that fuss, we all forget things!"'

I laughed, and tried to explain to her that calling herself a 'nutter' was rather counterproductive, but otherwise she was absolutely correct.

By the time we came to the point where we fixed the next appointment, it felt like there was very little to do.

'When would you like to come again?' I asked.

'Well, I don't know, doctor. For the first time I feel like I can manage without such regular appointments. Shall we leave it two months?'

'I shall be delighted to see you in two months – I am sure you will cope beautifully!'

After she'd gone, I couldn't help but shout 'Yes!' as I punched the air.

14

I had missed my lunch so I decided to go and buy a sandwich. As I left the building, I heard Anita call me. I turned to see her coming up the concrete stairs from her basement studio.

'I'm just off to see Johnny,' she said. 'Have you seen him today?'

I nodded, then opened the door for her as we walked together out of the building. As we went along the main road towards the shops and the Tube station, I started telling her about my visit. When I described my sketches about what happened to him, she laughed.

'I thought psychologists were always telling people they couldn't read their minds,' she said

'What do you mean?'

She stopped and swung her shoulder bag round to reach into it for her sketchpad. Flicking through the pages she came to the ones she wanted to show me. Over a few pages was a very beautiful series of pictures showing Johnny's accident and arrival at the hospital. Each drawing was intricate and detailed, with soft colours and hazy backgrounds. Her picture of Johnny had caught his likeness as had her final drawing of me sitting by the bed with my hand on his.

'You can't show him this. It looks so, so... unprofessional.'

'What do you mean? I was rather pleased with it,' she said, taking it back.

'No, the drawings are fantastic. Spot on. It's just that he ought not to know I was sitting there – and the hand, well, it's outside the guidelines.'

Anita's lips twitched and she raised her eyebrows. I turned to walk on but she took my arm and pulled me back to face her.

'Listen, Mike. It was perfectly OK that you touched his hand. You were communicating with him. No one will think there's anything wrong with that. But I'll tear it up if you want me to.'

I felt foolish. Maybe I was being a bit stuffy. But the drawing had captured my whole feelings at that moment when she had walked into the room and I had been talking to Johnny. How had she managed to convey such strong emotions in such a small sketch? She was some artist.

We reached Aldgate Underground and I realised I should have gone the other way. I hoped I could buy an edible sandwich at one of the kiosks.

'I'm going to grab something to eat, then I must get back,' I told Anita.

'I haven't eaten, either. Why don't we eat in the coffee shop on the corner, and, if we are careful about confidentiality, we can work out what to do with Johnny now he's more responsive.'

We crossed the road and went into the café with its brown leather-look seating. Between mouthfuls of French loaf with brie and salad, I told her more fully about

116

Johnny's condition, that he wouldn't be having an operation, and Shirley's attempts at speaking in Spanish. I asked her what she thought about getting an interpreter to assess his Spanish, in the first instance.

'How would they be able to do that?'

'I thought maybe if they had pictures of common objects then they could ask him to pick them out. The pictures could be more and more complex until we reached a point where he couldn't understand.'

'Where would the pictures come from? I suppose we could find a child's introduction to Spanish – one of those with the pictures and the vocabulary all around.'

I was glad she'd answered her own question – I hadn't thought that far ahead.

'Let's look in the bookshop now.'

Before I had a chance to answer, Anita grabbed her black coffee in its paper cup and began to move towards the glass door. I ate the last bite of my sandwich and followed her.

Shopping with Anita was not easy. She was a woman on a mission asking first one book shop assistant and then another until she tracked down the children's language books and was sure there were no others. They were pitifully few, but she found the Spanish ones and discarded all those without enough pictures. We were left with two – both of which reflected a child's world. Far too young for Johnny.

'These won't really do,' she said. 'We'll have to go to a bigger book shop or something.'

'There's a really good shop near the Westminster and Chelsea hospital, called Topsy's or something, it has loads of children's toys and books. I bet they have one there.'

As soon as I said it, the memories came back. This had been one of our favourite shops when Jamie was about four and I was working at the hospital. Ella would bring him to meet me sometimes and we would eat our packed lunch in the little gardens nearby and then have a good browse in an upmarket garden shop in Chelsea with Jamie having to sit on every garden seat and hide behind all the displayed bushes, and then his impatience would wear us down and we would set off down the road to the toyshop.

'Mike, are you listening? If you can remember what it's called I can find out if it's open when I've finished seeing Johnny, and nip round there.'

I pulled my mind back from the memory of Ella sitting on the beanbags with Jamie draped across her as she read to him, helping him choose between the three or four books he had picked up.

'Sorry, I can't for the moment. Topsy and Tina? No, that's the name of a book. Oh, maybe, I'm not sure.'

'Well, I'd better go now, anyway. I'll give you a ring later to see if you've remembered. Or you can ring me – I'll give you my number.'

She reached into her bag and tore the corner off a page of her sketchbook and scribbled her number down. It felt strange tucking it into my wallet, next to Jamie's photo. I had to remind myself that this was only a colleague's number, needed for work.

'I'd best go, too. I've got a trainee to supervise,' I said, glancing at my watch. I was going to be late again. Just one of those days.

When I got back to the office, Georgina was in the secretaries' room and the tenor of her voice sounded like she was having a moan. I walked in.

'Sorry I'm late, Georgina. Are you ready?'

She looked startled and uncomfortable. The conversation must have been about me, then. What had I done now? She gathered up her pile of files from the desk in front of her and followed me through to my office. She plonked the files onto my coffee table, took out one and, still standing, opened it. She looked at me with her chin slightly out and said, 'I've been leaving you messages, Mike, but you haven't replied.'

Why was it that when I started to feel I was getting things done, moving things forward, even, some measure of my own incompetency would leap up before me?

'Nothing worrying you, I hope.'

'Well, not really, sort of, yes there is. It's only that man who we decided should be taken over by you. He's started ringing to talk to me again.'

'I hope you haven't responded.'

'Well, that's the trouble – I answered the phone in the secretaries' office when they'd gone home the other day and it was him. He recognised my voice and asked me out. I refused, of course, but he said he'd wait for me.'

'What did he mean, "wait for you"?'

Georgina shuddered. She took a deep breath. 'I've been quite worried that he meant literally. So I've been bringing in packed lunches and leaving through the back entrance with Jane at the end of the day. But that's the reason why I haven't been able to go and see my agoraphobic lady, Lily Woodward. It's really difficult to organise someone to be with me all the time – even when I'm taking her out.'

'Sit down, Georgina; we need to talk this through.'

I was glad the anxious Mrs Bayton wasn't around for the next part of Georgina's supervision session. I really emphasised the risks and reinforced how wise she had been to keep well out of the way of what was obviously a stalker.

I summed up: 'Georgina, there is no positive slant to this situation, the man could be dangerous, we know that. You have been absolutely right to protect yourself. We need a plan.'

Georgina blew her nose loudly while I gained time, glancing through Miss Woodward's file. After all, that poor lady was a victim too – her psychology sessions had not materialised through no fault of her own.

I glanced up. Georgina was leaning forward. She looked at me now with steady, but slightly pink-rimmed eyes. I smiled. 'I think we have discovered the most suitable client for my observation of how you work. I shall have to come to all your sessions with Miss Woodward, and then take her over myself when you've finished your placement.'

Georgina sat back in the chair. She raised her shoulders, and then dropped them down. Her head moved from side to side as she released the tension in her back. 'That's such a relief to know I don't have to do those visits on my own. I shall be pleased to be observed!'

15

A few days later I woke with the strong impression that Ella was there, telling me to 'keep up the good work'. That phrase of hers; she used it all the time. When Jamie read his first reading book, when the doctors said they were getting on top of the leukaemia. It was like a refrain. She didn't say it in a stern, demanding way, but softly, with a smile. My hand crept across the pillow beside my own, even though I knew she wasn't there. Slowly, I pulled myself out of bed and wandered through to the kitchen to make myself a cup of tea, repeating a ritual for early mornings that Ella and I always had when we were together. I brought the steaming tea back to the bedroom, slipped back under the duvet, and sat there, propped on my pillows, thinking about her.

She'd been good fun. When we first met, it was her laughter that I heard as I sat on the grass talking to a bunch of my friends on a day-course from work. I turned to see where the gentle rolling sound came from and spotted her with other older students, her knees pulled up to her chin, hidden by a full, brightly coloured skirt. As I watched her, she glanced at me, still laughing. I could hardly keep my eyes away from her so as her group rose to go back into the college, I watched as she walked away, her long skirt blowing against her legs. When she turned and smiled I was on my feet in an instant, catching up with her to introduce myself. Over the following weeks we discovered so much we both liked such as *The Hitchhiker's Guide to the Galaxy* which led to long meandering discussions about the meaning of the universe.

Even then, Ella's faith was important to her; almost too important, from my angle. I was worried I didn't meet her criteria for a life partner because of my own weak and doubting beliefs. I started going to church with her and I loved the serious side of her. If faith is catching, then I caught it. We were a couple with God. Life felt good and I felt fulfilled.

We married, of course, because Ella would have it no other way. We carried on laughing and carried on loving. People thought we were the ideal couple. When we had rows, the making up was sweet, tender and beautiful. For four years we were content to have no children, but when she found out she was pregnant we celebrated with a Chinese takeaway that she brought up all over our new wool rug. She was sick throughout most of the pregnancy – but she smiled on through, totally delighted at God's gift of a child.

Thinking about her now made me aware of how much I'd lost. Not just Jamie, whom we both adored, but her. How could I let that happen? And I supposed I'd lost my faith as well. What did I believe in these days? Not a lot, really. I still believed that there was a God out there somewhere, but he no longer seemed personal or important. I wished I could tell Ella about this. She had been the only one I could talk to about spiritual matters.

Even once I was at work that day, back in my shabby office, I could not stop thinking about Ella. No longer was I angry and bitter when I thought about her. I missed her. And I felt ashamed. I had put her through a lot with my ranting and shouting after Jamie had died. She found a grief counsellor for herself and was using friends to help work things through, whereas I refused all help, saying that as a psychologist I knew about grief and I could cope. I thought back over the years and mentally contrasted my life then and now. Had I coped? No way. I was stuck in a flat that I rented on the spur of the moment and lived my life alone, surrounded by packing cases that I had only recently begun to empty.

I took a few breaths, told myself that at least I had a job where I could help other people and that I was improving now, and then walked out into the waiting area to collect my next patient. No one there. I walked into the general office and checked the message book by the secretary's desk to find that my client had cancelled. Also, there were a couple of scribbled lines from Anita in the book for all to see: 'Hi, Mike, have you remembered the name of that shop yet? A.' It looked like a personal note. I was aware that Rachel had stopped working on her computer and was watching me as I read it again. I dreaded to think what shop she thought Anita and I had been talking about. I made it clear:

'You don't happen to know the name of the big toyshop near the Brompton Hospital, do you? It has lots of children's books and we need one with a basic child's Spanish vocabulary for Johnny Two.'

Rachel looked puzzled for a moment. 'It's something like Rosie and Terry, I think.'

'I remember, it's Topsy and Terry. Thanks Rachel.'

I borrowed a phone book and looked it up. Then, back in my room, I rang Anita with the number.

She laughed. 'You were nearly right with Topsy and Tina. What a funny name for a shop. If you're happy to leave the choice with me, I can get over there at lunchtime to see what they've got. If I'm not sure, I can always ring you. Do you have any clients at lunchtime?'

Feeling cornered, I told her when I'd be free and cut the phone call short, explaining I had a lot of admin to do. I did, the desk was overcome with papers and notes to myself, mostly about clients. I purposefully put Johnny Two's file into the filing cabinet, turning my attention to the needs of other clients.

It was just as well Anita didn't ring at lunchtime, as I ended up eating a sandwich while I gave an informal supervision session preparing Georgina to see her new client, the lady with agoraphobia. I was working with an older lady with a similar condition. I listened carefully as Georgina showed me a beautiful plan, drawn up meticulously, with a hierarchy of small tasks graded towards her stepping out of the front door and walking down the street. I am always astounded at how often the trainees miss the point, despite their brains and academic training. It took me some time to help her think of all the things she should find out in her assessment. It had not occurred to Georgina that Miss Woodward might be reacting to a past traumatic event, in which case we would need to work on that before even thinking about the agoraphobia. The lady I was working with, Miss Drake, had made very slow progress until we had begun to work on an incident in her childhood that had impacted on her whole life.

There was no sign of Georgina's stalker as we left the building and made our way to take the Tube towards Crompton Road and Lily Woodward's home. The Tube was crowded and standing cramped with others I wondered whether we could still call it Miss Woodward's 'home' when she had not been out for fifteen years, or whether it deserved the name 'prison'. It was easy to find her Victorian semi but we had to step carefully over brambles growing through the cracks in the path to reach the weathered front door. The curtains were drawn and the house looked empty.

'It's like rescuing Sleeping Beauty,' said Georgina.

Georgina had knocked twice before we heard the sound of the door being unbolted. It was opened a crack and a white, tight face peered through the gap. There was still a chain across the door. Automatically, we both passed Miss Woodward our identity badges.

'Hello, Miss Woodward, I'm Georgina, we have an appointment.'

Miss Woodward mumbled something.

'Sorry, I can't hear you,' said Georgina.

'I said, "who's that man?"' Her voice was nearly a whisper and her gaze was darting around, taking in the street, then me, the street again and Georgina.

'He's my boss, Miss Woodward, I believe I told you in the appointment letter that he was coming too. He has to see how I work.'

'I didn't know he was a man.'

She closed the door. We waited.

'What should we do?' asked Georgina.

I was aware of being observed by a middle-aged lady who had stopped gardening in the house two doors away and an old gentleman on the other side of the road who had paused when his dog used the lamppost, but failed to walk on.

'Give her a moment or two, you never know.'

There was a spy-hole in the door and I sensed we were being weighed up. I turned to the watching neighbour.

'Good afternoon.'

'Afternoon.' She turned back to her weeding. The gentleman with the dog yanked at its lead and carried on down the road. Still we waited. Georgina repeatedly looked at her watch. She leaned back against the high garden wall and sighed. I absentmindedly flicked at one of the tall weeds and sent hundreds of fluffy seeds blowing in the air. I hoped the gardening neighbour hadn't noticed. We both heard Miss Woodward undo the chain and we became ready and alert. She opened the door just about wide enough for us to get in, keeping behind it as she did so.

The small hall was dark, with wallpaper that had probably not been replaced for several decades. A strong smell of polish almost covered the musty smell of decaying plaster. There was another smell, window cleaner perhaps, but the outsides of the windows were filthy.

Once we were in, Miss Woodward seemed to settle a little. She showed us into the immaculate front room. All was tidy and scrupulously clean as far as I could see in the dim light. I noticed her garden shrubs had grown higher than the window ledges, blocking out light. She bustled around us offering tea and biscuits. Pretty white china cups with a floral decoration were already on a tray with a milk jug and cubes of sugar, the tray sitting on a small, beautifully shiny, mahogany table in the centre of four high-backed upholstered chairs. We all sat down, with Georgina between me and Miss Woodward. I moved my chair back a bit, ready to observe.

'These were my mother's cups,' Lily Woodward told us, as she poured the tea, her hands slightly trembling. 'My mother lived in this house and her mother before her. I shall be the last of the family, I suppose. I shall die here on my own.'

'Why do you say that?' said Georgina. 'Once you are out and about again, you never know what will happen in the rest of your life.'

Miss Woodward responded with a small smile and a shake of her head.

'Let's just think about how good that would be, Miss Woodward, Lily; you have a lot to look forward to. We'll make a start today by getting to know a bit about each other.'

'Maybe.' She passed me the cup of tea and I noticed her moist eyes. She was still trembling enough to make the cup rattle against the saucer. With the style of clothes she wore she looked old, well, older than me. I was sure from her date of birth on the clinic notes folder that she was only thirty-two.

I was struck by the contrast between two women of fairly similar ages as I watched the young, well-groomed, fashionable, well-educated Georgina. She carefully spoke to Lily, leaning forward in her seat, interested.

'So what was life like when you were a child, Lily? The new houses at the end of the road weren't there, I suppose. Did you play out?'

'There was a stream at the bottom of a big field. My brother Robert and I used to fish in it. Not that we ever caught anything. He used worms on a bent pin to try to catch something. I hated the worms but he would tease me about them. I loved my brother, though, and I knew he cared about me.'

She paused, looking into the distance. We waited.

'Sometimes my brother would say, "Let's paddle in the stream," and I would go home with my skirt held away from my legs because it was all wet. Mummy would tell me off. There was only Mummy. I didn't know my father. He died soon after I was born.'

'Does your brother live near you now?'

Lily didn't reply but took a white lacy hanky from her dress pocket and began to dab the corners of her eyes. Georgina stroked her arm.

'Did something happen to your brother?'

There was a little nod behind the hanky. Then in a tremulous voice, Lily told us, 'He got ill and he died when I was eight.'

She was using the hanky to mop her running tears. I tried to concentrate, pulling myself away from the rising images of Jamie on the hospital bed. Georgina was carefully moving the subject along until Lily was on safer ground. With a few gentle prompts we learned about how she had been in the church choir and her love of singing.

'I still wanted to sing in the choir even when I stopped going to school.'

Georgina quietly asked her why she'd left school.

'I didn't like it.'

Lily crossed her arms and turned away from Georgina, but Georgina put her hand on her arm. 'I think it's important to tell me why not.'

Lily didn't turn round, but, after a few minutes she began to talk.

'It was fine at first. People were sad Robert had died. Then when I was still upset at school my best friend, Julia, told me I was a crybaby. I tried to stop, but I couldn't. Then the other girls said Robert died from embarrassment because he couldn't bear to be with such an ugly crybaby sister.'

I was scribbling all this down in my notebook. I had noticed that Georgina had stopped writing anything; she was concentrating solely on her client.

'That must have been really hard for you,' she prompted.

'My best friend said sorry when the other girls were horrid. But I was not keeping up with my work. So she tried to improve me. Sometimes she crossed out all my homework and made me do it again. She was worse than a teacher.' Lily's voice was rising. 'One day the other girls drew in my homework book and I had to go to the headmaster. I was told off. But that wasn't the worst. When Julia wasn't with me, the other girls tried to push me onto the level crossing when a train was coming. I ran home and told Mummy I would never go to school again.'

Carefully Georgina encouraged her to recall how her mother had hidden her, telling the school she was moving to live with her aunt. Lily didn't answer the door to anyone after that and kept out of sight when her friends tried to peer in the window to see if she had really gone.

'They had lost the right to be called your friends, don't you think?' said Georgina, softly.

Lily Woodward wept quietly into her hanky.

'I didn't have any others, and I missed Julia,' she said.

Georgina sat still, waiting until Miss Woodward's sobs subsided.

'Why do you want help now, Lily?' asked Georgina. A good question, I thought.

'I've got toothache and I would like to be helped to go to see a dentist.'

'I'll help you do that,' said Georgina. 'Is there anything else you want to do?'

Lily's voice became high when she said, 'I want to feed the ducks in the park, that's silly, isn't it?'

The lacy hanky was too wet for the tears that followed. Georgina silently passed her a small packet of tissues.

16

All the way back to the office Georgina bubbled with thoughts about how to help Lily, who she referred to as 'Miss W'. I watched the reaction of the people on the Tube while I listened to her. One slightly balding man in a smart pinstripe suit put down his *Financial Times* to openly watch her and listen.

'I just can't imagine it, being locked away for all that time. How do you think she will cope once she's out? She'll not know the first thing about modern life – although I expect she watches television – probably the old stuff, though, Miss Marple or something. Maybe she thinks that everything is like that. I must ask her next time.'

Georgina leaned down to her briefcase, which she had anchored between her feet, and for a moment I thought she would totally breach confidentiality and take the file out. Instead, she drew out a bright pink pencil case and from it took a tiny flowery notebook. These little props made her look like a teenager. I expected her to find a pink pencil with a fluffy wavy bit on the top of it, to match, but the pen she took out was an ordinary workaday biro. As she scribbled she talked.

'I think I should find out more about her likes and dislikes. We know she likes the park – didn't she sound young when she said she wanted to feed the ducks? And she seems to have a very old-fashioned taste in clothes – unless she dare not order things from catalogues. Did you see a phone? I'll find out if there's a phone number or whether calls go to a neighbour. She wouldn't be able to post a letter. I wonder how she pays her bills – she'll have water rates etc. Do you think she left the house for her mother's funeral? She must have organised the funeral, or someone did.'

The man with the folded *Financial Times* moved slightly closer. I half-smiled at Georgina as she noticed him. Even so, I don't think she was quite prepared for what I said next.

'I'm not sure there was anyone else to organise a funeral. Do you suppose there was one, or is the body still in the house, all these years later?'

I could see Georgina was trying to look serious as our interloper's mouth dropped open.

'I'll make a note to ask her when we next visit,' she said.

When we got back to the department, we hit lunchtime. Rachel and Anita were in the kitchen waiting for the kettle to boil. They stopped talking as I entered the small room and Rachel took her prepared sandwiches out of the fridge. I remembered I had meant to buy some on our way back, but had failed to do so. Anita reached into a cupboard and found a packet of fruit teabags. She dropped one into a mug covered in a bold abstract design.

'Do you want a coffee, Mike? The kettle's almost boiling. Black, isn't it?' She already knew I never said 'No' to a coffee. I looked in the communal biscuit barrel and found two old chipped custard creams. Not much of a lunch but maybe it would have to do.

'I've got a spare apple if you are trying to find something to eat,' offered Anita.

'Well, thanks. Yes, that's good. I'm a bit short of time today.'

I took my meagre lunch and hurried into my room, closing the door firmly. Why had I taken her apple? I should have popped out for a sandwich. It was the smell of the coffee that had tempted me to stay. Oh, well, I did have plenty to do.

I scribbled a few notes in Georgina's supervision file. She had done well with Miss Woodward overall and she was definitely enthused by the case. I found two papers from psychology journals: one about cognitive behavioural work with people living alone who were agoraphobic and the other about the effects of past trauma as a contributing factor, both published recently. In fact, I found a whole issue dedicated to aspects of trauma, so, taking Johnny Two's file out of the cabinet, I did a little research for my own client. By the time I had read three of the articles I had made separate notes for three other people as well as Johnny. It was years since my mind had worked like this. It felt like an excellent use of my lunchbreak.

I realised my coffee was now very cold and the custard creams and apple had lost their appeal, so still with twenty minutes to spare before my appointment, I decided to nip out to buy a sandwich and a drink. At the bottom of the stairs, Anita was crouched down, picking up magazines and brochures from the floor.

'Oh, sorry, Mike, am I in your way? I've dropped this lot – the covers are a bit slippery.'

I helped her gather up what turned out to be travel brochures for Cyprus and Greece.

'Oh, going away?' I said.

'Hopefully. I haven't been abroad for a couple of years so when my friend said he'd always wanted to go to Greece, I thought it was an excellent idea. Cyprus seems a bit cheaper, so it might be there. Probably we'll go in May next year.'

'Sounds good. Ella and I went to Cyprus before Jamie was born. We had a fantastic time. We went in the autumn, October I think, but the weather was still warm. There were oranges on the trees, left rotting.'

'That sounds a bit off-putting!'

'No, quite the opposite. You could smell oranges wherever you walked! You'd enjoy Cyprus, I'm sure.'

I carried on thinking about Cyprus while I hurried down the road to the sandwich bar. The small hotel we had stayed in provided 'entertainment' every evening and the one event that particularly stuck in my mind was a fashion show put on by the local dress shop. Ella was persuaded to join the girls who were modelling the clothes. The local girls strolled across the floor with their heads thrown back and their feet crossing over as they affected long strides with big swings of the hips. They looked terrible. Then came Ella, with a natural, beautiful stroll along the makeshift catwalk, making the ill-fitting dark jacket and cream slacks she was wearing look like designer wear. They sold a few of those that evening, but not much else.

I was smiling as I bought my liver sausage and tomato sandwich. As I walked back I remembered our last holiday together had been in a camper van, loaned to us by Ella's parents. It was not my kind of holiday, really. I felt too out-of-sorts and cramped. I kept bumping my head as I climbed into the small van and losing my belongings because Ella had tidied them away to make the most of the space. It was pre-diagnosis, so Jamie must have been under five. He had loved the whole experience – squirrelling found objects into his sleeping bag and reading in the bunk by torchlight. Ella seemed to enjoy cooking on two calor gas rings, with no oven, and concocted enormous breakfasts and incredible meals to keep us going. She'd done a lot of camping as a child, so this seemed like a step up for her.

I did enjoy the warm days and sitting in the sun, reading. Jamie and I played French cricket on the beach and went crabbing. I had a wonderful photo of him showing me his bucket-full of crabs.

All afternoon, between clients, I kept remembering that holiday. We'd had better holidays but that one was particularly about Jamie. By the end of the afternoon I knew I had to find that photo.

Back in the flat that evening, I started the hunt. In the bottom of the largest packing case I tackled there were a few pictures of Jamie in frames. I tried to remember whether I had any others. I thought back to the day when I moved out. I certainly hadn't been methodical in what I had taken from home. I had wandered around the house, unsure of what to do and what I should pack, then ended up in my study. That's where I had taken the photos from, along with most of the other stuff stored in the packing cases. I knew I had a right to everything in my study. I was not interested in dividing possessions. I was only leaving because I thought I needed space before Ella and I destroyed each other.

Ella. Here was my favourite picture of her, in a highly coloured frame that she had made out of papier mâché, with Jamie. She smiled out at me, looking young and bright-eyed. This photo was taken at her sister's wedding and she wore a huge pale blue hat with her long straight fair hair hanging down each side, disappearing out of the picture. I wondered if her hair was still long. It had been when I left, although she mostly wore it tied back with some sort of black velvet ribbon thing that shouted to me that she was still in mourning, whatever other bright colours she wore.

How was she? I needed to know. And I needed to find more pictures of Jamie, especially the crab one. I paced around my flat, trying to decide whether to ring her. I made another coffee and put it on my makeshift coffee table, covered with the piece of cloth Ella had hated. Ironically, this spurred me into action.

As I rang the familiar number of my old home, I began to have misgivings. Supposing she was with someone else. Supposing she was angry with me. Supposing she had moved away. What was I going to say?

The phone was answered. Not by Ella. A gruff male voice said the number. My pause before I responded was long enough for the man to speak again.

'Who do you want to talk to?'

'Is that the number for Ella Lewis?'

136

'Well, yeah.'

I swallowed.

'Is she there?'

'No. Sorry, she's not here.'

She must have moved on then. I swallowed again. I was now desperate to talk to her. She couldn't just disappear.

'Do you have an address for her? A forwarding address or something?'

The chap sounded slightly irritated.

'Who is this? Do you need to speak to her in a hurry?'

'It's Mike, her... um... husband, separated.'

'Oh, the elusive Mike. Nice to hear the voice to the name.'

He knew about me? Not the next owner of the house, then. Oh no, he couldn't be, I owned it. I felt confused.

'Who am I speaking to?' I asked.

'That's not really your business, mate,' he laughed, 'but I'll tell you. I'm Liam, a friend of hers.'

'Is Ella coming back? I wanted to collect a few photos.'

'Well, yeah, I hope so. But she plans to move to Australia. She's out there now having an interview. She'll be pleased you've been in contact because of the house. Tell you what, I'll pass on your number. I'm not sure I'm at liberty to give you her mobile number.'

I was having trouble taking all this in. This stranger was shielding my wife from me. My wife was moving to Australia and I didn't know. She wanted to get rid of the house. I gave him the number of my home phone, feeling as if I was putting my whole future into the hands of someone who might be my wife's lover.

Within a few minutes of putting the phone down, it rang. My heart started to become somewhat erratic and I found myself swallowing again. I tried to calm my breath as I answered.

'Mike? Are you all right? You sound sort of breathless.' It was Anita. What was she doing, ringing me at home? I'd have to get her off the phone quickly – suppose Ella was trying to get hold of me?

'Oh, hello, Anita. Sorry, I was expecting another call. You surprised me, that's all. What can I do for you?'

'Oh, I only wanted to tell you I had found a basic Spanish book for Johnny. I wondered whether I could pop it round to you sometime over the weekend because I know you're going to see him on Monday.'

If I hadn't been waiting for a call from Ella, I might have been pleased if Anita came round. As it was, I tried to back off without hurting her feelings and probably made a mess of it.

'I'm afraid I'm up to my eyes in it this weekend. What about leaving it in the office for me on Monday? I'll be going in before I go to see Johnny for the allocation meeting. I'm not sure I'll need it anyway, because I can't think what I will do with it.'

'Oh, all right. I thought there was some urgency. Monday it is, then. See you at work.'

She rang off and I sat looking at the phone, willing it to ring. I went over in my mind the conversation I'd had with that Liam fellow. Why was Ella going to Australia, and who with? Did he say? And did he say when he would be talking to her anyway?

I realised I had no idea what time it was in Australia. Weren't they seven hours ahead or was it behind? I did the sums and decided that if it was ahead then Ella would be asleep for another three or four hours. And I didn't know when Liam would call her. I went and brewed some fresh coffee.

I was on tenterhooks all evening but it was lunchtime on Saturday when the phone rang again. I'd been taking the rubbish out and raced up the steps, scrambling to reach it on time. The sound of Ella's voice brought back the smell of her freshly washed hair and the curve of her lips. She sounded confident, happy.

'Mike – how are you? Liam said you rang.'

'I'm fine. Much better. Improving, I think. What about you?'

I wanted to tell her I missed her, I loved her, I wanted her, I wanted us. I did not dare.

'I'm moving on, Mike. It's been too long since Jamie went. It's time I got on with my life.'

'Liam told me you're moving to Australia.'

'Well, that's the plan. I'm sorry someone else told you. I've recently hired a private detective to try to find you but he hasn't come up with your address yet.'

'What? Why a private detective? What's wrong with contacting work?'

'I've tried before, Mike. But as you've never replied, I didn't know if you were getting the messages or whether you were still there.'

'I remember one, but that was early on. Oh, Ella, we've moved offices. You wouldn't know that.'

Neither of us said anything for a moment. I was thinking about what might have been. It had never occurred to me that Ella was trying to contact me. She was probably thinking I was a stupid idiot not to let her know or call her or something.

Her voice sounded distant when she spoke.

'Anyway, Liam said something about some photos you wanted. Feel free to go and get them. I haven't changed the locks so you can use your key, or if you'd rather, go in the evenings – Liam's usually there. It would be good if you only take the ones where there are duplicates. Put any others to one side and I'll get copies for you.'

'I could wait until you're home.'

'No, it's OK. I trust you. Have a look around and think about what else there is of ours that you'd like, because I'll be selling more or less everything if I move out here.'

I wanted to ask her what would make her stay. I know it was only the fear of being rejected that stopped me. Why would she think I cared about her? I hadn't even answered her message. I couldn't think what to say.

'Mike, are you still there? We'll need to talk about things. I'll be back on the fifteenth, so ring me after that. OK?'

'Yes – we'll need to meet up, I think. If that would be all right.'

'We'll talk when I'm back. Take care, Mike. Bye.'

She was gone. I was left saying goodbye to a silent phone and found myself saying out loud all the things I wanted to tell her. Mostly that I missed her and was sorry. Back when I left, she had told me to go and sort myself out, but all I did was go. Now it seemed it was too late to sort myself out. Too late for us. I picked up her photo in its gaudy frame.

'What have I done, Ella? What have I done?'

17

The following Monday I picked up the picture book of Spanish/English words from my pigeonhole before going to the allocation meeting. Anita wasn't there but the other members of the team were all eager to know how I was progressing with Johnny Two. I did not feel in the mood to talk about him, having spent most of the weekend worrying about Ella and the end of our relationship. Anita had left me notes from her last visit to Johnny so I was able to report that he was now alert, able to use his right arm to draw and seemed to be understanding as much as he did before the accident. I showed them the book Anita had bought but the more I tried to explain that it was to establish how much Spanish he understood, to see if he could cope with any testing in Spanish, the more disillusioned with the whole idea I became.

I asked for ideas from the team. Georgina had many, but not a full grasp of the situation.

'Can't you just ask him what he understands?'

'How will he tell me?'

'Well, he'll nod, I suppose.'

'Will he nod to agree with the question, to answer in the affirmative or to try to please me? And does a nod in his native language equal a nod in ours?'

There followed a lively discussion of cross-cultural non-verbal sign language. This included the occupational therapist demonstrating several rude signs which were actually quite polite in Argentina. The meeting deteriorated into areas we should have kept away from. I decided to bring matters back to order.

'Well, I'll discuss the communication problems with Anita and we'll see if we can think of something better than the picture book.'

'You could speak to a speech therapist as well,' said Georgina. 'Aren't they meant to be communication therapists these days?'

'Excellent idea. Now on to the new referrals.'

It was quite easy, having assumed command, to distribute the referrals to others. I could have taken one more, but with my new-found enthusiasm to research cases, I thought I would prefer to concentrate on the ones I already had.

It was nearly ten o'clock by the time I set off for the hospital. The short journey took me longer than usual, so the doctor had finished his round. I looked in the notes before going into see Johnny.

The doctor had recommended discharge. I was so surprised I had to read it several times to be sure of what it said – but there it was, at the end of his last notes: 'Plan for patient: Discharge asap'. Then I realised I had not seen Johnny for nearly a week.

'Looks like he's going to be sent back to his lodgings, then,' I said to the blonde nurse.

'Not if the social worker has anything to do with it. She had a right go at Dr Smeedson this morning. She was really angry that he should suggest Johnny went home. She's still here somewhere – using the phone in Sister's office, I think.'

I found Shirley, obviously battling with someone on the other end of the line.

'But there has to be somewhere. The doctor says he needs someone with him… no, not full nursing care… he's on medication for fits and he has his leg in plaster.' Shirley gave me a rueful smile, raising her eyebrows and shaking her head despairingly. She mouthed 'Problems' as she listened to whoever was on the phone. I mouthed back 'I'll leave you to it' and went to see Johnny.

As soon as I walked into the room I could see the improvement in him. He was sitting up and a slow smile spread across his face when he saw me. He leaned forward to pull his over-bed table towards him and, with his good arm, shuffled papers on there until he found one for me. It was a picture of Shirley – a child-like drawing but the subject easily identified by the flowery trousers and heavy shoes.

'Did you do this?' I asked, using the Makaton sign for 'you' and indicating the picture. He smiled, and nodded. Maybe Georgina was right, and we could use nods – that definitely looked like an affirmative.

I took the picture from him – intending to take it to the nurses' station and use the photocopier so that I could have one for my file. As I turned to go, Johnny made a noise. Just a grunt – but a clear noise. When I looked at him, he shook his head, so I handed him back the picture. I'd have to take a copy later.

I pulled up a chair and sat down by him. I opened up his psychology file and made a few notes about how he was and the nodding and shaking of his head. Perhaps he'd learned that from the nurses here or had known it already from the Spanish crew of the *Margarita*. I was about to produce the Spanish/English picture book from my briefcase, with no clear idea of what I was going to do with it, when Shirley bustled in. She was smiling smugly.

'I've found somewhere,' she said. 'It's not ideal, but it's the best I can do for now. It's a Cheshire home for the chronic disabled. They can take him tomorrow on a temporary basis.'

'It's certainly not ideal. I'd say it's completely unsuitable,' I said. I was sure that a traumatised youngster and yet another strange, unknown environment would not mix. How would he understand that he was not in the home for good? And would there be anyone else there his sort of age? If so, would they be too disabled to communicate with him?

I tried to explain to Shirley – to help her imagine she was Johnny and had experienced some of the changes that he had coped with.

'Well, he must be able to manage with some more, then,' she said.

Johnny was looking wide-eyed from one to the other of us. The atmosphere in the room had become difficult and he was clearly not comfortable. I changed my tone of voice.

'I'll help you find somewhere better for him,' I said. 'Let's go and have a think, but don't cancel the place at the Cheshire home until we've found somewhere else.'

We left Johnny and walked down to the canteen. I discovered something in common with Shirley when I went to buy our drinks – we both liked black coffee. I had brought Johnny's file with me so I extracted a blank history sheet and suggested we brainstorm some ideas.

'What do you think I've been doing since yesterday?' said Shirley. 'Anyway, you don't use the term "brainstorm" any more, it's not PC.'

'OK – we'll call it "mind-mapping", although that might be something different. Two minds are better than one, so they say, so let's see what we can think of together.'

Shirley shuffled around on the rickety café style seat, and sighed heavily.

'I'm sorry, Shirley, I know you think I'm being picky here, but we have got to be careful not to confuse Johnny more. I have to help him reach the stage where he can tell us, or at least indicate to us, what has happened to him.'

Shirley leaned forward and tapped the table slowly as she spoke.

'What you don't realise, Mike, is how few options there are.'

'Look, I know you've worked hard to find a place for him and you have done well to come up with something. Let's give it a bit of thought together to see if there's something better.'

She sighed. 'All right, then. I've got half an hour and then I must get to my next client.'

We began our task. Shirley listed where her search had taken her. She had already tried psychiatric wards and inpatient units. She had also tried some old people's homes and a convalescent home for the elderly. The one convalescent home she had on her list for adults was full until next weekend and anyway was in Brighton.

Her list exhausted, Shirley leaned back in her chair and crossed her arms.

'Now do you understand the problem? Can you come up with anything better?'

'You've been pretty thorough,' I admitted, feeling very grateful that no one would take him into a psychiatric unit or somewhere designed for the over seventy-fives. What would Johnny have made of that?

Shirley nodded, obviously thinking that was the end of the matter, but I continued, 'You've certainly covered all the facilities for adults and older people. But Johnny might only be sixteen – we don't actually know his age. Are there any facilities for teenagers?'

'Foster homes. Small group homes. Assessment units. I suppose there might even be convalescent homes for children and young people. I don't know. I could ring the office and see if anyone working with kids has got any ideas. If you're sure he's young enough. I had assumed he was nineteen or twenty.'

I showed Shirley the original referral on the psychology file. As this had come from the immigration medical officer and stated quite clearly 'age unknown' we decided we'd give it a go.

Shirley rang on her mobile immediately. She is one of those people who shout on the phone, so we lost all confidentiality. I glanced around the canteen to see if any of those reporter chaps were around – but if they were, they were not obvious. I thought it probable that now Johnny was improving, someone else was more newsworthy.

Shirley's colleague came up with a few suggestions including a small group home where one of the youngsters had recently been removed following a court hearing. It didn't sound too promising, but I only hoped that some of the young people would be there because of circumstances, not because they were in trouble with the law.

'She's going to ring them now, and see what they say. I told her it would have to be today or tomorrow at the latest. I'm going to have problems finding time to take him on either day, so that will be the next difficulty.'

I tried to think what was in my diary for the rest of the day. Then I stopped myself. I was the psychologist; not the social worker.

'Is there anyone you can cancel today?' I asked. 'After all, you won't have to fit in coming to see Johnny tomorrow if he's settled somewhere.'

'Oh, I don't know, my whole life seems to be fitting extra things in and changing stuff I've already sorted.' She glanced at her watch. 'Oh, look, I'm late for my next appointment, as usual. I always seem to be chasing my tail.'

'Can you ring me to let me know where he goes to?'

'Sure, I'd better do that. You've still got to assess him.'

When I went back to Johnny's room, Anita was sitting by Johnny's bed. She had the picture book in her hand and was talking to him. She was reading words in Spanish with a pronunciation that did not sound quite right. Johnny was leaning forward, peering at the pictures.

Anita turned and smiled up at me.

'I'm not sure this is working terribly well, because I don't know any Spanish. Where's our Shirley? She spoke some Spanish, didn't she?'

'She's had to go to see her next client. We've been trying to work out where Johnny's going to next because he's ready for discharge.'

I brought Anita up to date on the search for the next place for Johnny. She agreed with me about the home for the chronic disabled. I watched Johnny carefully while we spoke – he didn't seem to understand anything. He was concentrating on the picture book, looking at a picture of a bedroom. As he did so, he was looking around the room obviously matching the pictures to the real objects.

'You know, Anita, Johnny might be better learning some English words. I wonder what he knows already?'

'Let's find out,' said Anita.

She sat by the side of his bed with the bedroom picture open. She started with the word 'window' – showing him the window in the picture, then pointing at the window in the room. Then she said 'door' and Johnny pointed to the picture. She looked around the room saying 'door' and Johnny pointed to the door of the room. We were on to something.

We gave up using the pictures and I spoke the words. He showed us he understood 'bed', 'table' and 'floor'. That was it, though. I tried reading the Spanish words and he then indicated his Spanish was better. He could understand curtain, drink, flowers and book. As he recognised each one, I gave him the English for the word. It was all very encouraging, but his English vocabulary at least was far from the standard needed for testing.

Anita said 'man'. At first he looked blank, but when she said it again he pointed at me. For some reason Anita and I laughed. Johnny looked smug.

'I'll see you tomorrow,' I told Johnny, as I gathered up my briefcase and put his psychology folder into it. He looked puzzled but when I said '*Mañana*' he treated me to a thumbs-up sign.

Anita followed me into the corridor.

'However did we miss that?' she asked.

'Maybe he was too traumatised to respond to the Spanish when we first worked with him,' I suggested.

'Yes, and for the same reason he's been slow picking up English. I think I'll see what else he understands, although not for long, he's looking rather tired.' We glanced back through the open door. 'On the other hand, perhaps that's for another day,' she said.

Johnny had his head back on the pillow and his eyes closed.

'Perhaps you could draw a series of pictures of him moving to somewhere new? He may need that today or tomorrow. If he wakes while you're here, would you show him?'

As I walked down the corridor I reflected on what a brilliant asset Anita had been on this case. I would still need a speech therapist, though; understanding was just not the same as talking.

18

When I arrived back at the clinic, the departmental secretary told me Shirley had left a brief phone message. Johnny would be installed at Rosemount Youth Assessment Unit tomorrow. No address. I rang Shirley's mobile number.

'Hi there, Shirley – I need to know where to find the assessment unit.'

'Oh, sorry, Mike, hang on.' I heard the sound of papers being moved around. 'Yes, got it. Here it is.' She gave me an address in Crystal Palace, which I scribbled on a blank piece of pink paper that had found its way among the general clutter on my desk. I was surprised the hostel was so far out of the city.

'Have you tried telling Johnny where he's going?' I asked.

I thought I heard her habitual sigh before she told me slowly, 'There's not much point, is there? He won't understand. He'll need to work out what's happening himself.'

Ignoring the sarcasm in her tone, I described Johnny's response to the picture book and his better understanding of Spanish.

'He might understand even more than we think. Perhaps you could try telling him about the move when you go to collect him tomorrow?'

This time her exasperated sigh was clearly audible.

'It might not be me – I'm very busy at the moment.'

I tried not to be judgemental as once again I embarked on reminding her what it might be like for Johnny, adding how important she seemed to be to him. I asked her if she'd seen the picture he had drawn of her.

'No,' she said, with a lift in her voice, 'are you sure it was me?'

'I'm sure. I recognised who it was immediately,' I said, stopping myself from describing his faithful replication of the gaudy trousers.

There was a pause. I waited, until she spoke again. 'Look, I'll try to get in early and have a go at telling him what's going on, if you think it's really important.'

'That's an excellent plan, Shirley, and will help Johnny greatly, I know.'

I came off the phone and began a search through the piles on my desk for Johnny's file, before remembering it was in my briefcase. As I stapled the pink paper onto the inside of the front cover I wondered how I'd got into all this. Surely pushing social workers to do their job was not really part of my remit? The only other thing I could do to try to make her recognise her responsibilities was put in a formal complaint, but I was not sure that was appropriate or in Johnny's best interests. I realised that I had forgotten to ask Shirley about new court dates – we had lost nearly a month because of the accident and I had made little progress in assessing him.

Making a note in my diary to ring Shirley again later, I rang Rosemount to fix a time to see Johnny once he had moved there. There followed a frustrating ten minutes as I was passed from secretary to keyworker to manager, at each stage having to state who I was and why I was ringing. Finally, I reached Mrs Graves, assistant manager and team leader.

'I'm sorry, Dr Lewis; we only carry out our own assessments here. You won't be able to assess him on our premises.' She emphasised the 'our' with a tone of possessiveness. 'Also, we will need to be given full details of any tests you have used or intend to use, to avoid duplication.'

'Surely he isn't coming to you for assessment?' I asked.

'We are an assessment centre, Dr Lewis. There is no other reason why he would be a resident here.'

'Ah, no. Of course not.'

So Shirley had asked for an assessment. A clever tactic, given the urgency of finding him somewhere to go, but it was going to create problems. Perhaps that's why she was reluctant to take him to the unit. She was probably afraid of being asked awkward questions. I decided to make the best of the situation,

'It would be very helpful to me to know what he's being assessed for. I may need some of that information for the court report I have to prepare. Perhaps we could work together on this case?'

I really did not want to bring him all the way into the city to my office, when I only lived up the road in Sydenham. It seemed totally unnecessary and rather cruel, when he had only just come out of hospital.

'The reason for the assessment is confidential information, Dr Lewis, but I can tell you that most of our youngsters are assessed to establish their risk to the community.'

Whatever had Shirley told them? About her alleged abuse by him on the Underground, maybe. I was becoming concerned now.

'That's not a problem with Johnny Two,' I ventured. 'He's no threat to anyone.'

'Well, we'll have to see about that, won't we?'

'Who assesses him?' I asked

'The Youth Offending Team – perhaps you'd like to speak to them?'

Of course I would! She gave me the number, before abruptly excusing herself and hanging up the phone.

I sat there for a while, trying to decide my next move. Johnny needed a safe place and this was the best on offer so far. Still, it seemed to be for assessing offenders, which was hardly appropriate and may well damage his case. The very fact that he'd been admitted into a centre to assess his risk to others could suggest to any outsider that he posed a threat of some kind.

I couldn't get hold of Shirley – so I left a message on her mobile expressing my disquiet. My next job would be to talk to the Youth Offending Team. I really needed a name of someone to write to. Did the YOT have psychologists or counsellors, or perhaps probation officers? I had no idea who formed the team. I would have to risk being passed from person to person again and hope I ended up talking to a clinician. I decided I needed a summary of Johnny's case so far, before I spoke to anyone. After a rummage around, I found a pen and a couple sheets of fresh paper and started to write:

CLINICAL PSYCHOLOGY ASSESSMENT

Given name: *Johnny Two (real name not known)*

Estimated age: *Fifteen – twenty-three*

Nationality/ethnicity: *Unknown, Afro-Caribbean appearance*

Language: *Language of birth unknown, understands some Spanish and is beginning to understand a little English*

Intelligence level: *Not formally tested, but appears to be of at least average intelligence. Good grasp of many new situations despite language barrier and inability to speak. Ability to learn new languages demonstrated.*

Other strengths and abilities: *Quickly learned how to draw. Appears to have some natural ability.*

Emotions: *Johnny appears threatened by some new situations. Has been seen to panic. When panicking clings to safety, e. g. grabbing Shirley Hills, social worker, on what was probably his first Underground journey. Observed to have generalised anxiety and probably post-traumatic stress disorder. Symptoms include alert watchfulness, fear, trembling, overbreathing, withdrawing into self or standing 'frozen' with eyes widened. Appears to be more wary with men than with women.*

Social skills: *With the few adults Johnny has begun to trust he has good eye contact and will initiate communication with them, through pointing or, recently, a small grunt. He reacts appropriately to the tone of voice and appears to be aware of disagreements. In his hostel he seemed to settle in with a group of asylum seekers of about his age and a little older.*

Communication: *Johnny has been described as a 'selective mute'. This psychiatric description of a person who cannot speak unfortunately carries the wrong suggestion that Johnny refuses to speak. There have been occasions when he desperately tried to make himself understood. His muteness is likely to be the result of a trauma which has caused him such internal pain that he is unable to express himself verbally. He uses some signs and appears to understand a little English but more Spanish. He is beginning to use art as a form of communication.*

Needs: *Therapeutic needs – to receive treatment for post-traumatic stress disorder and generalised anxiety. These to include learning relaxation techniques and how to control panic. The guidelines for clinical excellence suggest a cognitive therapy approach would be helpful for a person of his intelligence, but at present his communication difficulties prohibit this. His lack of speech also presents a barrier for other forms of therapy, such as Eye Movement De-sensitisation. Art therapy appears to be the most useful means of treating him at present.*

I wondered whether to put in my notes that I intended to try to use some subtests from a WISC to assess him. This set of intelligence scales contained some things that could possibly be demonstrated to Johnny, so that he could do them. As suggested by Georgina, the blocks test, with its set of identical cubes in white and red, could be used to make patterns to copy those in the test material. What would this tell me, though? Only a little more about his intelligence, and it would be a very rough assessment anyway, as I would be guessing his age. But, the only thing we really needed to focus on was helping him tell us what happened. Everything hinged on being able to understand his trauma.

I'd been jotting down notes as I was thinking and now had in front of me a mass of random words linked by arrows; 'blocks', 'speech therapy', 'Anita', 'art', 'pooling ideas', 'communication', 'culture', 'unknowns', 'drawing tests', 'Anita', 'Spanish v. English', 'copying designs', 'artistic skill?', 'ask Anita'. When I looked at the page, I wondered again whose client Johnny was.

I wrote myself a Post-it note, reminding myself 'Need to speak to Anita PRONTO' and stuck it on my diary.

19

Georgina had left a note for me in the message book in the departmental office. Time to see her agoraphobic lady again, and had I remembered? I hadn't, of course, and it wasn't in my diary, so I was in the office trying to rearrange appointments with Rachel when Anita arrived. She seemed to blush slightly when she saw me – I couldn't think why – was she cross with me for something?

I couldn't miss the little half-smile that passed between the secretary and Anita. Was this because I always seemed to get myself in a muddle? I decided to ignore them and turned back to the complexities of moving three of my clients and finding different times for them, so that I could fit in one home visit. But Anita wouldn't be ignored.

'How's Johnny, Mike?'

'Umm – hang on a minute – I'm very near to sorting out these appointments. I do need to talk to you, though.'

'I thought you did,' she said, laughing.

The secretary sniggered. 'I think that's obvious, Mike.'

'What's the matter with you two?' I was feeling a bit uncomfortable by now.

'Surely you know what you've put on your tie, Mike.'

There, stuck on my chest for all to see, was my Post-it note, reminding me that I needed to speak to Anita PRONTO.

I pulled it off, crumpled it and threw it into the wastepaper bin, missing the target. I bent down to pick it up off the floor, glad of the few seconds to think of something to say.

'I stuck that on my diary,' I began to explain. But I'd lost my audience, who were busy talking to each other about posting up their every desire for anyone to see, and the time when Anita as a teenager had unfortunately written SWALK –_ 'sealed with a loving kiss' – on the back of an envelope containing a letter to her father and 'C U Dad x' on one posted at the same time to her latest boyfriend. The boyfriend never replied. I stood and watched them; Anita, older than Rachel by at least fifteen years, yet suddenly looking really young and so vital. She must be great fun to spend time with socially. She turned to me.

'Anyway, after all that, what can I do for you, Mike?'

Her teasing smile and the way she asked the question took me off guard for a moment, but I recovered enough to say, 'Oh, I need to pull together a few loose strands about Johnny. He should be installed at the Youth Assessment Centre by now, and apparently they are going to assess him there with their own team.'

'That will be interesting!'

'My very thought. I'm not sure where that leaves me with my report, but I need a definite plan to see how we can dovetail any assessments together. I wondered if you'd think about your role in that?'

'OK, no problem. We'll sort out a time to bring it all together in the next couple of days. I contacted the speech therapists but I had to leave a message. Perhaps they've left one for me today.'

'They did, Anita,' said Rachel. 'I took a message just before you came into the office, it's in your pigeonhole.'

'Hang on, then, Mike, let's see what they say,' said Anita. She stood and read the note and passed it to me. I read that two speech therapists would meet with us, but only to discuss strategies. They listed possible times, all a few weeks ahead.

'I think we'd better choose a time now that we can both manage and accept we can't meet them sooner,' I said.

Anita's diary was in the art room, so we turned to go there together. As I went, Rachel called out, 'Hang on a minute, Georgina wanted me to give you Miss Woodward's file.'

I took it from her and Anita and I carried on down to the basement. I opened the door of the art room for her and she picked up her diary, absentmindedly wiping wet paint off its cover with a painting shirt that was lying on the table beside it.

'While we're looking at diaries, Mike, I wondered if you are busy tonight?'

I didn't need to look at my diary before responding.

'No, not washing my beard or anything.'

'Well, I wondered if you would like to join myself and a few friends? We are meeting in the Robin Hood in Upper Norwood at about 7.30 and then going off for eats somewhere.'

I thought of the alternative – probably a kebab in front of the TV.

'Yes, thank you. That would be good.'

'Great. You'll know one or two people because they are from work. It's just a bit of a social gathering, you know.'

'That will be good,' I repeated vaguely as I turned to go, my attention taken by the note from Georgina asking me to check her letter to the GP which was clipped to Lily Woodward's file.

It was later that day, when I was sat in a rather upright floral armchair, observing Georgina in Lily Woodward's gloomy sitting room, that I realised my work with Johnny was interfering with other cases. My mind kept wandering back to him, while Georgina was very efficiently explaining how a hierarchy could help Lily overcome her agoraphobia. I forced myself to watch her and to concentrate on how she dealt with this case.

'Here's a list of some of the things you find difficult at the moment, Lily.' Lily read through the list slowly, her eyes becoming moist. Her hand reached into the pocket of her skirt for a lace hanky and she carefully mopped the corners of her eyes. Georgina quietly waited. Lily gave a small nod and passed the list back.

'We can work on these, Lily, but not all at once. Just a little bit towards the easy ones for now. Are there more things you would like to be able to do?'

Afraid this might open the floodgates, I leaned forward ready to suggest that the ten items that were on the list might be a good starting point, but Lily answered with only two wishes: 'I would like to be able to hang out some washing. And it would be good to open a bedroom window.'

I had to stifle an irrational urge to leap over and lift up this self-imprisoned lady to carry her out of the stuffy house into the sunshine.

Georgina explained a gentler approach than my fantasy of flooding her with new experiences. Together they would work on the list, grading the tasks from the easiest (Lily to look out of the window ten times a day) to the most difficult (to go to the dentist on her own).

I began to wonder how Georgina was practically going to fit in all of the tasks with her, and how I would find time to accompany Georgina to every session. I was not sure that she would be safe from her stalker if he saw her with Miss Woodward. I only hoped I wasn't going to be needed for what looked like a very long drawn-out process. My thoughts were echoed by the client.

'How long will all this take?' asked Lily. Her lower lip was wobbling as she looked at Georgina.

'As long as you need,' replied Georgina, glancing quickly at me. I gave up thoughts of squirming out of my responsibilities.

'Yes,' I added, 'and if Georgina has moved placements before you're quite there, I shall help you with the rest. You will be well looked after.'

'What do you mean, is Georgina going?'

I looked at Georgina, surprised that Lily Woodward didn't realise she was on a time limited placement.

'Do you remember that when I wrote to you I told you I'm training as a clinical psychologist? Well, my placement comes to an end in March. That gives us over three months.

Dr Lewis, here, Mike, will know you very well by then so it will be easy for you to work with him.'

Lily obviously didn't think so. With a 'harrumph' that made her sound about seventy she gathered up the dirty cups and we heard her banging them down onto the kitchen surface.

'Somehow I don't think I will be an acceptable substitute,' I said.

Georgina went through to the kitchen to book the next appointment. I was eager to leave – I had noticed heavy clouds and Miss Woodward's windows were rattling. I was sure Georgina only had a short jacket and I'd left my raincoat in the office.

As we made our way up the weedy path, large drops of rain began to fall and we could hear the rumble of thunder. We bent our heads against the wind.

20

Later, on the way home on the train to Sydenham, I was thinking about Lily Woodward and contrasting her life with my own. Well, trying to contrast. I was amazed and horrified by some of the similarities. Lily was shut in her house, never, ever went out, and was too afraid to. I went out to work, all right, and to buy the odd paper or a takeaway, but otherwise I mostly stayed in my flat. I didn't do a lot there either, apart from the little flurry of unpacking boxes and a splash of housework a few weeks ago. That week had seemed like a great turning point in my personal life – but proved to be nothing more than a blip in a flat landscape of staleness. The flat wasn't my own, the furniture was junk shop stuff, the food was always bland and uninteresting, the walls magnolia. At least Lily Woodward had interesting heirlooms in her house – apart from Jamie's photo, my most interesting item was a piece of cloth bought on a long-forgotten holiday. Lily was trapped, though, by her own fear. In theory, I wasn't. I was a miserable sloth, nothing less.

I had wanted so much to talk to Ella, but I hadn't contacted her again. She would have been home from Australia for nearly a week. Once more, I was the one dragging my feet – reluctant to talk, yet wanting to be together. Hey, where did that thought come from – did I want us to be together? I had no idea. I wanted something different. Something that was not me here now, but a new me. Maybe it was Anita I wanted?

I scrambled off the train, nodding to a couple of familiar faces. We all knew each other by sight, but never exchanged a word. Now we all adopted an identical pose, heads down, shoulders hunched, as the weather caught us. In a few moments we were all in a battle, working our way into the push of the strong wind. The old station buildings were creaking and polythene bags and bits of newspaper buffeted in the air, like balloons and streamers. It wasn't quite so bad out of the station, but everyone seemed to need to walk in a slightly sideways manner until we reached the bridge where I turned right to be blown into Upper Sydenham. Trees from the leafy gardens beside me were bending over the pavement, and I could see there were twigs and branches strewn across the close-cropped lawn of the old people's home. The noise of the wind seemed louder than the traffic, as nature with its raw elements reduced all those walking to mere playthings. It was exhilarating – I forgot I had intended to buy food and let the wind buffet me back to my flat. I stood in the shelter of my porch, my back pushed to the front door while I found my key. Dustbins clonked along the road – those rectangular ones just aren't up to properly rolling – and a child's trampoline lifted and moved two metres down the next front garden. There was a dog under the hedge by our gate. He stared at me, unflinching.

'Don't worry, old thing – I won't push you out from there. Shelter as long as you like,' I shouted into the wind.

Wildness had hit our suburb and reduced all creatures to cowering beasts.

Inside the flat, the wind was muted by the double-glazing. The bay windows drew me to them and as I took my coat off, I watched the tall conifers in the park dancing and jostling with each other, bowing to the atmospheric force. Pliant and supportive they moved together, then apart, stood confidently tall, then bowed and swayed.

As I watched, from beneath the trees there emerged a small girl, trying to push a bike. Her coat billowed, looking as if she was about to rise up into the wind, which was whipping her long brown hair round her face. She didn't seem to be getting very far as she tried to cross the park diagonally, to reach the bottom entrance. She was struggling to stand. For a moment she let go of the bike, which stood up for a few seconds before falling back onto her. It knocked her over; she didn't get up but sat up beside it, pulling her navy coat around her knees. I reached for my parka and grabbed my identity card – if I was going to rescue small girls in parks I'd better be able to prove who I was.

She was still there after I had fought my way across the road and up the steps to the park. She looked very young, maybe seven or eight, and her thin pale face was streaked with tears.

'Hi there,' I shouted, above the wind.

Two enormous frightened eyes focused on me and she scrambled backwards.

'It's OK, I only want to help you – perhaps push your bike home for you?'

Not a smart thing to say – she looked even more frightened and shook her head vigorously.

'OK, then, if you don't want me to help, I'll just put my phone here and you can ring your mum or a friend to help you. All you need to do is punch in the number and press the green button, then it will ring.'

I put my phone on the ground between us, nearly within her reach, and let the wind take me further away. She watched me as she retrieved the phone and didn't stop staring at me all the time she put the numbers in. She kept pushing her hair out of her eyes while she spoke. Then she leaned forward to put the phone down, scrambling back by her bike again. I noticed her leg was bleeding. I waited till she was back, then fetched the phone, put it in my pocket and retreated again. I paused, trying to think what to do next.

'Do you want me to go now?' I shouted, expecting her to nod. Instead she eyed me gravely before shaking her head slowly. The kid looked frozen but I did not dare lend her my coat.

I set my back against a tree some thirty metres away from the kid. I glanced at her every now and then and was rewarded with a lopsided smile. Absolutely no one else was around, and I began to feel as vulnerable as she obviously had. Suppose this kid said anything had happened, or that I had looked at her in a funny way or something? There were some strange people around these days.

We hadn't waited more than five minutes before a stocky man in a leather jacket and a thin woman without a coat hurried into the park from the bottom gate. The woman rushed up to the little girl who hugged her and cried. With scarcely a glance at his daughter, the man strode straight over to me. I moved forward to meet him.

'You the bloke that lent her the phone?' he asked. His voice was guarded, gruff, made fiercer perhaps as he shouted against the wind.

'Yes, I saw her out of my window. Top flat, over there.' I pointed at my window. 'She was struggling with her bike. I couldn't very well leave her.'

'Got kids yourself, have you?'

'Well, yes, well, no.'

He pushed his face nearer to mine – I could see large pores on his nose. He was panting heavily and his breath smelled of vinegar. I instinctively stepped back.

'Have you? Or haven't you?'

I shouted the raw facts of my fatherhood status against the noise.

'He died. Aged six. Leukaemia.' My voice felt distorted.

A flash of pity softened the stranger's face.

'Sorry, mate. Just checking.'

I no longer cared – I needed to get back to the flat.

'You'd best get your kid home,' I said, turning away.

Back in the flat once more, I sank into the sofa with my coat still on. Jamie's photo smiled cheerfully at me. I picked it up, running my finger round his little face and yearned for him to be struggling with his bike, hugging me in the wind, sitting by me. The more I yearned for him the stronger the feeling came that I should be doing this with Ella. I blew my nose and dialled her number. I felt my heart pounding through my being as I waited for her to answer.

'Ella,' I said as I listened to the dialling tone, 'I need you.'

21

Ella answered with a cheerful, 'Hello, Ella here.'

Hearing her voice was soothing. I suddenly felt rather foolish ringing her.

'It's Mike here, Ella. Do you have a minute to talk?'

'Sure, what's the matter?'

She listened as I told her about the girl in the park and coming back to the flat. It seemed so easy, talking to her. I had a mental image of her sat on the bottom stair, twirling the flex of the cream phone in her hand as she spoke. I paused, as I reached the bit about coming back into the flat.

'So why are you ringing, Mike. What happened?'

'It was when I came in and there was Jamie's photo, and, well – if only it had been him in the park. Oh, I don't know. Sorry – I'm being ridiculous.'

'You are not, Mike. Definitely not. I help with a kids' club and every boy seems to remind me of him.'

'What do you do?' I asked. I was trying to keep my voice steady.

'I have to keep remembering the good times,' she said.

If only it were that easy, I was about to say, but Ella carried on, 'Do you remember the time we took him to the zoo, when he was, oh, I don't know, about three, perhaps?

He was amazed at the elephants. He kept saying 'the *big* elephants', with his hands stretched out.'

'I remember – he kept wanting to go back to see them, again and again.'

'Yes, I've got the photo I took somewhere, of him standing on your shoulders to see them better. I took loads that day.'

I remembered his shoes digging into the top of my shoulders as he almost danced up there, with his excitement. It was a really cold day, but he wouldn't go into the café, whatever we offered him by way of reward. Ella and I were stamping our feet and Ella was rubbing her hands together, laughing at Jamie.

'I'd love to see the photos,' I stammered. I had to blow my nose. I hoped Ella didn't hear.

'Then come round, Mike. Come and join Shaun and me one evening for a meal and we can look at all the photos afterwards.'

Shaun, not Liam then. Oh, my goodness, couldn't her new man have a nice solid name like George? It wasn't the counsellor, either. I couldn't remember his name, but it certainly wasn't Shaun.

'I'm not sure about that, maybe one day.'

There was silence at the other end of the line – I thought I'd lost the connection when Ella said, 'Mike…'

'Oh, I thought you'd gone,' I said, foolishly.

'Mike, you do know who Shaun is, do you?'

'Someone famous, I suppose,' I thought to myself.

'No. I do not know who Shaun is. Should I?' I tried to curb the sarcasm in my voice.

'Plainly you don't know, Mike. Shaun is an adult I am fostering. He has learning difficulties.'

For a moment I could not sort it out at all. Was Ella in a relationship with someone and they were fostering together? Then I twigged. I must have gone quiet while I figured all this out and realised that my Ella did not have a man – at least not a live-in one.

'You still there, Mike?'

'Yes, sorry. I'm trying to work out who it was who told me you were away, when I rang before.'

'That's the sitter – Liam. If I go away, someone comes in to look after Shaun.'

'If I were there, I could do that.'

Ella's laugh had not changed a bit. It was gentle and wavery; it sent shivers down my spine exactly as it had when I had first met her.

'But, Mike, you're not here. You decided to move out.'

How could she say that? I answered as gently as I could.

'You sent me away.'

'Sorry?'

'You asked me to go.'

The phone went quiet, then Ella spoke softly. 'I didn't want you to go, Mike. I was so upset when you left.'

'But you told me to leave you.'

'What? When?'

'That night when you started throwing things. You said, "Leave me, Mike. Leave me alone. Just go." I'll never forget that night, Ella. I was so miserable.'

I could hear Ella had started to cry.

'Ella? Are you all right? Ella.'

All I could hear were sobs.

172

'Ella, I'm coming over. OK?'

She didn't answer.

I didn't bother to change, or clean up, or anything. I was still wearing the same stuff I had come home in, with my old tweed jacket and baggy cord trousers. I would have dressed up a bit, with warning, and found some clothes I knew she liked.

It took forty-five minutes to reach Selsdon. I had to go by bus, changing at Croydon. The wind had dropped a bit, but it was raining heavily. I peered out at the people running for shelter and wondered what I was running into. I knew that by the time I arrived, Ella would have calmed down and been totally together and probably rather annoyed at having cried on the phone to her ex. But, I said I was coming, so I was. The same thoughts went round in my head until I was standing on my own front doorstep – I suppose I did still own half the house. I straightened my tie and tried to smooth down my damp beard.

The door opened a crack and I saw half a face. A round face with slanting eyes and sticking-up dark hair. Shaun.

'Hello,' he said. 'What's your name?'

'I'm Mike,' I said. 'Are you Shaun?'

'I'm Shaun and you're Mike. Do you want to come in, Mike?'

'Yes, please, Shaun. I've come to see Ella.'

'Ella's nice. She looks after me.'

'I know. Can I come in?'

Shaun walked away from the door, the chain was still on it, so I had no choice but to wait. I smiled at the strangeness of it all as I heard him calling, 'Ella, I saw Mike. He's at the door.'

I could hear odd snatches of her answer

'That's my husband... talk... polite... lay the table...'

Then she was coming up the hall and unchaining the door.

'Sorry, Mike, I've been working really hard to stop him inviting everyone into the house.'

She looked up at me with that enigmatic half-smile of hers and I was lost. Before I could help myself, I had gathered her up into the most enormous hug. Her body felt so small and fragile and her hair smelled of shampoo – she was wearing the perfume she always asked for at Christmas – Chanel something or other. I breathed in the scent of her and held her close.

'Hey, Mike, steady.'

She was struggling in a half-hearted way. I loosened my hold, but then snatched her hands before she could go.

'I can't believe I'm here. You look so wonderful.' Apart from her blonde hair being shorter, she looked the same. She was wearing a single tear-shaped amethyst on a chain round her neck – one I remembered buying her to match her eyes.

She gently pulled her hands away from mine, avoiding my gaze. She turned away, saying, 'Come on, I've cooked supper. There should be enough for three of us if you'd like something to eat.'

I followed Ella through the lounge and into the dining room. Shaun had bounced ahead and was sat at the head of the table, where I used to sit. I hesitated. It all felt too familiar. Ella still had the old farmhouse dresser – the shelves doubling up as a bookcase, still overflowing with books and half-finished projects. Her sewing machine was almost falling off the far end, with a huge basket next to it. I remembered how that basket was crammed full of pieces of material and every time she had wanted to make something small, all the contents were tipped out and there would be a kaleidoscope of colours and textures all over the floor. There was a day when Jamie, aged about four, swooped in on bright fabric pieces to make his bear a patchwork waistcoat. Ella sewed it for him – covering it with embroidery and sequins, taking as much care as if she were making a waistcoat for a pageboy. I wondered if she had kept it.

Ella pulled out one of the oak dining chairs that had once belonged to her grandmother. I remembered borrowing a trailer and collecting them from Yorkshire a few days after her grandmother's funeral.

'Why don't you sit here, Mike? Shaun has rather taken a fancy to that end of the table.'

I tried to smile and sat down, feeling like a guest, a stranger, a ghost. All this had stayed the same while I was away – the tablecloth, the cutlery, Ella's favourite casserole dish with the little chip in the handle that you could hardly see. I knew it was there, it was me who had knocked it against the tap when I was washing-up once.

'We are having spaghetti,' said Shaun, 'it's my favourite.'

'Mine too,' I told him.

There was a time before Jamie was born when Ella and I had gone to a little Italian restaurant. We both had spaghetti – hers was vegetarian but I went for the meat. We

175

were celebrating something – maybe buying this house – and we were on a high. I laughed so much that I splattered the sauce all over the pristine white tablecloth. It didn't matter. We both thought it was really funny.

Shaun was tucking a big checked napkin in at his neck.

'Mustn't make a mess,' he said. I couldn't remember napkins being used before; maybe they were essential with Shaun. The one by my place was pale blue and matched the familiar tablecloth – I never knew we even had them. I spread it out over my lap.

'That's right,' said Shaun, 'mustn't make a mess.'

Ella came through from the kitchen with a large bowl of steaming spaghetti. She stayed standing as she scooped it onto the three plates.

'Help yourself to the sauce, Mike. I'll fetch the garlic bread.'

The Bolognese sauce smelled delicious – I took some and then added some to the other plates. I passed one to Shaun.

'No good,' said Shaun. 'I like them not together.' He folded his arms and pushed his chair back away from the table.

'I'm sorry Shaun. I didn't know.'

Shaun pushed the plate further away.

Ella came back with the garlic bread. I mouthed a 'sorry' towards her.

'Oops,' was all she said.

Shaun was frowning at the floor.

'I'll show you a trick, Shaun. If you turn your plate this way, you can eat just the spaghetti and if you turn it that way, you can reach the meat. You try.'

I turned the side with the most spaghetti towards him.

'You try it, Shaun,' said Ella, 'then you can have some garlic bread.'

Shaun reluctantly pulled his plate back towards him and pulled up a long strand of spaghetti with his fork. As if orchestrated, Ella and I began to earnestly eat and chatter about the food. I remembered a small Jamie refusing to eat broccoli – I made it into trees in his mashed potato and Ella promised a pudding. We had both pretended it was very ordinary when he began to eat.

Ella poured me some wine. I was already feeling heady with the surfacing memories, the familiarity, the strangeness. I was becoming aware that being here with Ella and feeling so intimate towards her made me long for what had been.

Shaun was experimenting with the spaghetti. He was holding it high with his head back, looking at us for our reaction. Ella's glances to me were friendly, warm, yet with a tinge of apprehension. I was trying to push Jamie out of my mind. I was desperate to talk to Ella on her own.

Maybe she felt the same. 'Shaun, it's time for your programme. Do you want some dessert, or do you want to go and watch your programme now?'

'Time for my programme. I'll watch my programme now.' Shaun smiled and nodded at me.

'Thank you for my dinner, Ella,' he said, as he left the room. We heard him running up the stairs and then footsteps overhead and a loud bump which seemed to shake the ceiling – perhaps he had jumped onto his bed – followed by the noise of television, so loud that we could almost hear the words of the programme.

'He's very polite,' I said.

'We're working on it,' said Ella. 'He was rather institutionalised when he came here. He had no idea how to behave in company. He has done very well with you today. He's improving with every visitor.'

'He is certainly quite a character. How long has he been with you?' It felt safe to be talking about Shaun.

'Ten months. It's quite hard work, sometimes. But it's rewarding, too. Better than being on my own...' Ella paused. 'I'm sorry,' she said. 'I didn't mean it to come out like that.'

'I'm miserable on my own, too.'

'But you went.'

'I thought that was what you wanted. I didn't know what else to do.'

We looked at each other. Could it be possible that those years on my own could have been totally unnecessary? Surely I hadn't moved out on a misunderstanding?

'Mind you, it was a relief at first,' she said.

'What do you mean?'

'I could only just cope with Jamie having died, but not with you blaming yourself and the doctors. You were so angry, Mike. And sad as well. But I had nothing to give you to help you through it. I was in such a state as well. Then you started all that stuff about Henry and that was one thing too many. That's why I became so angry with you.'

Henry. Ah, yes, that was the counsellor's name.

'It worried me that you could talk to Henry when you couldn't talk to me.'

'Of course I could, Henry was outside the situation, with no experience of a child who had died. If I started to talk to you, then I had to deal with your grief as well.'

'I wish we'd been able to talk about this at the time.'

'So do I.'

I felt my eyes begin to moisten and fought to control myself. Ella's hand covered mine on the blue tablecloth. I took hold of her slim fingers. She still wore her wedding ring.

'I'm sorry,' I said. 'I'm still that same miserable old guy now. I haven't really grieved for Jamie properly. I've only recently begun to look at his photo.'

'Then it's a good job I'm ahead of you – we can work through this together, if that's what you want.'

I resisted the urge to lift her fingers to my lips to kiss them. Instead, I stroked them, as I spoke.

'I would like that very much,' I said. My voice wavered a bit.

'Hey, steady, Mike. Let's just talk for now. I'm too hurt by you leaving to ever risk it again.'

I looked her in the eyes. I wanted to argue, to defend myself, but I held back. We both sat in silence until I couldn't stop myself from saying something.

'Well, if that's how you want it. But, Ella, I really wouldn't have left if I hadn't thought that was what you wanted. I really think we ought to try again.'

'I really don't know. I think not.' But she held my fingers in hers and gave them a little squeeze before letting go.

By the time Shaun had come back downstairs from watching 'his programme', Ella and I were sat on the sofa looking at piles of photos – some loose and others neatly labelled in albums. Ella found the one of Jamie on my shoulders at the zoo. I was looking at it, remembering the day, when Shaun came and sat by me on the settee and leaned forward to see.

'Ella's boy is on your back,' he said.

I glanced over to Ella, surprised.

'He knows all about Jamie. In fact, he knows quite a lot about you. But I wasn't sure the connection had been made.' She turned to Shaun. 'Do you remember I told you how my husband, Mike, used to live in this house with me, but now he lived in his own place?'

'Mike,' Shaun said, pointing at me.

'Yes, Shaun. This is Mike who used to live here. Do you remember that I said my husband was coming? Well, this is Mike who is my husband.'

'Is he sleeping here?'

I smiled at Ella. She kept her cool, obviously used to Shaun being embarrassing.

'No, we are going to carry on looking at some photos of Jamie, our little boy, and then Mike will go home to his flat.'

'Come back?'

Ella glanced at me before answering slowly, 'Yes, I think he'll come back. If he wants to. We are friends.'

'OK. I like Mike. Can I have a yoghurt?'

'Yes, take one from the fridge. But make sure you shut the fridge door.'

'To keep it cold.'

'That's right. To keep it cold and to keep the food fresh.'

'OK.'

Shaun grinned at me, made a thumbs-up sign and swaggered through to the kitchen.

'You are very good with him,' I said.

'It can be very tiring, sometimes.'

'You were a wonderful mother, you know.'

'Was I? I always felt there was more I could have done for Jamie, to have made his short life more fulfilling.'

'You did everything any mother could.'

'I couldn't stop him dying, though.'

'Nor could I. No one could.'

'It's not fair, is it?'

I forgot all about only agreeing to be friends as I moved over to put my arms around her and pull her close to me. For a moment she stiffened, and then I felt her relax as she rested her head on my chest. We held each other for a few minutes, then she raised her head and gave me a kiss on the cheek.

'Thanks Mike, I needed that hug.' She stood up and started to clear away the photos.

'Would you like a coffee before you go?' she asked, as she left the room with her arms full of albums.

Ella had retaken control of herself by the time she'd made some strong Brazilian coffee. She carried the mugs in on the tray we bought as a reminder of our Cyprus holiday. She ignored the seat next to me on the brown leather sofa and sat on the rocking chair opposite.

'Well, how's work then, anyway?' she asked.

We found ourselves discussing our professional selves and old friends in a rather formal way. I told her a little about Johnny Two, but it felt like performing and my story faltered. Probably just as well, in case she had seen the original news item and realised who I was talking about. She told me that she was now teaching three days a week and had a terrible class. I learned that our friends Nick and Janie had moved to Canada. But we had lost the comfortable feeling we had when we were looking at the photos. I was worried that I had overstepped the mark with her.

I drank down my coffee and suggested it was time I went back to the flat. I couldn't say 'home'; this place felt like home. Ella went to find an envelope for the photos she had selected for me, while I fetched my coat.

'Goodbye, Ella. Thanks for the meal.' I didn't dare say, thanks for being there, thanks for being you, thanks for letting me know you didn't send me away. 'Thanks for everything.'

'That's all right. You're welcome.' She sounded like any polite hostess, anywhere. I moved forward to hug her again, but she stepped back, offering me her hand. It was very firmly a smiles and handshake-only goodbye.

'I'll give you a call,' I suggested. 'If that's all right?'

She smiled. 'Yes, Mike. We'll have to meet up again.'

It was nearly midnight when I arrived back at the flat. Despite the strange ending to the evening, I was still feeling elated. My mind was full of pictures of Jamie, Ella caring for her lodger, Ella being close to me. I was feeling content for the first time in months, maybe years. I was suddenly hopeful, seeing a variety of possible futures.

My answerphone was bleeping – four messages. I pressed the button on it as I passed; the first message was blank, the second Anita's voice: 'Mike – we're about to order without you – we can't wait any longer.'

I was puzzled for a brief moment and then, as I remembered Anita's invitation, I sat on the stool by the answer machine, hardly daring to listen to the next message. What had I done? The first time I was meeting up with her and her friends and I hadn't shown up. She didn't deserve this. I pressed the button on the machine, another blank, then Anita again.

'I hope you're OK, Mike – we had a great evening without you, after the initial embarrassment. You have the honour of being the first person who has ever stood me up. I can't say I'm pleased. Maybe you'll give me a ring before Monday so that we don't have to sort this out at work.'

I looked at my watch – probably far too late to ring. Feeling an absolute swine, I wrote myself a note – *'Ring Anita'*. I had completely mucked things up there – I wasn't sure what I'd tell her– the truth seemed so callous; *I decided to stay and eat with my ex-wife* – how could I tell her that?

The bubble of my reunion with Ella had burst – I went to bed feeling miserable.

The next day, I put off ringing Anita until nearly lunchtime. I was relieved when I heard her answer machine. I put down my phone and thought about the message I would leave, then phoned again. This time she answered.

'Hello, Mike – are you all right?'

'Yes, and no – I'm really sorry I let you down. It's all my fault.'

'Well, do you have an acceptable reason?' Anita's voice sounded tight, controlled. It would have been easier to apologise to the answerphone.

I took a deep breath and tried to explain. 'Something happened soon after work that really upset me – made me think about Jamie. I was in quite a state, so I rang Ella. Then she was upset and I felt I had to go round there. It was all very emotional and I ended up staying – for a meal, I mean, just a meal...'

There was a silence.

'With her and her lodger,' I added, feebly.

Still silence.

'Anita, I'm sorry. I didn't think. I forgot – oh hell, I wouldn't have done this to you for the world.'

'But you did, Mike, and as I see it, you have now used your grief to excuse yourself from dumping a friend on her birthday without even so much as a phone call.'

'Your birthday?'

'Yes, Mike, my birthday, and my group of friends – all in couples. But I guess you and I had a different idea about our friendship. So perhaps we had better draw a line under it now.'

'Look, Ella, I am really sorry. Can I make it up to you in some way?'

Anita's laugh did not sound like Anita.

'You just called me Ella, Mike. I don't think there is any way you can make it up to me. Goodbye.'

I heard the click as she finished the call. I stood there holding the phone, feeling like a complete idiot. However did I manage to call her Ella? I didn't even know if there was going to be any future with Ella and myself, except perhaps as friends, and Anita had invited me out with her friends on her birthday. It dawned on me that Anita had asked me for a date.

It was far too early, I know, but I went to find a whisky.

22

I didn't hear from Anita again that weekend but she was the first person I came across in the secretary's office on Monday. She hardly lifted her eyes as she said 'Excuse me, Mike', coming out of the room as I went in. I expected disapproval from her, of course, but not from Rachel, who greeted me with a shake of the head.

'What have you done, Mike? Anita is really upset.'

'It was a mistake, Rachel. Just a mistake. I'm not perfect. And how was I expected to know it was her birthday?'

Rachel pointed to the noticeboard. There was a huge office year calendar with all our names, neatly written against the date of our respective birthdays.

'How long has that been there?'

'Four years, Mike. Ever since we moved to this building. Don't say you haven't noticed it!'

I didn't dare admit it, but I hadn't.

I grabbed my messages from my pigeonhole, and without a word, I scurried back to the office.

Once there, I tried to work out what to do to appease Anita. A part of me was beginning to excuse myself, because I realised that if I had turned up, I would still have let Anita down. I would have had no flowers or card, therefore she would still have been embarrassed in front of her friends. I knew my reasoning was faulty, though. It must have taken courage for her to invite me in the first place when I might have said 'no'. I scribbled a little note to leave in her pigeonhole: 'Anita, I am so sorry. I hadn't even realised it was your birthday or I may have made a much better mental note of the proposed' – I crossed out proposed, it carried too many overtones – 'of the invite to a social gathering. Perhaps I could take you out to a meal to make up for my social gaffe?'

There were three versions of the same message screwed up and thrown away before I produced nearly the same wording and decided it would have to do. By then I was thinking that a note would be a bit risky. The pigeonhole was rather a public place. I thought Rachel was probably a little too interfering not to turn it over to read it. If I put it in an envelope, it would seem too formal.

The phone rang. A frosty Patricia, this time.

'Are you aware, Mike, that you have a client waiting to see you?'

I put the note to one side, selected the appropriate file and hurried into the waiting area to apologise to a very anxious Mrs Barnes who was pacing up and down the small space between the low armchairs.

I had a busy morning – with my clients not having done anything spectacular since I saw them last, and feeling generally out-of-sorts with myself. I decided I had better go early to see Johnny and not stay in the office over my lunch hour. I was desperate for a coffee but didn't dare risk going to make one in case I bumped into Anita before I had put things right with her.

It seemed strange going on the same train that I usually took home when I was only having a quick sandwich before going to see a client.

As I went into the flat I headed straight into the kitchen to make myself a cheese sandwich with some rather stale bread. I found the last clean plate, and took the food through to sit in the less messy living room. I flipped on the answer phone as I passed it.

I listened again to Anita's messages from Friday and felt guilty that I hadn't done anything about putting things right, yet. There were more messages, left today. The first was Anita: 'I'm sorry, Mike. It was very rude of me to ignore you this morning. Rachel said you hadn't realised it was my birthday. I expect you are assessing Johnny at the moment, so I wanted to reassure you that anything difficult between us personally will not affect our professional relationship.'

I listened to it again, feeling wretched. I should have rung her. If I rung work now, could I get through to her without having to go via the main office? I wasn't sure.

I pressed the button to hear the final message. It was from Ella.

'Mike, it was really good to have you round yesterday. It helped me a lot. But I feel it's only fair to tell you I have been offered a post in Perth. That's Australia, not Scotland. I want to be free to think and pray about this without any pressure, so it may be best if you give me a few weeks to do this.'

I felt as if someone had hit me round the head. I listened to the message again, then once more. However hard I had tried not to get my expectations up, I had hoped that we could at least have talked about our relationship together. This was a huge decision she was about to make, and I wasn't to be included in that. Would she be talking to that counsellor chap, Henry? I had to do something, but what? My mind bombarded with thoughts, I reached for the phone.

Her answer phone responded. I hated talking to those things. I hung up. I put my head in my hands, trying to think. I tried to breathe more slowly, think more clearly. I dialled again. Her message: 'Hi there – you've reached Ella. Sorry I can't take your call right now, please leave a message after the beep.'

I started speaking immediately: 'Ella, we must...' when it beeped. I cleared my throat and started again. 'Ella. Hi. Mike here. I don't want to put pressure on you. But just for the record I want you to know that if you were to go to Australia, I would like to talk things over with you before you go and we could together decide whether I should seek a job out there too.'

I don't know how long I sat by the phone, mentally trying to imagine a world without even the possibility of being close to Ella again, when it rang.

'Mike, what are you doing home at this time?' asked Ella.

'I'm en route to a visit in Crystal Palace and I popped in for some lunch,' I replied, looking at my cold black coffee with a film on the top and the stale, uneaten cheese sandwich.

'Well, I wanted to tell you that of course we can talk before I go. If I go, that is. The job is absolutely perfect for me, and you know how I love warm weather. But there's a lot to think about.'

'What would happen with Shaun?'

'I am part of the preparation for him to live independently. It is hoped that he will move into a flat with a warden within the next few months. Of course, I would have liked to be around to visit and offer advice, etc. But that's one of the things in the melting pot.'

I gulped a couple of times before I could say, 'I'd like to be in that melting pot, too.'

'You're being unfair, Mike. I haven't existed for you for nearly five years – it will take more than one visit for me to be convinced that you want to become part of my life again.'

'I know, I'm sorry. But you have existed for me. I just lacked the courage to do anything about it. You must make your decision, and then we will talk.'

'You pray about it too, Mike, use your faith to decide what you should be doing, not just what you think is right at the moment.'

Me – praying about a decision? There was a novel thought. I'd certainly grumbled at God since Jamie had gone. And shouted; I was so angry. Did that count? I wasn't sure.

'I'll do my best.'

'You'd better go, Mike, if you are on your way to see a client.'

'Ah, yes. I'll talk to you soon. I hope.'

'Bye, Mike, take care.'

'Yes, you take care. Bye, Ella.'

As I put down the phone I realised I was trembling. I tried to tell myself I would persuade her to stay. I thought that highly unlikely. Feeling useless and helpless, I picked up my briefcase and left the flat to take the bus up the road to Crystal Palace.

By the time I arrived at the assessment centre, I managed to pull my mind round to focus on Johnny. I was required to state my name and business into an intercom, before the door to a small lobby was opened. There was a hatch beside the door, with a glass screen. The middle-aged woman the other side kept me waiting while she finished a call. She scribbled notes before turning to me. Her disinterested face looked me up and down before she said, 'Can I help you?'

After a great deal of explaining who I was, including showing my badge and being asked for two other items of identification, which I did not have, I was shown into a communal recreation room. There was a large television up one end, which was on. No one was watching it. There were two lads – one tall, the other short and sturdy, playing snooker on a very battered table, with the felt ripped off in a large streak across the middle. The shorter one appeared to be the better player but the other one was making all the noise with a great deal of use of the 'f' word. He glared at me each time he walked around the table, so I got out my diary and began to make some notes to remind me about things I had to do.

Unfortunately, this attracted more attention than when I had been sitting there doing nothing. He came over.

'You a social worker?'

'No.'

'What are you then?'

Difficult question, that. If I confessed I was a psychologist, then it could cause trouble for Johnny. Not many people can sort out the difference between a psychologist and a psychiatrist, so he'd be labelled as a 'nutter' in a place like this.

'A problem solver. I help those who've got a difficulty they need sorting out.'

He seemed satisfied, which was good. I was feeling a bit hot and bothered with him leaning over me, snooker cue in his hand. I was hoping I would be able to talk to Johnny somewhere else.

A large woman in a bright green dress came in. She stood looking down at me, a little too close for me to stand up. A formidable figure.

'Are you Dr Lewis? I'm Nancy Armitage, warden here. You can use my office to talk to John.'

Relieved, I followed her into a small room near to reception. It was overcome with papers and untidy piles of files and I felt quite at home. I moved two files out of the way from two upright padded chairs, and waited for Johnny.

It was so long since I had seen him upright, I was quite surprised when Johnny appeared on crutches. He was being guided through the door by a black girl, who helped him sit down on the vacant chair before turning to me.

'Hello, I'm Margaret, Johnny's key worker. He hasn't really settled in yet, he's still quite worried about things. Aren't you, dear?' she added, turning to him. He looked at her, uncomprehending.

'If you don't mind me asking, doctor, how are you going to communicate with him?'

'I'm not sure, Margaret. I have used drawing before, with the assistance of the art therapist. I may not spend long with him today, but perhaps I could talk to you as soon as I have finished?'

'Of course, I'd be pleased to help.'

She left the room and I turned to Johnny. He was wearing a white T-shirt that proclaimed 'Just do it!!!!' in bright red, and a pair of denim jeans. For once, his clothes fitted but without the baggy tracksuit, his thinness was even more evident. He was watching me with large eyes, waiting.

I asked him if he liked it here, signing with Makaton. He shrugged, perhaps to show he did not understand. I tried again. 'Is the food good here?' Despite my best mime of eating, he did not understand. I got out blank paper and my fountain pen, and began to draw.

I made a passable attempt at depicting a plate of food then drew two faces, roughly like Johnny's own, one smiling and one with a downturned mouth. I then repeated my question, pointing at the food and indicating here by waving my arms around. Somehow he understood and pointed at the smiley face. That set me off on asking about his bed, his clothes and the carers. It was quite a challenge to draw the green-clad warden, until I found my green biro – he didn't like her – and easy to draw the smiling Margaret, who he did like.

There was a crash in the corridor outside the room, followed by shouting and swearing. Visibly startled, Johnny folded his arms around himself. He began to shake.

'It's OK, Johnny. You're safe.' His breathing was really fast, so I matched it, gradually slowing mine down. He concentrated on my breathing and I had him steadied again.

'Well done,' I said, showing him again a nice slow breathing pace, by gently blowing. He was no longer trembling. I was running out of things to do and decided I had better find Margaret and have that talk with her.

'It's time to go, Johnny.' I said. I started to get up.

Johnny stretched out one skinny hand and grabbed my jacket. He was making a strange guttural noise in his throat. I sat down again.

'Are you trying to talk, Johnny?' I asked, indicating talking by touching my lips and moving my hand forward.

Johnny nodded.

I showed him breathing again, and took his breathing even slower. Then I made a noise from the back of my throat, similar to the one he had been making. He made a guttural noise again. I then tried other sounds and gradually he improved, with a passable go at 'ooo'. He was looking frantic and had tears in his eyes. I motioned to him to stop.

'It's OK, Johnny. I will come again. Just relax.' Together we slowed our breathing and I drew a stick man cartoon, showing him that I would walk out of the door – then a clock and that I would walk back in the door. I don't know what he made of that, but this time he let me get up. I handed him his crutches and helped him stand, then he followed me out of the room.

I was unable to find Margaret, but Johnny showed me his room and I left him at the door, then returned to reception. The receptionist rang around the building trying to locate Margaret, finally finding she had been called into an emergency meeting. There was nothing to do except leave a message requesting to speak to her before my next appointment with Johnny.

23

Arriving back at my flat at 5.15pm, I threw off my coat and immediately rang the office in the hope that Anita was still there. Rachel answered, and replied to my request to be put through to Anita. 'I will see if she is available to talk to you.'

Her tone was not friendly. I waited, thinking that this was a stupid idea – I suspect the line was quiet for only a minute or two but it seemed longer. I sat on my lumpy sofa, pulling at my beard and feeling very uncomfortable in the limbo land between personal and professional. I knew I should have apologised to Anita when she passed me in the morning. I needed to make things up to her, but I couldn't think how to do it without looking as if I were interested in her. She was an attractive, intelligent lady and I really enjoyed her company, but I was still married. If I took her out for a meal clearly on the basis that I owed her an apology, surely that would put things right. I was about to give up and put the receiver down, when Anita's voice answered. She sounded brusque, impersonal, business-like. 'Hello, Mike. What can I do for you?'

I cleared my throat. 'Well, first I wanted to apologise for last night and ask you if you would like to come out for a meal on Saturday.' There, I'd said it. But had I made it clear? There was a brief pause.

'No, I'm sorry, I am busy on Saturday. Maybe some other time.'

I detected, rightly or wrongly, an edge of anger in her response. I couldn't leave things like that. 'OK, some other time. Maybe one day next week?'

'I'm not sure. Is there anything else?'

I disguised the irritation I was feeling at her response, managing to click into professional mode as I pulled Johnny's file from my briefcase and flicked it open.

'Well, I've been to see Johnny today – do you have time for a quick update?'

'Yes, of course. How was he?'

I gave her a rundown of the appointment, telling her about his nervousness and the general atmosphere of the place, including a brief description of the other youngsters. I'd only seen two, of course, but the shouting in the corridor had sounded aggressive and controlling.

'Are you sure he's in the right place, Mike?'

'He's in the only place we could find. It will have to do for now.'

'Do you think he feels safe there?'

'I don't know – but the appointment was very successful. Johnny tried to speak.'

'What do you mean?'

'He was making a guttural noise, and definitely trying to speak. I tried to relax him, slowing down his breathing, so that he could get more from his voice.'

'That's one of the things we must discuss with the speech therapists. I wonder if they have any tips? What made you think of the relaxing breathing?'

'Instinct, I guess, or maybe the fact that I worked with someone with a speech impediment at one stage. The circumstances were different but I used relaxation with him. But from what I remember about people with selective mutism, Johnny will have trouble moving on from mere sounds to words if he is still traumatised.'

'I have pencilled him in for tomorrow afternoon – will the assessment centre let me do art therapy with him, do you think?'

I remembered the warden in green. It was hard to tell.

'Margaret someone is his key worker. She seems to have a good understanding of him. Perhaps if you spoke to the warden, Nancy Armitage, and suggested that Margaret stay throughout?'

'Maybe you should ring and talk to her.'

Anita's suggestion sounded a little more like a command than a request. Under the circumstances, I agreed, 'All right, I'll see if I can get hold of anyone today and let you know in the morning.'

'Thank you.'

The phone call ended with a click. No goodbye, or other niceties. I looked around at my shabby flat, with its bare dirty floorboards, lonely, wilting plant and tea chest for a coffee table. I picked up the cup of cold coffee and stale cheese sandwich from lunchtime and took them into the kitchen. There wasn't even room in the sink to stack the plate and mug. The evening I had spent back at my real home had made me even more aware of my unwelcoming living conditions. Would I be on my own forever? I wished I had someone to talk to.

I felt completely bereft. Had I left it too late with my Ella, and lost Anita's friendship? I felt too sorry for myself to think about it – I picked up the TV controls and started flicking down the channels until I found a mindless late afternoon quiz game to watch.

Later, when I had remembered I had eaten virtually nothing all day, I decided to make myself go and get a kebab. It felt better to be out of the flat. Sydenham High Street was busy, with a sudden rush of commuters leaving the station as I passed. In some vague search for a familiar face, I scanned those around me to see if any of these passengers usually travelled back, or into London, on the same train as me. I recognised no one, but there was a group of black lads in smart public school blazers. One of them looked a little bit like Johnny, which set me making mental comparisons as I stood in the queue, waiting for my kebab. Those rich boys; privileged, in private education, well-spoken, probably never lacking anything, and Johnny; alone, homeless, not even owning the clothes he wore, and in a world where incomprehensible things happened to him that were totally out of his control. Despite all that, he had at least gained in confidence since I first met him as that frightened, shaking boy who could not leave Shirley Hills' side.

Shirley. I realised I hadn't spoken to her about my meeting with Johnny. I had been furious when she didn't keep me informed – now I was doing it to her.

As soon as my kebab was ready, I hurried up through the crowded street, back to my flat. I knew that somewhere I had Shirley's home number and it didn't take too long to locate it. I punched in the numbers. She answered almost immediately.

'Hello, hello. Butch, will you quieten down! Sorry, sorry.'

The barking was getting even louder. I shouted, 'It's me, Mike. Mike Lewis.'

Above the crescendo of canine exuberance, Shirley heard me.

'Oh, hello, Mike. Sorry, dog again. Hang on, I'll put him in the kitchen.'

I waited, imagining her dragging an enormous creature through a cluttered house. I was probably doing her an injustice, but I bet her house was as chintzy as her clothes, even if it wasn't cluttered.

'Mike? Are you still there? We should get some peace now. Any news?'

'Yes, that's why I am ringing. I saw Johnny this afternoon so I thought I should keep you up to date. It can wait until the morning if you are very busy.'

'No, that's fine, I often take evening work calls.'

'I'll try not to take too much of your time. I used drawings to communicate with Johnny, plus a few basic words and signs. In some ways he seems to be settling in, but he is still very nervy – anxious – and startles easily.'

'It's a bit of a rough crowd there, I think.'

'Yes, it's natural that he is a bit on the alert, especially considering his probable history. On the plus side, I was pleased to see he was getting about on crutches.'

'He's a bit wobbly on them. I spoke to the warden, emphasising that he needs to be kept away from those lads who might give him a shove.'

By now, I was quite impressed with Shirley's change of attitude towards Johnny.

'Good move. Another plus today was the fact that he made definite attempts to talk.'

'Did he?'

'Yes, he was mouthing words and managing a guttural noise. Of course, we don't know whether his first language is guttural.'

'What do you mean?'

'Some languages use more of the back of the throat to make the sounds. He was certainly trying to get words out, but not succeeding. I helped him slow down his breathing but he became anxious again trying to talk, so we left it for today.'

'Is there anything I can do to help?'

I was amazed. Shirley seemed to be really trying with Johnny now. Perhaps she felt sorry for him or maybe she had finally realised that he could have acted out of panic the day she frightened him on the Tube.

'Yes. You can use some of your Spanish when you talk to him, but always give the English as well. And if he tries to talk to you and you see his breaths speed up, see if you can relax him a little by first matching his breathing rate in an exaggerated way, then slowing yours down.'

'How does that help?'

'I did it today with him, and he matched my slower breathing and seemed calmer.'

'Well, that sounds a bit technical to me. But I'll try.'

We then discussed what to do if he did say anything and she added, 'Well, I shall look forward to seeing him, then. I go tomorrow morning.'

'Anita will be working with him in the afternoon, if I can sort that out with the warden.'

'Will you be going too?'

My full diary flashed into my mind like a reminder of who I was. A girl with obsessive compulsive behaviour to visit, a depressed mother to work with and a group for the whole afternoon.

'No, not tomorrow. I am rather booked up, but anyway, I think two visits will be enough for Johnny.'

I felt quite satisfied that I had everything covered by the time I had finished talking to Shirley. I peeled the paper off the kebab that had been waiting for me. It looked cold and unappetising. I walked towards the pedal bin, then stopped myself. I scooped out the salad, put the meat and chips onto a separate plate and reheated them in the microwave.

Only as I was eating the rubbery result did I remember that I had said I would sort out Anita's visit with the warden but had forgotten. I would have to ring the centre first thing in the morning.

24

Chasing dreams again – me chasing Ella – Ella elusive, disappearing out of my reach. I had those dreams when I first moved out into this flat, plus the one where we were with Jamie.

Even when I arrived at work, I couldn't get the dream out of my head. I knew I was working at a minimal level. Everything my clients said seemed in some way connected – I had Jenny Drake first. Jenny had really changed of late, but still struggled to get to sessions. She was writing notes when I went to collect her from the waiting room.

She was obviously doing well. She sat immediately into one of my chairs – it usually seemed a bit of an effort – and launched into filling me in on all she had been doing since I last saw her. I knew some of it, because she had written and sent me a tape of her thoughts. But even her accounts of all she had been managing since I last saw her were not sufficient to control my thoughts. When I set her a task and waited for her to complete it, immediately my mind wandered to Jamie's big floppy toy dog that went everywhere with him when he was about two. It had been part of his life until the end, gradually moving from his bed to a windowsill then a shelf and finally tucked away in the top of his wardrobe. I wondered where it was now, if Ella's visitors were using the room. Even as my client talked about her progress, that toy invaded my thoughts. I imagined it thrown carelessly into a cardboard box in the loft – maybe even eaten by mice – or worse. Maybe it had gone into a bag of items for the charity shop.

I rallied enough to complete the appointment and set Jenny more to do. It wasn't really necessary, she was totally self-motivated. Helped perhaps by making a new friend.

The next appointment ran itself, because I was observing Georgina doing a cognitive therapy session with a depressed twenty-year-old lad. I was impressed. Georgina was gaining in confidence every day and could already easily pass as a fully trained clinical psychologist. In fact, I had a lesson in how to do a near perfect session.

After the session we discussed the client's progress. I had little to add to Georgina's plan and as I became hungry I was battling to control my Jamie thoughts again, which were now around wondering what he would like eating if he were alive. I suggested Georgina went and had her lunch.

I sat in my room, and thought. There were bits I couldn't remember about Jamie's life and I began to wish I had gone through all of this when he had first died and written it all down so that the memories were trapped on paper, or in photos. I took a sheet of paper and began a sort of spidergraph, scribbling down his likes and dislikes, friends and favourite people. I couldn't remember. I needed to talk to Ella.

My sandwiches lay uneaten as I started a separate list of things I wanted to know about my son and his possessions. I knew I had let go of him too soon – but maybe I had never let go of him in the first place? The memories had become squashed as I had tried to pretend that nothing had happened, and get on with my life. I had squeezed them tight until they had become fuzzy and useless when I could have kept them alive by talking to Ella.

I jumped when someone knocked on my office door. Before I had a chance to shout 'Come in' Anita opened the door, walked in and carefully closed it behind her. I watched her cross her arms across her chest and take a deep breath.

'We need to talk.'

'Yes.'

'Is that all you have to say?'

'No, no. I'm agreeing with you, that's all.'

Images of toys in the attic and memories being lost left me as I realised that she was doing what I should be doing, and trying to straighten things out between us.

'I'm sorry,' we both said together. She smiled. I carried on talking, 'No, I am the one who should be sorry. I didn't think. I'd taken your suggestion of getting together as only that, so the importance of it hadn't registered. And I honestly had no idea it was your birthday. I thought we were just, you know, meeting up with colleagues after work. Which is maybe why I forgot.'

'But you did forget.'

'I know, there's no excuse really.'

'You told me what happened and I am sorry I didn't accept your apology when you gave it.'

'I was rather self-absorbed. It was the child in the park that sparked my memories. I'm a bit of a mess now.'

'Child in the park?'

I told her as briefly as I could about the little girl struggling with her bike. I hadn't really talked properly about it but now that I was explaining the incident to Anita, it was beginning to feel like a vital turning point.

'You're a nice man, Mike, to try to help in that way. But it is a bit of a risky thing to do in this day and age, with child protection being such a huge issue.'

'I know. Even as I lent her my phone I was worried about that. But I am sure if anyone could see us they would know that I wasn't going to hurt her.'

'Have you done anything about it since?'

'What do you mean?'

'To protect yourself if it ever comes to court.'

'What?'

'I don't suppose it would, but maybe make some notes about it somewhere. Perhaps you could tell Shirley about it and ask her if you should have done anything different.'

I considered this for a moment. If that suggestion had been made maybe three days ago, I would have laughed. But the last phone call I had with her had shown me a side of Shirley that I hadn't expected.

'Maybe.'

'Not maybe – do it!'

I remembered that phrase and tone of voice from when I was with Ella. Anita was bossing me about! Things felt back to normal, except... except I didn't feel excited that she was taking an interest in me at all. She was the wrong person.

'Can I just ask you something, Mike?'

I nodded, wondering what was coming.

'Are you finished with Ella, or is she still a vital part of your life?'

I felt myself go hot and cold. I knew that Anita would ask me something like this, so when I first let her down I had rehearsed the answer many times over. But even the last few minutes had made me change my mind.

'Ella will always be part of my past and I will always have feelings for her. It is unlikely that we have a future together. I may have to accept I have lost her as well as losing Jamie.'

Anita stood quietly. Her hand hovered uncertainly around her mouth, then she regained her composure.

'I understand.' She smiled quickly then glanced at her watch. 'I'd better get on. I'll let you know how things go with Johnny.'

As she left the room I realised I had forgotten to speak to the warden. I lifted the phone and searched for the number which was somewhere in the pile of papers on my desk. I found it, then gathered up the notes and bits of papers about Johnny to put them all together in his file before ringing the number.

The lunchtime conversation with Anita had been difficult, but strangely it had begun to pull me out of my thoughts and memories of Jamie and my fears for the future with regard to Ella. Anita's response, or lack of it, had helped me enormously. Having discovered and articulated my feelings for Ella, I no longer felt locked in a quandary of my own making. I was now determined to take action.

On the way home in the train that day I felt strangely light-headed. I knew now that I needed to grieve for Jamie and that there was only one person who I wanted to help me, if she could cope herself. Despite the fact that she might go to Australia, I was curiously optimistic that the woman I had rejected in her grief may understand enough to help me overcome mine.

But I had no plan. I could scarcely just ring her up and ask her to be my counsellor while I talked about the loss of our son. Nor could I make presumptions and start talking about it. Shared memories were fine, but what about my feelings? Could I bare all to Ella and risk losing any chance with her because of a need to help myself out of this enormous hole?

I wondered through to the kitchen which still smelled of stale kebab, probably because the paper from it was poking out of an overstuffed bin. I thought about Ella coming to the flat to talk to me. This was even more disturbing than when I considered the possibility of Anita coming, when she had wanted to drop the book round. I emptied the sink of its dirty crockery and set to, first tackling the washing up.

I had finished in the kitchen and took the damp cloth through to the living room. It didn't dust very well but was ideal for wiping away coffee mug stains on the windowsills. I puffed up a few cushions and straightened the Spanish material on my substitute coffee table. The place needed vacuuming, but it wasn't too bad.

The doorbell rang. I couldn't actually think what it was and picked up my phone before I realised. I went to the door and had to rub off dust across the peephole to peer through. I couldn't remember ever checking in this way before. I didn't recognise the couple on the other side. I opened the door carefully. A small woman in an olive-coloured coat was nearest to me, a burly man who looked familiar stood behind her.

The woman spoke in a middle-class accent. 'Excuse me; we think you are the gentleman who helped a little girl in the park the other day.'

Anita's concerns about child-protection issues flashed into my mind and caused me to think the worst. I felt cold and clammy.

'Yes, she was struggling in the wind.'

'May we come in?'

I stepped to one side and let them through. They walked past me and stood by the sofa. I stayed by the door with it held open before realising that it looked like I was about to dash off. I closed the door and motioned for them to sit down. I fetched a dining chair and sat opposite them. I could hear my heart pounding as if I were in the head teacher's study but I had the presence of mind to try to take hold of the situation.

'Are you her parents?'

'No, we're not, actually.' Social workers then, or police. I shuddered.

'Well, how can I help you?'

'We are going to need a written account of the episode from you.'

I looked at them, they didn't seem hostile. Just matter-of-fact.

'I'm sorry – I can't discuss this with you unless you explain who you are and why you need an account.'

The man spoke.

'Sorry, mate. Thought you recognised us. I came and fetched her. I'm Fred Bannister and this is my wife, Fiona.'

Fiona Bannister leaned forward. 'We're her carers. We're in trouble with the social workers over the incident.'

'Ah, social workers.' The statement left me without thinking. I was so relieved that it wasn't me trying to save my reputation. Unfortunately it appeared to have the effect of startling the couple who glanced at each other with obvious concern. I hastened to explain, 'I work with social workers sometimes and their job is to keep children safe. That's probably why a man helping a child is frowned upon. I'm sure it won't be a problem.'

'I hope not, it has taken us so long to help Jackie settle. I really think it would be awful if she were moved to a new placement.'

'Bit of a problem, mate, making them realise you had no bad intentions. And we don't want to lose the kid – we're both very fond of her.'

The couple were leaning forward on their chairs, worry lines across their foreheads. Fred was sweating slightly and Fiona had her hands up the opposite sleeves of her coat. Anxious maybe, or cold. I moved across to switch on the fan heater. As I did so, I imagined the child being forced to move because I went to help her. It seemed ridiculous – what was I supposed to do, leave her there? My reputation was nothing compared to the effect of this on a small child.

'I'll get pen and paper and write down what happened. Then you can send it off to them and I'll speak to them as well, if you like. But make sure you tell them I'm a psychologist and am police checked.'

They looked at each other and smiled.

'Thank you so much, that should really help,' said Fiona, and her hands left her sleeves as she moved closer to her husband.

By the time I had written the best account I could of the incident, Fiona had made us all some black coffee and admired my Spanish throw while Fred and I had decided the best jazz musician of all time was Dave Brubeck.

We got on so well I almost found myself inviting them round another time with Jackie. Instead I waved them off, reminding them that they were free to come back if necessary.

25

The next afternoon clinic only had one person booked in, so by 2.15 or so, I was free to concentrate on Johnny's report. I looked at my previous draft. It said very little that was not known before I first saw Johnny. I wondered what other people wrote when assessing mute asylum seekers – I had no idea. Probably there was a little about the intelligence of the client and his ability to tell the truth. I could make a supposition or two about the former, although I still hadn't used any assessments on him. I started listing items from the WISC, the children's version of the WAIS. By now I was pretty certain he must be under sixteen, so they would be the most useful. Then I began to doubt myself and decided I must use both the test for adults and the one for children, but only where there was no obvious overlap to create a result affected by practice.

I had started to doodle in the margins of the papers in front of me. I had nothing to write. This wasn't going to be easy.

My biggest problem was still the same as the one when I first met him. I was really unsure about what had happened to him. There was no proof that the picture he had painted with Anita was really a small child being attacked with an axe. It was clear he was traumatised by something, but that could be anything that had happened on his journey to Britain, not in his home country, wherever that was. My report would be pathetic. I had simply bounced along in a reactive way from incident to incident, trying to befriend him and reduce his anxiety. Glancing through his file, I saw that all my notes reflected this ad hoc approach. It was like a hardly started jigsaw puzzle.

I needed to see other psychological reports on asylum seekers, to identify anything that I could do without speech. I should talk to Anita about it first, of course, and compare files so that we pooled information. I could ask her to write a separate report, and add it as an addendum. Somehow all I did seemed futile because I could not explain it, or draw conclusions from it. Although, clearly Johnny was making some progress.

I picked up the phone to talk to Anita, but then put it down again, realising she would be busy with one of her groups. I tried going on Psychlit to track down some other immigration reports – I couldn't find anything at all, so then wondered if I should ask Georgina to find me information. Trainees seemed able to find out anything that they needed and it would probably be interesting for her. Was this using her, or was it a justifiable use of her time? I rang through to the office.

'When is Georgina next in? I would like her to do a search for me.'

'Not until next Wednesday – the placement days have been changed next week. Didn't she tell you?' Patricia's tone was brusque, impatient. I still wasn't flavour of the month with either of the secretaries.

'Oh, she may have done. Thank you, anyway.'

I went through my own stock of old clinic materials, trying to find anything useful. Eventually I found some exercises for use with a man recovering from cancer in the throat. I could remember the case, although not the name of the man. His speech had been almost non-existent, but those exercises, coupled with anxiety management, had started him building his confidence again. The speech therapist took over once he was brave enough to make a few sounds. I gave up thinking about the report and instead started to prepare for my next appointment with Johnny, drawing a few scenarios that may or may not be relevant to him. My stick men were not too beautiful, but I thought the situations were recognisable. Someone shouting, someone holding a knife to him, a sort of picture of him in the hold of the *Margarita*, then one of him being run over. I then decided it was all too terrifying, so added him eating at a table, drawing with Anita and seeing me. I then tried drawing a scale with my version of 'The Scream' at the top of it and a smiling Johnny at the bottom. I had no idea what I was doing, really, but I hoped Johnny would cotton on and recognise what I wanted for him. Would it stand up in court, or would it be considered priming him? I would have to go with it. But the more I looked at my effort at preparing a fear hierarchy, the more I thought it was futile. It was upside down for a start – much better to put the aimed-for result at the top of the page. I tore it up.

I sat thinking, desperately trying to come up with a better idea, until I realised I was doodling on the cover of Johnny's file. Six days until Georgina could be asked to do the search and all that time wasted, I thought. I had my elbows on my pile of papers and my head in my hands, when there was a knock on my door.

As I lifted my head, Georgina looked in.

'Were you looking for me Mike, or are you trying to plan something for next week?'

Those secretaries – why didn't they tell me she was in today? I hadn't seen her and Thursday certainly wasn't a usual day. Within five minutes we had sorted out what I needed to know and she had left my room with the file, appearing very eager to find out everything she could.

In celebration and probably because I felt quite relieved that Georgina was on the case, I turned my attention away from Johnny and began a sort out of my cluttered desk. By the end of the afternoon I had dictated four outstanding letters and made three bookings for new clients, plus created space to work by putting away a huge pile of files.

For once I left the office feeling that I had done a day's work. It was only when I was on the train that I realised it was my appointment with Johnny next morning. I was going straight there since it was only a short distance from my home, and my file was with Georgina. In it was the page of speech exercises and my carefully drawn scenarios for Johnny to make sense of what happened to him.

There was a delay on the train to Sydenham, so I was late back. Despite my hunger, I stopped myself from going into the kebab shop but walked further down the high street to buy eggs, cheese, potatoes, bread and mushrooms. I let myself into my flat and stepped over a large white envelope which had been pushed under the door. Putting my shopping and briefcase down, I looked at it carefully.

It didn't look like anything official, and had no name on the front. I opened it and was mystified to see a card obviously made by a child. My heart turned over as I briefly thought it was from Jamie.

The card had a picture drawn on the front of bent trees and a bicycle. So I realised who had drawn it before I opened it. Inside was a big 'Thank You' in orange and blue letters and 'love Jackie' in purple and pink with a row of kisses. There was a letter as well, handwritten on good quality writing paper.

> *Dear Mike*
> *It was lovely to meet you last night. We have phoned our social worker and read out your description of what happened. I think it's all going to be all right. They said they may contact you at some time but all they did was tell us off for letting Jackie come home on her own in that gale. We didn't, of course, she was meant to be at school choir practice and forgot to go!*
> *But thank you for your intervention. It is a sad world when a good deed is met with such suspicion.*
> *Yours*
> *Fiona and Fred*

I smiled as I went into the kitchen to make a coffee and get on with preparing my meal. I noticed the answer phone was blinking, but ignored it as I set to making a cheese omelette. I took my meal back into the living room and placed it on my Spanish throw. I then listened to my phone messages.

The first one was from Georgina, who had realised I was seeing Johnny and gave me her home phone number in case I needed anything from the file. 'Smart girl,' I thought. Then it was Ella.

'Hi, Mike, it's Ella. I'm on my own this evening if you need to talk. Feel free to come for a meal. Give me a ring. Bye.'

By now it was eight o'clock and my mouth was watering for the rapidly cooling omelette. I took it back in the kitchen, hovering over the bin to throw it away, then realised she had probably eaten ages ago.

I rang Ella's number.

'Hello, Ella here.'

'I've just listened to your message, I was late home. Is it too late to come?'

'Well, I did a large shepherd's pie, in case you did, but I have eaten mine. Are you hungry?'

'I am, yes.'

'I'll pop it in the oven and watch you eat when you arrive, then.'

I laughed. I was feeling extraordinarily happy. Talk about a day of chaotic emotions.

'I'm on my way!'

I took two bites out of the omelette and ate the mushrooms before confining the rest to the bin. At least it would stop my stomach rumbling. As I changed my shirt, I remembered I had Johnny's hierarchy to prepare again. I mustn't be too late back. But even Johnny seemed less important than the fact that my wife had invited me to dinner. I knew I should go carefully this time and not rush her. But my heart was pounding with the hope that this was the evening that would renew our courtship.

26

Ella greeted me at the door with a broad smile, brief hug and a telling off.

'Your beard looks really straggly, Mike. It needs a trim. Come on through, I'll serve your meal.'

I gave her a quick hug back.

'I just can't find a decent barber these days!'

She laughed. I remembered the towel round my neck and trying to make her giggle as she stood over me and tut-tutted at the mess my beard was in. She was forever telling me to shave it off and save her a job, but I think she liked it really.

I followed her through to the dining room, feeling calm and comfortable.

The table was set as before, but this time with two places opposite each other, cloth napkins by the cutlery and a candle in the middle. I hung my jacket on the back of the chair, recognising my status as a visitor, not the part-owner of this house which still took a fair amount of my salary in mortgage repayments. While I waited for her, I watched the candle, wondering whether this was a romantic dinner, until I remembered that Ella always lit candles when we were together, even after Jamie was born. I wondered why there wasn't one last time we came. Maybe it was too much of a risk with her lodger.

The shepherd's pie was covered in cheese and there was a pile of broccoli, carrot and courgettes on the plate as well. I remembered our old ritual of helping ourselves and was a bit surprised that she had not brought the food through in bowls. Maybe she would have done if we had eaten properly together. I regretted the snatched mouthfuls of mushroom and omelette; this looked like too much to eat.

Ella had brought a minute portion for herself. 'I couldn't let you eat alone,' she said as she sat down opposite me.

'This is nice,' I said and then thought to myself, 'That sounded pathetic!'

'Umm,' said Ella. She pulled herself up straight in the chair and looked straight at me. My mind stopped, waiting for something. It came.

'I'm sorry to bring you round here but I do need to talk to you about one or two practical things.'

My first thought was that she must have decided she was going to Australia and the house would need to be sold. That would account for Shaun's absence – he must be trying out sheltered housing or something. The beautiful shepherd's pie felt like rubbish in my mouth. I put down my knife and fork.

'You're selling the house.' My voice sounded flat, hostile maybe.

Ella gave me a quizzical look. 'Whatever made you think that?'

'You said you might be taking up a post in Australia.'

'Oh, that. No, I've become rather unsure about what to do. I've asked for them to give me a few months before I give my answer. It's probably only an escapism dream. I might leave it a year or so and see if there's anything then. Meanwhile, I want to convert the loft.'

I must have let out a sigh of relief. Ella reached over and touched my arm.

'Sorry, I startled you. I didn't mean to. I didn't know the house meant so much to you, anyway.'

'No, it's not the house.' I looked at her and I couldn't explain. Her eyes were large in the candlelight and I longed to go round and hug her, kiss her and ask if I could come back home. Too soon. I focused on my plate and started to eat again.

'Well, what do you think about me converting the loft?'

'Yes, go ahead. But what for? Haven't you got enough space for the two of you here? And won't Shaun be leaving you soon?'

'I want it as an investment. I can have two lodgers and maybe you won't feel obliged to pay the mortgage. I've worked it all out.'

This shepherd's pie was now sawdust again. Everything was slipping away.

'I want to pay the mortgage. I'm used to paying the mortgage. There's no need to convert the loft for that.'

'But where do you live, Mike? In a one-bedroomed flat, probably without much furniture and in a not very good area. It's not fair on you.'

The slipping away feeling was so powerful I had to make a move.

'Ella, I was hoping that I would be able to come home one day. I haven't even unpacked everything.'

Ella looked down. She said nothing. She wiped the corner of her mouth with her napkin, although I hadn't seen her eat a thing. I started to curse myself for breaking my own rule about rushing her. How long would it take to do a loft extension anyway, and fill up the house with another lodger? I had plenty of time and yet I had pushed myself forward again.

'So that's a "no" to the extension, is it?'

I was flummoxed. Hadn't she heard me? My voice was flat when I answered her.

'No, it's not a "no". If you think you need the extension, then I'll help you fund it. After all, it is *our* house at the moment.'

'Thank you. I did hear what you said, Mike, but I really don't know what to do about that. I need to be moving forward in my life and for now I can't take on anything too emotional.'

'I need to sort out my grief.' Even as I said this, I was surprised I had managed to express it. I had been denying it to myself for so long.

'I know you do. But I'm not the one to help you, if you were thinking that. Find a counsellor or one of your colleagues and see if you can do something about it.'

I nodded and tried another mouthful of shepherd's pie. It was going down all right but I couldn't leave things too uncertain. I took a deep breath and asked her, 'So that's not a "no" to a future together, then, is it?'

Ella laughed, maybe a little too brightly. 'I don't know, Mike. You see if you can get some help with your grief for Jamie, and we'll see where we go from there.'

We both looked at where Jamie used to sit. I remembered him smiling at us and the broccoli trees. He would always be there with us, however much counselling I had and however much I accepted the fact that he was gone. I was just about to say this when Ella looked at me. Her eyes were glistening and she was blinking.

'Your counsellor may tell you to get over me as well,' she said.

I couldn't look at her as I took another mouthful of sawdust and tried to listen as she immediately turned the conversation to her plans for the loft conversion.

27

I slept so late the next morning that I was certainly not prepared for Johnny. I scrambled to get ready and then rang the home to say I was delayed and would be half an hour late. I used the last ten minutes before I left for my new deadline to scribble notes in a small notepad, detailing my drawings of the day before. I found some A4 sheets, a pencil, scissors, sellotape and a red pen and threw them into my nearly empty briefcase. I felt rather at sea without Johnny's file and so little equipment, but felt it would have to do.

In my rush, I had forgotten my badge, which I discovered when I was trying to sign myself in. It was very embarrassing as I was asked for proof of my identity and found I had none. I had a sense of déjà vu as I ran my hands through all my pockets trying to find anything to show who I was. I was despairing and thinking I would have to go home when Margaret, Johnny's key worker, recognised me and came over to the reception window.

'Hello, Dr Lewis, how are you this morning? Are you having difficulties?'

'I seem to have arrived without my identity badge.'

Margaret turned to the receptionist and introduced me. The girl sullenly pushed the button under her desk. The door swung open in front of me.

'Thank you so very much,' I said as I walked in with Margaret.

For the first time I was asked to leave my briefcase in the locker and only take in anything that could not be used as a weapon. I was let through the second doors with my strange assortment of notebook, paper, pencils, sellotape and a single pen. I was not allowed to take the scissors. A member of staff, who looked as if he should be in the army, explained that there had been an incident involving home-made weapons the night before. I was very pleased to see Johnny, when I was shown into a visitors' room where he was waiting for me, with no obvious signs of being the person who had been attacked with any sort of weapon. The door was locked behind me. I shuddered. I have never liked closed spaces very much.

Johnny was sitting down, his damaged leg stretched out in front of him on a small stool. He greeted me with an effort to speak. I slowed him down and he began again. He was definitely making an M sound. It took me some time to realise he was saying 'me' and then I was surprised he was speaking English. I don't know why, when everyone had been speaking English to him for the last few months. I sat down opposite him, mimicking what he was saying. He repeated it several times until he was clearly articulating 'me' and pointing at himself, over and over again, only interrupted by his need to smile. I was about to introduce him to another word when a long drawn-out 'u' filled the room. He was pointing at me while he said it. I laughed and pointed at him, saying 'you'. I tried to get him to say 'table' and 'chair'. Both were beyond him but he made an effort.

I looked around for something else to teach him. There was nothing else in the room. I wondered where his crutches were. There were no pictures on the white wall, the vinyl chairs were screwed to the floor and so was the heavy coffee table. I had glanced into this room the time before but hadn't noticed how bare it was; everything was a slightly softer version of a prison. I wondered if the feeling of being locked in was helping Johnny feel safe enough to speak, but doubted it considering his panic during our last appointment. Maybe he was beginning to feel safe with us – Anita and myself. Whatever it was, I needed to get on with reinforcing his efforts at speaking. Johnny was waiting, his large eyes watching me. 'Ear,' I said, tugging at my own.

'Ear'. It was nearly perfect – I stopped myself from hugging him.

'Nose,' I tried.

Johnny's mouth moved round trying to create the shape of mine; after a few times he gave up and looked at his feet. I wanted to encourage him.

'Johnny, I am really pleased. You are trying out your English on me. Can you speak in your own language?'

He looked at me blankly. I tried to think of another way of asking. I pointed to my tongue, then him and said 'you'. He shrugged and looked down again. I decided I would have to involve a speech therapist, or a linguist. I was out of my depth. I resolved to turn back to what I knew.

'I'm going to draw something with you, Johnny, so that I can understand what makes you frightened.'

I began to draw again the situations I could remember from the ones I had worked on the day before. Having no scissors, I tore around the edge of them as each one was finished. Then I handed the little slips of paper to Johnny. My intention had been to finish a few scenarios and help him put them in an order of fearfulness. Johnny took them one by one and looked at them closely. He seemed to understand what they were, these scruffy little sketches, and when he had worked them out he put them on the coffee table. I was so busy drawing and watching him scrutinise the pictures that I made a mistake. Without thinking, I handed him a picture of a person with an axe. He took it from me and looked at it closely.

One repeated word escaped from his mouth as he shuddered and crawled to a corner, dragging his leg.

'No, no, no.'

It took around forty minutes of trying to engage Johnny enough to calm him down. He said no more words, but by the time I left he had drawn some smiling faces, recognisable as Margaret, his key worker, Shirley, Anita and myself. The picture of the man with the axe was in my pocket – I planned not to let him look at it again until he was ready and able to work on the trauma.

I travelled into work feeling quite optimistic. With the carriage to myself at this later hour, I was able to look at the morning's notes and draw up a bit of a plan. The first thing to do was to contact the speech therapy department and see if anyone could come on board yet, to work with Johnny. Or maybe assess him and give me some ideas.

Then we would begin to address the problem of finding his first language, perhaps. This was out of my experience. I would have to take advice from the immigration service. Did they have a multilinguist who could identify languages? By now, Johnny would probably be able to respond in a way that would indicate that he understood a particular language.

I made one or two notes and sat thinking about it, being so engrossed in my planning that I was surprised when the train arrived at London Bridge. I stuffed my papers in the briefcase and hurried on my journey.

Once I was back at the office I waved to the secretaries, then went into my room. I found the nearest speech therapy department and dialled the number. My request to the head of department was met with almost ridicule. All the speech therapists were very busy with long waiting lists. Same story at the next hospital. Then I remembered I hadn't asked about paediatric speech therapy, so I phoned the same two departments again. The same derision for my first call, but I got nowhere with the second call because the head of department was now in a meeting. I wondered if the immigration service would fund a private referral. After all, they wanted a report soon and I would be far less hampered if Johnny was able to talk to me.

There was a knock on my door. It was Rachel.

'Mike, you do know your next client is waiting, do you?'

'Oh, I don't think I have anyone in my diary.'

I flicked it open to prove my point, only to see a long-term client's name.

'Oh no, I am sorry, I should have seen her half an hour ago.'

Rachel tutted and left the room. I quickly did a little bit of a tidy-up, including putting the dirty mugs on my desk into the bottom drawer of the filing cupboard. I noticed that the ones in there already had signs of mould beginning to grow. I found the right file, and opening it saw that I had promised to send some notes from the last meeting. I didn't recall doing so. Feeling wrong-footed, I tried to pull my thoughts into some sort of order, ready to help this lady begin to live her life without my support.

Shirley rang with good news for Johnny later in the afternoon. She had used all her social worker's know-how to track down a foster carer with a vacant space that relished the opportunity of looking after an asylum seeker with a broken leg.

'Shirley, that's great. When will he go?'

'Well, Mike, I could move him on Monday, but then he won't know what's happening. I am not able to get away this afternoon to see him. Do you have any time at all to get over to Crystal Palace and somehow see if you can help him understand that he will be moving?'

'The time isn't important, Shirley. I don't mind seeing him this evening, but I am really unsure about how to convey the information to him.'

'Maybe Anita could draw something to help?'

I was glad she'd said that. Because she thought Anita and I were more than work colleagues, I had hesitated to suggest that I might need her help.

'If she's free, I'll see if she can draw me a cartoon to illustrate what's happening. Otherwise I will try with my scribbles. Will you be picking him up tomorrow? If so, what time? And who is he going to? And how will he get there?'

By the time she had rung off, I had all the information I needed. I rang the internal number for Anita, realising, as I did so, that she hadn't told me about her meeting with Johnny. In fact, I didn't even know whether it had happened.

When she answered, I asked, 'I'm sorry to ask you to fit in something extra, Anita, but please could you draw me a cartoon strip of Johnny moving to a family home? I need it to take round this evening to prepare him.'

'No problem, Mike. Anything for Johnny. I had arranged to see him on Monday, but obviously that won't happen now. I'll be straight up with the materials I need to draw a sequence of pictures to prepare him, then you can tell me exactly what's happening and how we need to get it through to him.'

With a sigh of relief, I thanked her and put down the phone. It was so good to be working in tandem again. I knew that whatever happened, we had strengthened our professional relationship through sharing our skills. I prayed that would continue.

It was quite late when I left the office armed with the most exquisite cartoon strip clearly depicting Johnny moving house. The names of the new carers were Jodie and Mark Hartley. They had three children of their own, one grown-up and gone and the other two in their early teens. Twin boy and girl. The picture Anita had drawn of them all welcoming him may have been a little fanciful as they all stood with open arms, but I had known from the address the sort of house it was likely to be. I hoped I was right. We had managed to check one or two bits and pieces about the family with Shirley, but then Shirley had been due in a meeting and switched her phone off.

Instead of my usual train home, I took the train direct to Crystal Palace. This time I had my identity badge with me, the materials I needed and Johnny's file which Georgina had left ready in the secretaries' office. I arrived, more or less on time, and Shirley had let them know I was coming. It took Margaret a few minutes to find Johnny and bring him into the visitors' room.

'Sorry,' she said. 'He was helping in the art room.'

'Helping?'

'Yes, he's been helping the volunteer to sort out the stock. He catches on very quickly, despite the language barrier.'

Johnny was smiling as she said this. I had two thoughts. First, were we actually panicking and taking him away from a place where in fact he was happy? Second, did Johnny understand her, or was he only picking up that she was pleased with him? I decided his understanding must be pretty good when she added, 'You know, I shall really miss him when he moves. He is such a breath of fresh air here. He isn't aggressive, or demanding or depressed. He is really helpful. Aren't you, Johnny?'

Johnny was looking at her quizzically, his head on one side and his eyebrows slightly raised. He nodded at her question but then turned to me, the query still over his face. I forgot about the beautifully drawn cartoon strip and said to him, 'Yes, Johnny. We thought you might not be safe here. Your keyworker is very good at protecting you but some of the other lads might hurt you. We want to move you to a family.'

Johnny looked at Margaret.

'It will be better than here, Johnny. You won't be locked in.' He didn't appear to understand, so she went to the door and unlocked it. He moved towards it.

'No, you stay here Johnny,' I said. 'Come and look at Anita's drawings.'

He came and sat on the vinyl chair next to me in the barren little room.

'I'll sit out of the way, Mike,' said Margaret, as she took a seat in the corner. Johnny looked up and gave her a thumbs-up sign, then turned his attention to me.

I spread the cartoon open across the coffee table, rolling out the first section. It was a bit too long – Anita had insisted that it should be written in one strip so that there was no confusion about the order. So she had cut two A3 sheets of white thin card into three and stuck the sections together lengthways. To make it easier for me to carry it, she had rolled it and put some cord around it. The end fell off the table and unrolled as it reached the floor.

Meanwhile, Johnny had already begun to scrutinise the pictures. He was recognising himself and said 'me' several times over as he looked at the first few drawings. The initial one had me in it too: it was a picture of the both of us in the same room looking at the cartoon strip. He grinned broadly.

Anita had then drawn Margaret taking him from the room, him having his meal with the other boys, and then him in bed. It was looking as if he understood all this.

There was a picture of him getting up and eating breakfast. Then he was back in this room, but with Shirley.

Johnny was shaking his head. I thought about the number of moves he had already had – from the asylum centre to the lodgings in Silk Row, then into hospital, then here and now he was on the move once more. I wondered again whether we were doing the right thing.

The next cartoon was him in a taxi with Shirley. He looked at it and shook his head. I pointed to the following picture of two adults, with two fairly tall children stood beside them in a doorway. All were smiling and the taxi was just coming into the picture. The colour on the cartoon was enough to indicate that the man was black and the woman white, with the children somewhere in between. The next illustration showed Johnny and Shirley getting out of the taxi, followed by the family greeting Johnny with open arms.

I moved the cartoon strip across the table. Johnny seemed to have understood everything so far. I had been talking about it as I went on so somehow he had come to the right conclusions.

It had been a bit difficult for Anita to draw the inside of the house, but she had indicated a room with a sofa and a television, which was good. Then she had drawn an upstairs room, from near the top of the stairs, where you could see Johnny sat on the bed.

I waited for Johnny to come to the final pictures. There was a night-time view of the room with curtains closed and lights out. Then a glimmer of light through the curtains and an alarm clock ringing and the final picture showed Johnny sat at the breakfast table with the family.

Johnny's finger was following the pictures. He spent longer over some than over the others. I didn't know what he understood but he looked at me with a slight furrow between his brows for the first bedroom picture. After he had studied the other two and he moved onto the picture of the breakfast table, it was as if he suddenly saw what it was all about.

Johnny looked at Margaret, then at me, then at the picture. He nodded. But he did not smile.

When I was back in work on Monday, my morning was peppered with meetings. Patricia called me out of the second one, telling me that Margaret had phoned. I expected that the arrangements had not come together and that Johnny was not coping.

'Hello, Mike, you asked me to ring with any news so I thought I'd fill you in with the progress so far.'

'Yes, thank you.'

She then began to tell me how Johnny had spent the evening in his room, pouring over the cartoon strip.

'I became a little concerned that he may be brooding,' she added, 'so I then took him to one of the quiet rooms for a chat, just to make sure he understood what was happening. With signals and odd words that he could say he took me through the whole process. I was very impressed. They are great pictures.'

'Yes, I think Anita did an excellent job. How was he when he went through them? Did he seem upset to be going?'

'Oh no, quite the contrary. When he came to the last few pictures he used both hands to point at the drawings of himself and his new foster father and to say "me", pointing at his own face. I thought he seemed very excited to be going to a family where at least one member looked like him.'

I felt annoyed with myself that I hadn't really taken on board the importance of racial similarity earlier. Margaret was finishing her description of the morning.

'Shirley arrived soon after he had finished breakfast. He'd packed his bag as soon as he got up, so he was sat on the bed waiting, clutching the rolled-up cartoon. Although he hadn't spoken to them, I thought I should take him through to reception via the day room. Three of the lads were there and they crowded round him saying their goodbyes.'

'I hadn't realised he had made friends already.'

'He was liked, well enough. One of the boys who said goodbye was a big lad who had been taunting Johnny. He came over to shake his hand saying, "Bye mate. No hard feelings, eh?" I don't know if Johnny understood.'

Margaret then told me how pleased Johnny was when Shirley came. Everything was a little hurried because Shirley had asked her taxi to wait, so hastily bustled him out and told him to get in. Margaret managed to say 'goodbye' as she followed them out of the building.

But, there had been a bit of a hiccup. Anita had drawn a typical London taxi, but this was an ordinary car. Johnny stood by the car, then, with his bag on his back, walked back towards Margaret. Shirley had the presence of mind to get him to unroll his cartoon. Between Margaret and Shirley he gradually realised that this was indeed a taxi, so he did get in.

'He did look very sad as the taxi drew away,' said Margaret. 'I do hope he'll be all right with his new people. I know he'll be safe, but will anyone really care about what happens to him?'

'That's the problem,' I thought, as I finished the phone call and made my way back to the family room for the rest of the meeting. 'He is being moved around, from pillar to post with no real plan.'

I expected a phone call from Shirley within the next hour. I had back-to-back meetings, and I knew my mind was elsewhere. I wasn't sure why this move seemed so much more crucial than the others. Perhaps it was because he had started trying to communicate and I was worried that he might give up if there were too many changes in his life.

It was lunchtime before I heard anything. I was interrupted from a hastily arranged meeting with the occupational therapist about a client who had become psychotic. We were struggling with the need to involve psychiatry and the fact that when he was not in a psychotic state he was responding well to rebuilding his life after a long depressive episode.

When the call was transferred to my office, I scarcely had time to say hello before Shirley was telling me about the morning.

'Johnny has coped so well. I think we have finally found somewhere that is good for him.'

'I'm very pleased to hear that.'

'We arrived in West Wickham and the house was very similar to the cartoon. We knocked on the door and Johnny's face dropped. His new foster mother took him indoors and then Johnny unrolled his cartoon to show the picture.'

'Oh, so we made another mistake there. He was expecting all the family.'

'Yes, but it didn't matter. She yelled upstairs and down came the foster dad. His colouring was virtually the same as Johnny's and they both sat there poring over the cartoons with wide smiles on their faces.'

'Well, that's a relief; we thought we might be taking a gamble with making the shading so close.'

'No, it was perfect. But it's a shame the children weren't there. They were at school.'

'Of course! We hadn't thought of that.'

'Plainly not.' I thought I detected a little criticism in her voice.

'Anyway,' she continued, 'his foster mother showed him a photo of them both. He took it and looked at it closely, then passed it back to her, smiling.'

'How did he manage with his leg in plaster?'

'Oh, didn't I say? The dad is disabled. The room is all clear for his wheelchair and Johnny was fine getting around on his crutches. There's a stairlift, which he seemed to cope with well.'

'Good job Johnny is adaptable,' I thought, 'because there's another mistake in the cartoon.'

'I stayed for about half an hour, during which Johnny was trying to say things to his new foster dad and they were both drawing when they couldn't make each other understand. At one point Johnny laughed.'

I felt a little envious – I had so longed to hear him laugh and had thought I would be the first to do so. I remembered missing Jamie's first steps and having the same feeling. What was the matter with me? I had never felt like this about a client before. I was definitely getting too involved.

'Mike, are you still there?'

I realised I had stopped listening.

'Yes, Shirley, I'm sorry, I lost you for a bit there. You'd said he laughed.'

'And I said please thank Anita for me, Mike. Those pictures really helped.'

'Anita will be very pleased they were so useful.'

'They were. I think we may have had a very reluctant young man if we hadn't had those pictures, you know. As it was, he seems to have totally accepted the change.'

'Well, that's great. Let's hope he continues to feel settled.'

'I'm sure he will, Mike, that couple have an excellent reputation.'

By the time I had finished speaking to her I was feeling pretty pleased too. The drawings put together so beautifully by Anita turned out to be pretty near the mark. I rang to tell her.

Anita and I became very excited on the phone, talking about Johnny and throwing ideas around. In fact, I forgot I was trying to hold back and it may have been me that suggested that after work we went and had a drink.

'Well, thank you, Mike. That would be good. Not quite a birthday meal, but a drink would help!'

I felt instantly guilty about the mess I had made of meeting up with her on her birthday.

'I could probably stretch to a meal. We'll have to see. What time do you finish tonight?'

Only after I had put the phone down did I realise I had actually made a sort of date with Anita. Then I felt guilty about Ella. There was no winning! I liked Anita as a friend and colleague but my hopes for the future were with Ella. I wasn't sure what to do. Be careful, I suppose.

We left work together at 6pm. I was hoping we weren't attracting attention to ourselves, but suspected we probably were. I wasn't really sure which way to turn when we came out of the office. I hadn't been to the pub for some time after work – years, probably.

'Where are we going, Mike?'

'I'm not really sure. Any ideas?'

'I know a place near Leicester Square. It's a nice friendly pub with decent food if we decide to eat.'

With no better idea, I was in no position to argue.

'That sounds good,' I mumbled.

'OK, come on then.' Anita strode purposefully towards the Underground and I hurried to keep up.

Taking a tube ride in the rush hour forced us into a proximity for which I was not prepared. I remembered the day we all got caught in a rainstorm after taking Johnny to the gallery. We had dived into the Tube, mostly for shelter. I had enjoyed being with her then. Now I felt guilty. In fact, now I really felt married again. Even though Ella and myself were not together, the very fact that she was prepared to see me and help me made me realise that I was linked to her in a very strong way.

'Penny for them, Mike.'

'What? Oh, sorry, I was miles away. I was thinking about Johnny and the first time he went to the Tate.'

'Tate Modern, you mean.'

'Yes, I do. It was absolutely pouring when we came out.'

'And you got cross because I started doing some work with him when we got back and forgot to ask your permission.'

'I didn't get cross.'

'Oh yes, you did!'

Anita made a face at me and then smiled.

'I forgive you,' she said.

I felt uncomfortable. I had wondered what had happened to them, but I was sure I wasn't cross. At least, if I was, I didn't show it.

'Come on, it's our stop.' Anita took my arm and steered me out of the train. In a way, it was just as well she did, because it was so crowded that I wasn't sure how we would have kept together otherwise. She let go as we went up the escalator, but I took hold of her arm when we were back in the crush as we went through the ticket barriers. It was a relief to be out in the fresh air.

'This way, Mike,' said Anita. I followed her closely, with the street still busy. I was beginning to feel like a child on an outing. It occurred to me that I was one of Anita's projects. She was throwing herself into this outing in the same way she threw herself into running women's groups and teaching Johnny to communicate. Wholehearted. Was that what I liked about her, the way she just went for it? I slowed my pace. I wasn't sure I wanted her going for me. I didn't know what I wanted. This quiet celebration drink had turned into something different. I felt unkempt, unconfident and unsure. I was out of my depth.

There was a crowd now, between Anita and me. A thought went through my mind about turning off down one of the side alleys and making my way back to the Tube. I saw Anita stop ahead of me, turning slowly round, scanning the crush, looking worried. I couldn't do that to her. I would have to make it clear where our boundaries were. I pushed my way through the bunch of tourists in front of me and caught her up.

'Are you sure this is a good idea? I had rather thought we were going to have a little celebratory drink.'

'Sorry. But you did say "I could probably stretch to a meal", so this is the nearest place I knew that would do both.' Anita didn't sound sorry, she sounded hurt.

'Of course. I thought there would be somewhere nearer, that's all. But I don't often go out these days, as you know.'

Anita laughed. 'Perhaps this wasn't such a good idea of yours! You haven't just remembered you are meeting your ex-wife, have you?'

'No, no, nothing like that.' I attempted a grin. 'I'm all yours.'

Anita smiled and put her arm in mine. 'Come on, then, let's go and have our celebratory meal.'

Somehow I got through the meal. I was fine toasting Johnny and our excellent work with him. I was uncomfortable when Anita asked for the menu, but then I had said I was 'all hers'. What a stupid thing to say. I was Ella's and Jamie's. I felt the familiar pang of loneliness and loss. Meanwhile, Anita was choosing what she would like to eat and more or less chose mine. I was feeling more and more like a child. I took myself off to the gents.

I was gone a long time, trying to work out what to do. In the end I went out of the back and phoned Ella.

'Hi there, Mike, what can I do for you?' She sounded pleased that I had rung.

'I wanted to know how you are, really. I've ended up in a pub with Anita and it is making me remember things we used to do. I've nipped out while waiting for our order to come.'

'Just Anita?'

'Yes.' I felt pathetic.

'Look, she's someone you work with, isn't she? What's the problem?'

'I think she sees it as more than a meeting of two colleagues.'

There was a slight pause before she said anything.

'And do you see it like that?'

'No, I feel a bit cornered.'

A pause again.

'Look Mike, I don't know how you feel. But if you are attracted to her, then don't let me stand in your way.'

'She's attractive, but I really don't think...' I didn't know what to say.

'Be honest with her, Mike. Go and eat your meal and try to talk to her.'

'I am sorry I rang you, Ella. I suppose it's because I feel a bit stuck.'

'I can't live your life for you, Mike. Go on, go and eat!'

'Well, bye, then, Ella. Speak to you soon.'

'Bye, Mike.'

There was a cough behind me. I turned round. Anita was there. I don't know what she heard.

'The food's on the table, Mike. I thought you must be on the phone somewhere – or dead in the loo.' Her voice sounded flat.

'Sorry, Anita. That's the trouble with spontaneous outings; you forget you have phone calls to make! Let's go and eat.'

I felt really sorry that I may have upset her yet again, so I put my arm gently round her shoulder as we walked back to our table. I proposed a toast with our Sauvignon Blanc before we started eating, 'To us. The developers of the most creative and crazy therapeutic approach for mutism.'

Anita smiled a little. 'Perhaps we had better write a paper about it together.'

'Maybe we should. Complete with your drawings.'

'What's the stuffiest journal to submit it to? And should we do a few keynote addresses to promote it?'

Within a few minutes we were laughing as we imagined presenting the paper to several of the most stodgy and traditional leaders of our respective professions, including the bits about Shirley's initial fear that he tried to abuse her and my other less professional attempts at reaching him. If Anita had overheard that I was talking to Ella on the phone, she didn't say. But the evening went well and we remained strictly colleagues as we ate our respective fish dishes.

I admired Anita for her composure; she is quite some woman.

28

When I got back to the flat, I phoned Ella. It was only 10.30pm, but it sounded as though she had been asleep.

'Is that you, Mike? What time is it?'

'Sorry, did I wake you?'

'Yes. How did your evening go?'

'Thank you, it went well. Anita and I have decided we might write a paper together about the asylum seeker case.'

'Sounds good.' I heard her yawn. 'How's that going?'

'Look, I've woken you up. I'm sorry. Let's talk about it some other time. I'd love to pop round if I can.'

'Yes. Ring me tomorrow, we'll sort something. Or I can get a sitter for Shaun and come to you.'

I glanced round my messy flat.

'Maybe. But it's always a bit of a mess and I wouldn't like you to think you had to sort me out.'

It was only afterwards that I realised why she laughed.

Another early start to go and see Johnny. Anita had set it up with his new carers and I was up early enough to take a number 194 bus to West Wickham. I knew I could order a cab, but I never remembered to claim for these journeys so the bus was cheaper.

The bus was crowded with schoolchildren and college students, mainly. There was an empty seat upstairs. A young man not unlike Johnny followed me and sat sideways on the left of my seat with his back to me, to shout to his friends on the opposite side and further down the bus. The general noise level was awful and some of the language very unwholesome. I made a mental note to myself to stand downstairs in preference next time.

Eventually I clambered over backpacks and sports bags to get out at my stop. I stood on the pavement and wished I had brought my A–Z. I didn't even know if I still had one. I couldn't remember when I last used it.

The houses were all like the one Anita had drawn. Semi-detached, bay windows, arched porch. Probably built immediately post-war; I was unsure, I'm not good at architecture. I set off in what I discovered was the wrong direction so it took me twenty minutes to reach the house, which was probably only about five from the bus stop. It didn't seem to matter too much; the greeting from the new foster mother was warm and inviting.

'Dr Lewis, how good to meet you. Are you the person who drew the beautiful cartoon strip?' She was tall and fair-haired with a lovely smile.

I smiled back as I answered, 'Oh no, I'm no artist. The art therapist and I have both been involved with helping Johnny. For the cartoon, I worked out the most likely scenario and she did the artwork.'

'I think it is amazing. How did she know what our house looked like?'

'I knew what sort of houses they were along here because my wife and I were house-hunting in this area, maybe ten years ago. We looked at one along the street.' I didn't add that we wanted a house that didn't look the same as all the others in the neighbourhood. I knew they were great houses, though; just not for us.

'Well, what a good job you did. Johnny seems to have accepted us really well. Maybe there should be something like that for every foster child – well, certainly every child who may have difficulty understanding what is happening to them.'

'Maybe we should patent the idea. Is Johnny around?'

'I'll call him. He'll be doing something with his foster dad. Those two have really hit it off.'

'Well, let me go and find him. I'd love to see what they are doing.'

They were busy in the shed at the bottom of the garden. Mrs Hartley showed me where to go and then went back to a huge pile of ironing, which had obviously been abandoned when I rang the doorbell.

Before I reached the shed I could hear a deep voice talking, interrupted by the occasional grunt or attempt at a word. As I opened the door, Johnny was saying 'me', holding out his hand to have a turn at screwing a piece of wood to a crosspiece. Mark Hartley spun round in his wheelchair to see who had come in. His welcome was as warm as his wife's had been, as he stretched out to shake my hand.

'Hello, you must be the psychologist bloke. We were expecting you.'

'I'm very pleased to meet you. Yes, I'm Mike Lewis, the psychologist. Feel free to call me Mike.'

Johnny moved forward, squeezing into the small gap next to the wheelchair, squashed against the workbench. He looked very pleased to see me. He put out his hand too, so I shook it in the same way as I had with Mark. It was the first time I had seen Johnny with a male carer and he seemed totally at ease and was definitely taking his cue from the way Mark behaved.

'Johnny, pass Mike the stool please, so that he can have a seat.' Mark reached out to pat the stool and pointed to me. Johnny understood and with a little manoeuvring he managed to set it down by the door and then indicate to me that I should sit on it. I sat down, feeling rather guilty that he had a leg in plaster but was only leaning against the bench.

'How have you been, Johnny? Is it good here?' I asked, not expecting any answers.

'Good,' he said. At least, that was what I thought he said. Maybe he was only repeating the word I used.

'It's OK here, is it, Johnny?'

'Good. OK.'

I smiled at him. I still couldn't quite believe my ears.

'You are speaking really well today, Johnny.'

'I think he understands nearly everything,' said Mark. 'I've been chatting away to him and giving him instructions about how to do things and he has got on very well. Very well indeed, son, haven't you?'

Johnny was obviously listening and he nodded when Mark said this. I suspected that Johnny had been understanding a great deal before he ever attempted to talk, but I wouldn't have called it 'nearly everything'.

'What about speaking? I haven't heard him say "good" and "OK" before. Is he saying anything without having just heard it?'

'You have, haven't you, Johnny? Didn't you try to say "thanks" at breakfast?'

Johnny nodded. I made a mental note to try to include him more when I was talking about him. Mark was really good at it.

'What words are you trying to say, Johnny? Let's see, there's "me" and "you" and you tried to say "Jodie" and you did say "Mark". Then I was trying to teach you "nail", wasn't I? But you didn't really manage that. Early days, yet, eh, Johnny?'

Johnny was nodding.

'Can I hear you say some new words, Johnny? How about "wood"?' I pointed at the plank of wood.

Johnny's mouth didn't seem able to manage the 'w'. He made several attempts until I suggested a new word, then another and a few more. I had a list of twelve new words by the time we finished, all repeated and all simple sounds, but I was excited by his progress. I wanted to have a quiet word with Mark, but I decided to leave the shed and go to talk to Jodie. I would do my best without a speech therapist and create a list of words to leave with her.

Which is what I did. It was quite hard to identify easy words, but Jodie came up with a few she remembered from when her children were first speaking, so we concentrated on those. She also reminded me that he was using 'no' quite frequently but she hadn't heard him use 'yes'. By the time we finished we had twenty potential new words. I was fairly confident that he would find several of his own.

I took instructions from Jodie about how to get to West Wickham station to make my way into work. I felt strangely excited for the entire journey into the office. I was hoping Anita would be free so that I could share the great news with her.

29

I had a very busy clinic that afternoon which went well over time. The department was quiet when I said 'goodbye' to my last client. I made myself a strong coffee, taking it back to my room. Feeling revived enough to tackle some of my outstanding administration I set to work. For once I wasn't avoiding the weekend, I wanted to be organised for the following week.

When I eventually got home, I was aware of the bleep of the answer phone. I knew it would be Ella before I listened. Her voice sounded strange, a little high, maybe? Something was up.

'Mike, please ring me as soon as you're home. I have a problem with Shaun.'

I kept my coat on and rang her. She answered straightaway, obviously assuming it was me.

'He walked out soon after tea. Said he was going to the shop.'

'How long ago was that?'

'Nearly three hours.'

'Has he done anything like this before?'

'Only once, during daylight hours. The police won't let me report him as a missing person, despite his disability.'

'I'll be straight over.'

I regretted no longer having a car. As it was, I ran down the hill to Sydenham station where I knew I would find a taxi. I was soaked by the time I got there, but was quickly whisked off towards Selsdon.

Although Shaun was an adult in years, I was surprised that Ella had not been able to access more help from the police. His mental age must be about six, I reasoned, and he would be very vulnerable among certain groups of people. As I mopped my hair and beard uselessly with my hanky, I considered the chances of him being safe and well. Probably quite slim. I was worried he would be pushed and shoved by some of the lads who hung around the town centre in the evening. What would he do if he found himself in trouble? I thought of all the possible scenarios and how I would help Ella, whatever happened.

The taxi driver did well to arrive within twenty minutes. We drew up outside my old house. I felt immensely strong and powerful. This was the first time Ella had needed me for the whole of the time since Jamie had died. No, I was wrong. She had needed me but I was too distraught to realise, so she turned to others. Maybe I wouldn't let her down this time.

I paid for the cab and went to the front door – it was flung open by Ella, who looked rather wilder than her usual self. Despite my sodden appearance, she clutched my raincoat.

'The police told me to wait by the phone, which is ridiculous, he can't manage to ring the house phone. He does have his mobile with him and he might be able to ring me on my mobile if he's not panicking. He has managed once or twice before.'

'So what would you like to do? I could stay by the phone or go off for a search in a cab, or walking. Or we could both go and use your car.'

'Let's both go. I can't stay here any longer – I'm sick with worry.'

Ella grabbed a coat from the rack in the hall, and her keys.

'Have you got your mobile, Ella?'

'Heck, no. Hang on.'

She rushed into the kitchen and came out carrying a large handbag.

'I suppose it's in there somewhere,' I said. Even as I said it I remembered the jokes I used to make about the size of her handbag and the amount of unnecessary junk she carried about. I knew this was not the moment for such comments.

'I'd better check.'

Ella tipped out the whole contents onto the hall floor and sure enough, it was there. Clutching it in her mouth she bundled the mess of make-up, tissues, notebooks, pens, cheque book and other bits and pieces back in.

'You drive,' she said, handing me the keys.

'I can't, I'm not insured.' Why did I feel that my lack of driving was totally letting her down?

She took the keys back and gave me a disdainful look. I said nothing.

'I'll have to, then,' she said sullenly.

'I'll look out for him, you drive slowly. From the shop, I should think, then to all his usual haunts.'

'There aren't many of those.' Ella's voice was flat.

'Don't give up, we'll find him.'

I wasn't sure if I was right. It was an awful night; as we set off, the rain was streaking down, obscuring my vision. I strained to see through it. There seemed to be no one around. I clutched Ella's phone, realising I had no idea how to answer it if it did ring. I couldn't even look at it while watching the road.

The shop, a local twenty-four-hour affair, was still open. Ella drew up outside.

'I'll go in,' she said. 'They know me in there and will connect me with Shaun.'

She was gone for a few minutes while I fiddled with her phone, trying to sort out how I would answer a call. I was hopeless with these things. Other people seemed to get on fine with them but anything new-fangled took me a time to conquer. My own was extremely basic, but it had still taken me a long time in the shop to be taught how to work it.

Ella was back, climbing into the car. She was shaking. I didn't know if that was because of the rain or what she had heard.

'I spoke to the owner and his son. They both saw him in the shop at 7.30 and he was talking to a woman. She's always talked to him when she's in the shop. She must have asked him to carry her bags because he had one in each hand when they left.'

I didn't like the sound of this. Why did the woman always talk to Shaun? Was this innocent friendliness, or could it be something sinister? I didn't ask what Ella thought, she looked too frightened.

'Well, at least we have a lead. Does he know the woman's name or where she lives?'

'Not really, but the young lad in there said he did know someone who he thought might know her. He didn't know her name either but he's given me the address. It's just down the road from here.'

'I've had a thought, Ella. Doesn't he have a social worker – should she be told?'

'I've dialled her number, there's no reply. I left a message but I don't suppose she's in until Monday.'

'Perhaps we should ring the emergency social services number?'

'I really don't know. Look, let's go and find this address first.'

I peered out through the rain. It took us two rounds of the block until we spotted Olive Crescent. Then we were looking for number 32 which the owner's son had described as having a tall gate.

'Stop. It's here,' I said. 'The only one in the street with a high gate.'

'But that's 31.'

'It's probably the right one, with 30 next to it he may have assumed it would be 32, but there are no houses opposite.'

'I'll go and ask,' said Ella.

'No, you don't, I will.'

The gate creaked as I pushed it open and I could hear a dog barking in the house. I couldn't see a doorbell or knocker and the rain was dripping off the overhanging windows and down my neck. I banged on the door and waited, listening. There was no sound and I repeated the process twice before I heard some shuffling towards the door. It opened on a safety chain. I peered round the door and came almost face-to-face with an old woman in her nightdress and slippers, with her long grey hair hanging down her back.

'Sorry to disturb you, but apparently you have a friend who often chats to a young man with learning difficulty, in the shop up the road.'

She looked at me and started to close the door.

'No, please help. My wife's in the car, would you rather talk to her? Shaun, the young man, has gone missing and she's desperate with worry.'

The door was opened a little more again. She spoke. 'I don't know her full name. She's Barbara, or Babs, she likes to be called. Lives in the last house on the left.'

'Which way?' But I was too late, the door was closed and I heard the bolts go across.

I relayed the information to Ella as I climbed back into the car. We reasoned that her left would be further up the road.

'Come on,' said Ella. 'Let's find it.'

The last house in the road was a large Victorian place divided into flats. We stood on the tiled porch and peered at the bells, trying to make out the names in the dark. There was a porch light but it was not working.

'We'll have to ring one at random,' I said and pressed the bottom bell.

After a wait, the door was opened by a young man in a black T-shirt and jeans. There was a vague smell of cannabis.

'Yes?' he asked.

'Is there a lady named Barbara or Babs who lives in one of the flats?' I asked.

'Who's asking?'

Ella replied, 'I'm sorry, we should have explained. I am the foster carer for a young man with a learning disability who's gone missing. Barbara was talking to him in the shop and he hasn't been seen since.'

'Top flat. Ring the bell.'

The door was closed in front of us. I began to think this was a very unfriendly road. Ella rang the bell. We waited. She rang it again. Nothing happened.

'Let's try once more with that young man. Maybe he'll let us go and bang on the door. We've got to do something.'

Before we could do anything, an ambulance drew up outside on the road and a paramedic ran up to the door.

'Someone here called an ambulance – do you know anything about it?'

'No, what's happened?' Ella's hand had crept into mine. We were both jumping to the same conclusion – Shaun must be in there and he was hurt. Quickly she explained the situation to the paramedic.

'So do you know if it's him?' she said.

'Not him, an old lady had a fall is all I've got written down. They think a child rang in. Top flat. Excuse me.'

The paramedic rang the top bell and then several others. At last, the same young man we had already seen came to the door.

'Accident in top-floor flat,' said the paramedic and ran straight past him. I still had hold of Ella's hand and pulled her in and past the astonished hippy. We dashed up the stairs.

We reached the top landing. The paramedic was kneeling down, saying, 'Back a bit kid, it's OK now we're here. We'll take care of her.'

'Shaun, thank goodness.' Ella walked over to him and put her arm round him. 'What happened here, Shaun? Are you all right?'

Shaun was sniffing. 'Babs fell. Shopping bags.'

There was a voice from the floor.

'This your son?' She was breathing heavily, struggling to lift her head and get the words out. She appeared to be wincing with the pain. The paramedic was trying to give her some oxygen, but she pushed his hand away to say, 'He's a good boy. He learned how to call an ambulance. And he fetched blankets.' She put her head down again and let the paramedic put the mask over her face.

We moved aside while a second paramedic appeared with a stretcher.

'Is there anything we can do for you?' I asked Babs.

She shook her head.

'She'll be all right now we're here. We'll have to take her in because she's probably broken something. Looks like she's been here a while.'

'Shaun's been missing all evening.'

'Well, he's quite a hero, isn't he? Without him she could have laid here all night.'

Ella knelt down to speak to Barbara again. 'We'll sort out your shopping and take him home, then.'

There was a voice behind us. 'You go. I'll sort the stuff out. Glad you found him.'

'That's great, thank you,' I said to the young man from the bottom flat.

Ella still had her arm around Shaun's shoulders. I slipped off my coat and she wrapped it round him. He was still sniffing and rubbing his eyes with the back of his hand as we took him home.

30

I woke the next morning to the smell of bacon. I stretched out in the comfortable bed and realised I was sleeping in my underwear in Jamie's bedroom. I was at my old home, Ella's home. Gradually the events of last night unfolded in front of me as I remembered them.

It had been gone eleven by the time we arrived back at Ella's house. I helped her get Shaun into a warm bath and make him a hot drink before he went to bed. He was shuddering with cold. He wanted to talk, but seemed too tired to do so. Ella praised him for being such a hero and he said, 'Pick up the phone. Number 9 then number 9 then number 9. Say old lady on floor on top flat. Last house Olive…' he was wrinkling up his face, trying to remember.

'It's fine, Shaun. You don't have to remember the address any more. You go to sleep.'

He settled remarkably quickly. Ella went and got changed into some drier clothes and brought me down a jumper and pair of trousers.

'Are these mine?' I asked.

'Yes, you left quite a few things. These were probably in the ironing pile when you cleared out your wardrobe. I thought you might need them sometime.'

I went into the cloakroom and changed. The corduroy trousers were very loose. I transferred the belt from my soaking wet work trousers and tried to make myself look respectable. I looked in the mirror at my gaunt face and wondered how much weight I had lost. I looked a mess – wild-eyed and wild-haired. No wonder people wanted to shut the door on me. Despite having been in a warm house for half an hour, my head felt cold and damp so I rubbed it vigorously with the hand towel. There was a brush on the shelf over the basin, so I used it to smooth my beard and try to organise my hair. Feeling a little more together, I went back into the living room. Through the open door, I could see Ella was in the kitchen making hot drinks.

'I'm making hot chocolate, but perhaps you'd prefer wine,' she said.

I felt too weary to make the decision. 'Perhaps I'd better get back. I am very tired.'

'I could make you up a bed in Jamie's room. In fact, it's all made up already because Shaun's having a friend round to stay over tomorrow.'

'But you'll have to prepare the room again.'

'Don't worry about that. You're welcome to stay the night, if you like. We can have a slow start, it being Saturday.'

I didn't take much more persuading. The house was warm and comfortable and I was cold and in need of comfort. We were both exhausted, so we hardly spoke as we sipped sweet hot chocolate drinks and then went up to our separate beds.

So when I woke and remembered where I was, I felt a strange surge of excitement. Was this the start of something again? I lay in the bed and looked at the plastic stars on Jamie's ceiling, then let my eyes wander, taking in the odd ornament of his that Ella had left in the room. It felt comfortable, I wasn't sad at all.

There was a knock on the door and Ella looked round. 'I've brought you a clean towel and a cup of tea.'

'Tea – that's great. But I should have made you one! I always used to make the tea in the morning.'

Ella laughed. 'Well, if you ever stay again, I'll allow you to take over that duty.'

I grimaced. 'If?' I asked.

'Don't push it, Mike.' She put down the tea and I could smell her freshly shampooed hair. I longed to grab her and pull her into bed with me. I touched her hair briefly instead.

'You're making me feel very lazy,' I said. 'You look up and organised and I'm lolling around in bed.'

'Shaun had me up at 6am. He's rather a light sleeper.'

'Has he had breakfast? I can smell bacon.'

'He's eaten his, but I'll do our eggs when you're ready.' She had moved back to the door while we were talking, and now she gave me a cheeky smile and walked out of the room. All I wanted to do was move back here, be with her again.

I drank my tea slowly, savouring the moment. Then I got out of bed and picked up the towel. Wrapped up in it was a clean pair of pants, a T-shirt, shower gel and a toothbrush. Pleased to feel so cared for, I gathered up my clothes and went for a shower.

When I came out of the bathroom, Shaun was moving from one foot to another on the landing.

'You slept in David's room,' he said.

'David's room?'

'Yes. David's my friend.'

'He's coming tonight, right? He can sleep in this room.'

'David's room.'

'Yes, David's room tonight.'

I walked into Jamie's room and looked around. No, it must be how Shaun saw the world. This was still very much Jamie's room. To me it always would be. I went downstairs to have an enormous cooked breakfast with my rather special ex, desperately hoping we would one day be a couple again.

But breakfast felt a bit awkward. We hadn't eaten this meal together for so many years that we weren't sure how to behave. At first we ate in silence, with me giving Ella a grin every now and then which she half-returned. Then we both spoke together.

'How's work?'

I laughed uncertainly as I thought about Anita and her part in helping Johnny. Was she chasing me? I was surprised if she was.

'The stowaway case is working out pretty well.'

'I gathered that, from your phone call.'

So much had happened since that I had almost forgotten about that. I wondered briefly if Anita had heard what I had been saying to Ella. It didn't matter now; the evening had finished fine with me putting her in a taxi home while I took the Tube and train. We were friends and colleagues; I hoped that was all she had thought too.

Ella was looking at me, head to one side.

'What's the matter?' I asked, smoothing my hair in case she had noticed what a mess I was.

'She wasn't with you in the flat when I phoned, was she?'

'No, no way! She's never even been to my flat. We are work colleagues!'

'Sorry, it occurred to me that I might have upset something important to you.'

I looked at her. I knew she didn't want to be pressurised but I had to say something.

'No, I'm a one-woman man. You know that.'

She didn't reply. I didn't dare say anything else. I cleared up our plates and started washing up the dishes, which had often been my job at home.

Ella came and stood beside me.

'What would our lives have been like if we hadn't lost Jamie?' she asked.

I took her in my arms and we clung to each other for a minute or two before we heard Shaun clumping down the stairs.

'David coming. David's room.'

'You'd better go,' said Ella. 'He won't settle until he's seen the room ready for his friend David. They are both excited because I've promised we'll all go and buy a Christmas tree.'

'I don't mind helping,' I said, remembering untangling lights and putting a star on the top of a tree when Jamie was jumping up and down beside me.

'No, you go now. We'll talk another time. Here's a bag for your things.'

I took the carrier bag up to my room and gathered up the wet clothes. On impulse, I took the toothbrush through to the bathroom and put it in the tumbler with hers. I went downstairs.

Ella was in the hall and she passed me my now dry trench coat. As I was putting it on she gave me a photo album and a business card.

'Here you are, Mike. This is the name and contact for my counsellor. I phoned and there's a space to see you if you contact in the next few days. And I copied some photos of Jamie for you.'

I don't know whether it was her kindness, leaving her, or the fact that I now had a whole album of photos of Jamie, but I had to clear my throat before replying.

'Thank you, Ella. I'll ring you, if I may.'

'Thank you for all your help last night, Mike. You were wonderful.'

She reached up and kissed me on the cheek. My arms encircled her briefly before she moved away.

Fighting my instinct to stay, I walked out of the house.

31

I had the allocation meeting on Monday, followed by a full day of appointments, so my phone calls were jammed into small slots throughout the day. Among the messages left for me was a request from immigration to ask about the possibility of setting a new date for Johnny's hearing. I didn't even know for certain that he really was seeking asylum. I managed to ring speech therapy, who still didn't have anyone to see him, but who promised to send up some materials with instructions for use.

Anita rang at lunchtime to ask me to take a large amount of paper and other art materials to the foster home for Johnny to use. She couldn't see Johnny until Friday and was anxious that he should have freedom of expression through art at this difficult time. Otherwise that was all the contact I had with Anita since our meal. In fact, life had quietened down for a day or two and I was beginning to feel a bit more on an even keel.

There was one other thing I did right at the end of my day. I rang the counsellor, Henry. As I put in his number, I was remembering the extreme jealousy I felt when Ella was seeing him. He had taken so much of her time, at a crisis in my life when I couldn't even speak to Ella. I knew I was losing her but she seemed completely fixed on seeing him.

When I had told her I didn't think it was good for her to pile her grief onto a new person's shoulders, she was furious. In fact, she was more angry than I had ever seen her before. It was that which flipped things for her and for me. We totally lost our ability to communicate with each other. I became depressed and convinced that I no longer mattered to her, and in my misery I decided she meant it, when she told me to go. Now I was going to meet this man who had been part of the problem. I wasn't sure this was wise, but if it would bring me back to Ella, I would try.

When I rang the number it was a female who answered: 'Henry Langdon Counselling.'

I stuttered out my name to the receptionist and the fact that he'd been recommended and would fit me in if I rang soon, which I had.

There was a laugh at the other end of the line.

'I'm Henry Langdon,' she said. 'I'm sorry, everyone has always called me Henry – Henrietta is my given name.'

'Oh. I didn't know, I was expecting a man,' I then felt ridiculous for stating the obvious as well as sounding as if I wouldn't speak to a woman.

'Does it make any difference? I saw Ella after you lost Jamie and I am happy to work with you, too.'

My mind was reeling as I tried to sort out what had just happened. Henry was a woman – I had been jealous of my wife talking to a woman! I pulled my attention back to the conversation. 'No, that's fine.'

'How soon would you like an appointment? I can offer you an early appointment, 8.30am, on several days in the coming two weeks; otherwise I am rather fully booked.'

After a discussion we sorted out a day at 8.30am. Her counselling rooms were in Bromley and I only hoped I'd be able to get over there in time, see her and be at work before my first appointment, which was at 10.30. But at least I had made the call. I started to gather up all the items I had to take to my appointment with Johnny next day.

The next morning, I felt very organised. I had my fear index with me, which we still hadn't used, and picture cards from the speech therapist showing several objects which were fairly easy to pronounce. I was free to leave them with the carers for practice after showing them how to use them. I felt like a teacher in the reception class at primary school. I could remember Jamie bringing back easy words for reading, and playing all sorts of memory games with him, until he was proud of being able to read them with no help. For Johnny, I also had a large amount of paper, pens, oil pastels and crayons, courtesy of Anita.

I rang the doorbell and the door was opened by Mark even before the chiming tune had finished. Johnny stood behind him.

'Hello,' said Johnny. It was good to hear his voice. Typically adolescent, it sounded like a gruff soprano.

'Hello, Johnny, I'm so pleased to see you.'

'Mu-so-ke.'

'He's been telling us his name is Musoke,' explained Mark. 'He is speaking so well, aren't you?'

Mark had turned his wheelchair round and we all went into the living room. Jodie was there tackling yet another huge pile of ironing, but she immediately unplugged the iron and asked if I would like coffee and how I took it. She and Mark went off into the kitchen together.

Johnny, Musoke, was still stood up. I said, 'Sit down, Musoke, it is wonderful to know your name.'

'Musoke,' he said. 'Me, Musoke. You, Mike.'

The way he said 'Mike' was with a note of triumph in his voice. I tried to imagine what it must be like to be talking after all this time.

'You say Mike very well,' I said. 'I am really impressed.' I didn't know whether he understood but he smiled and nodded.

I sat down by him and took out the picture cards from the speech therapist to show them to him. In the course of a few days he had gone from having no voice to being able to tell me his name in his own language. I still had no idea what language it could be, so I noted in my file that I needed to discuss this with the immigration service as soon as possible. Then I set the file aside and turned my attention to Johnny, who made some good attempts at many of the words on the picture cards, imitating me. I went to fetch Jodie and show the cards to her.

'What's this one, Musoke?' she asked.

Johnny obviously knew, but not in English. He picked up card after card, saying their name in his own language. Some he put to one side – I wasn't sure why until I looked at them more closely. There was a mobile phone and a computer, plus an electric shaver. Perhaps these objects had not featured in his native tongue. I guessed that if we had a picture of an Underground train, he would not know the words for that either.

This was such an optimistic session that I slipped the fear index, with its pictures of difficult incidents, back into my briefcase. I didn't want to risk retraumatising him while he was progressing so well. He needed a week or two of healing. In his own good time he could work on the trauma with someone who could understand his language. Instead, I chatted with Johnny the best I could, using the cards and the words he knew, and a series of questions which he seemed to understand. By that means, I was able to discover that he wanted to stay 'here', and not go on a ship again. I didn't know if 'here' was the foster home, or the country, but at least it was a start for the yet-to-be-written report.

I left the art materials with Jodie, who promptly spread them out on a table in the conservatory ready for Johnny's use. All the way up to the office on the train, my mind was buzzing with ideas about how to help Musoke, who now had no need of his substitute name.

32

My mind was still full of Musoke and the excitement of the session when I arrived in the office, only a few minutes late for my next client. I was doing standard cognitive therapy with a very logical-thinking young man, so it was easy to stay on task and keep to a routine therapeutic approach. He was making better attempts at controlling his mood these days, but then I think I was a rather more focused therapist than I had been a year earlier, when I first saw him.

At lunchtime I sat with the phone in my hands for several minutes before I could decide whether to ring Ella or Anita to share the good news about Johnny's progress. In the end it was the internal number I rang, which was more appropriate in view of Anita's involvement with the case.

'Anita, I have some good news!'

I proceeded to tell her about the session and my excitement at Johnny telling Mark his real name. At that point she interrupted me. 'I'm sorry Mike, I'm in a meeting. I'll pop up for an update later. What time is best?'

'I'm afraid I don't have any gaps this afternoon.'

'What time do you finish?'

'Probably not until 6.30pm,' I gave her an out-of-hours time, thinking it would be highly unlikely for her to stay that long.

'That's no problem. I'll come up to your room then.'

I put down the phone and worried about the conversation. Where had I indicated to her that I must talk today? Why had she offered to come to talk to me when no one else was around? How could I not have come up with an excuse to put her off?

I realised I was twisting my wedding ring around my finger. Why didn't Anita realise I still considered myself married?

I rang Ella.

'Hi there, Mike, you're lucky to catch me, I'm not usually in at lunchtime.'

'I wanted to give you two bits of good news.'

'Which are?' Her voice sounded as if she was trying not to laugh.

'Well, the first is my client – you know, the boy. He is really starting to talk and has given me his real name in his own language.'

'What is it? Or shouldn't you tell me?'

Ella has always been more confidentially minded than I am.

'Perhaps not – but it was wonderful to use it. I don't know whether I am trying to teach him English now, or helping him speak. It has all become a bit of a muddle.'

'Perhaps it's an interpreter he needs now. It sounds like you've done your major work with him.'

She was right, of course, but I would miss this interesting client. I wanted to know what happened to him and see if I needed to help him with his trauma.

'We still don't know why he was so traumatised that he couldn't speak.'

'Will your referral cover extra work with him?'

'I don't know. I expect so. But I do have the report to write, anyway.'

'But what was your second piece of news?'

'I booked my appointment with the counsellor and I am going tomorrow.'

'That's excellent. I am pleased. What did you think?'

'About Henry, do you mean? Well, I was surprised she was a lady!'

'Surely you knew that? I was talking about my visits with her to you. You must have realised.'

'I didn't cotton on. To me it was "Henry this and Henry that", I never realised she wasn't a man.'

The phone went quiet. I wondered what to do. I wished I hadn't told her about my mistake.

'That accounts for a lot, Mike. I don't know what to think. We need to talk. Thursday, perhaps.'

Her tone had changed. Had I offended her? I hoped not. Trying to keep my own voice light, I arranged a time. Seeing her twice in one week was more than I could hope for, but I was troubled as we said goodbye.

My 1.30 was waiting, so I organised my desk, checked her file, wrote a note or two to remind me what I wanted to cover with her, and went to greet her in the waiting area, trying hard to put thoughts of Ella out of my mind. I managed, too, for that appointment and the one after.

I overran with my 2.30 appointment. As I showed her out, I realised there was no one waiting to see me. I popped into the secretaries' office.

'Has my 3.30 cancelled?' I asked Patricia.

'No, no messages at all for you today, Mike. Just a no-show, I should think.' She was polite and smiley again. I was back in favour. I thought I would try to enjoy it while it persisted, but suspected that once Anita realised that I was not interested in her, everything in the office may go frosty again. The ladies always seemed to stick together.

'I've got her down as a double appointment. It's strange that she's missed it.'

'I expect she's forgotten. Would you like me to ring her, to rearrange?'

'Yes, thank you. That would be most kind.'

I picked up my post, which I had failed to collect that morning, and went through to my office. Before opening it, I thought I'd make myself a drink. Somehow I hadn't had one, nor eaten any sandwiches, at lunchtime. I carried the dirty mugs from my bottom drawer into the kitchen and began washing them while the kettle was boiling. I heard the phone ring in the office. Patricia came to find me.

'It's immigration,' she hissed, as if it was the secret service or thought police. Drying my hands on the tea towel, I went to take the call.

'Dr Lewis? It's Dr Harding from the immigration service here. How are you getting on with our young stowaway?'

In my enthusiasm I probably told Dr Harding rather too much. He seemed to think that I would have no trouble assessing Musoke now and the report could be with him in less than two weeks.

I protested, 'I wouldn't be too sure. The number of assessments he can do which are not culture or language-specific are very small. It is an extremely difficult task to assess him. I will need an interpreter and will now be able to record some of his words to send a recording to you, if that will help.'

'Excellent idea. I'll see if we can delay court again, because if we can interrogate, I mean question him, as well, it will provide more information.' There was a slight pause before he said 'information', which worried me. Was he about to say evidence? And he certainly said interrogate. I knew enough about Musoke already to know he had been through some dreadful trauma and I was hoping my report would save him from more bad experiences.

'So far I do know that he has been through a trauma and had to run from his country to keep safe. And yesterday I established with him that he doesn't want to go on a ship again, and he wants to stay in this country.'

'How did you do that if the fellow has only recently started to speak?'

Being careful not to give too much away, I explained about the pictures and the terror they inspired in him. Also I mentioned the trip to the art gallery when we were trying to unblock him.

'Art therapy? That's a strange one. You psychologists certainly work in a most peculiar way. Extraordinary!'

'But effective,' I added.

'I shall be interested to see your report.' The phone went dead. I was left hoping I hadn't scuppered Musoke's chances of staying in this country because of the unorthodox method used for assessing him.

I packed up my briefcase, ready to go. It was only just gone half-four, but I felt like I'd had enough for the day and I had a lot of time to be taken in lieu. I went through to the office to leave a message for Anita.

'I wonder if you could let Anita know that I am going home. I've finished earlier than expected and am off now; I will catch up with her tomorrow re: Johnny.'

Patricia looked at me quizzically, 'She hasn't got anyone with her now. You could ring her yourself.'

'Oh, I thought she was busy this afternoon. I'll do that, then.'

I went back into the office and put down my briefcase with a sigh. I would have rather left a message, but then I didn't want to upset her again.

She answered the phone immediately.

'Hi, Anita. I've had a no-show, so I thought I'd pop off early. I thought I'd update you first, or we can talk tomorrow if you'd rather.'

'No, I'll come up now. I'm dying to know what's been happening.'

I took off my coat and went to make some coffee. I desperately wanted to be back at the flat in case Ella had rung. In fact, I could ring her when I got back because I had forgotten to ask after Shaun. He seemed fine on Saturday after his ordeal, but sometimes there may be a delayed effect.

Anita came into the room and sat herself down on one of the easy chairs. I thought about staying standing, but decided that would be churlish so went and sat on the other chair, moving it a couple of inches further away. I passed her the file.

'Look at my last notes,' I said.

She bent her head forward to read, and her hair flopped down. She had good hair, which I used to admire greatly, but now I thought it seemed to lack the shine and depth of colour that Ella's still had. I wondered if Ella dyed her hair. I hadn't noticed any sign of the grey hairs she had worried about when we were together.

Anita was saying 'that's exciting' and 'great' as she read. I waited and thought of Ella.

I was startled when Anita spoke. 'Aren't you going to tell me about it, then?' She waved her hand towards the file as I looked at her blankly. 'Your appointment, I can read your notes, but it's not like you telling me.'

'Oh yes, the appointment.' I proceeded to tell her about how Musoke looked when he said my name, and how proud he was to announce his. I explained that he seemed so happy that I didn't use the fear index and that Jodie had set all the art materials out for him. I described Mark and Jodie and how they were with Johnny and what the atmosphere was like. All the time I was talking, Anita's large eyes were fixed on me, lapping up every word.

'When are you next seeing him?' she asked.

'Thursday. In the afternoon. I shall go there and then go back to the flat, I should think.' As I said this, I realised it would be a straightforward journey on the bus from Johnny's new home to Selsdon, where I would be later in the evening. I started thinking of Ella again.

'What are you thinking, Mike?'

'Oh, sorry, it's just that Johnny's now living fairly close to where I used to live.'

'Is that where Ella still lives?'

I suddenly felt hot and uncomfortable. 'Yes.'

Anita surveyed me as if I were a client. She put her head to one side and thought.

'Then you'd better pop and see her and sort things out with her, Mike. You'll never forgive yourself if you don't try.'

I nearly hugged her.

'That's very good advice,' I said, as solemnly as I could.

33

Had I but known it, the last few days of working with Musoke were drawing closer. I went to see the counsellor on Wednesday at 8.30 in the morning. I had woken perhaps a little late, and arrived even later, so she was probably about to write 'did not attend' in her file. She was very polite, though.

She came to meet me in the waiting room, as soon as I arrived.

'Hello, you must be Mike. I'm Henry.' She was a very neat lady, barely five foot tall, I should think. She had a helmet of smooth, shiny blonde hair and understated make-up.

'I'm sorry I'm late.'

'Don't worry, I can only apologise that I had to give you such an appointment so early in the day. Within a month, I should probably have an early evening appointment, if that would suit you better.'

As I thanked her we walked into her consulting room. It was trim and tidy, exactly like her. There were two well-kept plants on the windowsill. The untidiest thing I could see in the room was a box of men's tissues by a glass of water on a low coffee table. It was all very calming. I made a mental note to sort out my office back at work.

We both sat down on comfortable armchairs and nothing happened. I hated this kind of therapy; was I meant to say something, or not? I was conscious the time was ticking away and time meant money on a private appointment. I began to talk. 'My wife, Ella, said I should come. She thinks I need to talk about when we lost our son, Jamie.'

'And do you?'

'Yes, but I'm not sure that with a counsellor is the best way for me. Not that I don't think you can be very helpful, I'm sure you can, but I'm usually on the other side of the desk.'

Wrong analogy, because she certainly wasn't sat the other side of any desk. She was sat in the correct 45 degree position, next to me but turned towards me. But I think she knew what I meant.

'Why does Ella think you should be here?'

'I was very shocked by Jamie's death and felt thoroughly hopeless and helpless. I felt I should have prevented it somehow, but I failed him and I failed Ella.'

'Did you seek any help at the time?'

'No. None. And I know I should have done. But now I feel I would be better talking to Ella about it all, perhaps sharing photos and memories.'

'That's certainly important, but for you to use Ella as your counsellor would be inappropriate in the circumstances.'

She probably noticed that I shifted in my seat and moved slightly away. I had become very uneasy. What circumstances was she talking about? What did she know that I didn't know? Was Ella seeing someone else, or had she told her she wanted nothing to do with me? I sat there, listening to Henry's clock ticking behind me, while I tried to figure out what to say. In the end I asked, 'What circumstances?'

'As far as I understand it, you have been separated for about five years.'

I nodded.

She continued, leaning forward in her chair, 'During that time Ella has built a life for herself. For her to be your shoulder to cry on, she must be ready and willing. Not only do you need to establish her willingness, you must also seek her permission. You will need to bear in mind that even if she says you may talk to her, she will be grieving too and it may be too hard for her.'

I knew it all, of course, so I'm not sure why I reached for a man tissue to mop my eyes. I found myself making a confession to Henry that I had made to no one.

'I was a fool to leave her. I love her and want to be with her for the rest of our lives. It wasn't Jamie who glued us together; it was us – our love and respect for each other.'

Henry looked directly at me. I managed to meet her gaze. She spoke softly, 'So you have respect and love for Ella. You desire a reunion. But you left her. Would you like to tell me about that?'

I forgot she had been Ella's counsellor and it seemed immaterial that I, the professional, was now the client. I talked. I told her about the sense of guilt when Jamie died, about my jealousy of Ella as she worked through her feelings with a counsellor, when I was imprisoned by my own. How frozen I felt. How trapped. Then Ella snapped that I should go away, so I did.

Henry listened. She moved her head to indicate the tissues when I needed them. She waited when I needed to pause. She prompted gently when I was lost for words. Finally, everything had poured out of me. I slumped back in her chair.

Henry spoke. 'So now you are ready to look at your feelings and work through them.'

'That's right.' I was regaining my composure again.

Henry outlined how she planned to work with me. I was impressed with her style and the way she deftly helped me to feel I was having a hand in her approach. I thought it must be quite a difficult session for her, she had been so involved with helping Ella, and here was the big, bad husband who ran away, asking for the same sort of help. I wondered if she would be able to remain objective in working with me.

She had finished talking and waited. I'd missed whatever she had just said.

'I'm sorry, what were you saying?'

'I am suggesting weekly sessions for three weeks, after which we will review to see if the sessions are helping.'

'Yes, thank you. That will be good.'

Suddenly eager to be away, I stood up a little too quickly and knocked the coffee table. The glass of water tumbled over slowly, but she reached out and put it upright just as it began to spill. With a tissue deftly dropped over the consequent small puddle, she showed me to the door.

'Well, it's been very good to meet you, Mike. I'll see you again at the same time next week.'

'Yes, thank you, Henry. I'll try to be on time!'

She smiled and slightly shook her head. I determined to be early for the next appointment.

As I left the building, I resisted the temptation to turn left to hop on a bus to go and see if Ella was home before I went back to the office. I wanted to apologise, I must have hurt her really badly. Was an apology needed after all this time? I felt such a heel for leaving her, it was the worst thing I could have done under the circumstances. She needed me and I deserted her, how could I even think that she might be willing to have me back now?

The questions about Ella and our relationship bothered me all the way to work. I had to consciously drown them with thoughts about my clients as I walked the several hundred yards from the Tube to the Mental Health Department.

By the time I arrived, I felt better prepared for the day. I had made good time from Bromley so I remembered to look in the message book in the secretaries' office before my first appointment. There was an apologetic message from Dr Harding from the immigration service to the effect that the court hearing would be in four weeks' time and I must file my report two weeks before. Dr Harding had added that he would almost certainly be able to supply me with a translator if I recorded a few sentences of Musoke speaking in his native tongue. When I finished reading the message, I looked up to see Patricia passing me an old Dictaphone.

'I think you might need this for your appointment tomorrow, Mike.'

'Good thinking, Patricia. That's very helpful, yes. Remind me how to use it.'

Patricia looked upwards in despair, but then smiled before explaining it.

'Leave the tape in there when you've finished,' she said. 'I will take it out and have a courier take it to Dr Harding first thing on Friday. You're going to be a bit time-pressured with this.'

'I'd better tell Anita, then she can make some notes for me to include in the report.'

'She's writing something now; I took the liberty of warning her.'

'You are so efficient.'

'I try,' she said, looking very smug.

With everything suddenly so urgent, my brain went into overdrive. I took Musoke's file home with me and poured over it all evening, looking for anything I had already found out to put into the report. I drew columns and boxes all over a large sheet of paper, until I had collected all I already knew with its evidence, and noted all I needed to know, plus a list of all tools I would need to assess him more thoroughly, divided into 'before translator' and 'with translator'.

It was nearly ten by the time I finished my work, and I hadn't eaten. I went down the road to buy a kebab, and then passed by the off-licence to get some malt whisky. I had no energy left, so scarcely touched either before falling into my bed. The sheets smelled stale and unsavoury and bore no comparison to the beautiful soft bed in my old house with the freshly laundered linen. My longing for Ella stayed with me as I fell into a fitful sleep.

I woke with the alarm and as I hurled things at it, I remembered the day I first heard about Johnny. I felt like a different person from then, in many ways, but yet here I was, still in a disgusting bedroom full of dust with unpacked storage boxes all around me. The room was musty, my clothes needed washing. I eventually found a clean shirt, but it had sat in the bottom of the wardrobe needing to be ironed for so long that it had long since given up trying to smell clean. I remembered I was seeing Ella later and resolved to go into Bromley after seeing Johnny in West Wickham to do some late-night shopping and kit myself out in something better before I saw her. Meanwhile, I hung the crumpled shirt in the bathroom while I showered, and hoped it would lose some of its creases with the steam.

Once in work, I forgot about clothes and appearance. I was on a mission to do my best for Johnny, Musoke. I raided the tests cupboard to find all the items I could use without a translator. I practised in my room between clients, being both Musoke and myself arranging blocks in patterns and timing myself, then copying squiggles and shapes from memory. This would be a real mess of tests and results, but at least it would be something. Now I knew he understood instructions with only a little help, it had opened up a whole new range of possibilities for testing. I did have one problem, though; I still had no idea how old he was. How would I find that out? The testing I could do without knowing, but scoring it depended on age. I took a gamble and took the tests for the up to eighteen years' age group. I was pretty sure he was younger than this, but immigration had sent him to an adult service in the first place, so they plainly had a different idea.

Meanwhile, I was seeing clients. Mrs B was back, still progressing well. To my surprise, my agoraphobic lady contacted to say she was in Devon so had cancelled. I was behind with observing Georgina, so that gap was quickly filled as I watched her progress with a lady with postnatal depression. I enjoyed my next client – a young university lecturer who was covering up his extreme anxiety with jokes in public and binge-eating in private. It was a breakthrough session where he finally talked about his feelings. The irony of the situation was not lost on me.

At lunchtime, Anita knocked on my door. She held out a long report outlining all her involvement with Musoke and her views as to his past. I thanked her and skimmed through it. It was tidy and together but lacked any real evidence.

'This looks very thorough, Anita. Thank you. I am going ahead with testing, too, because I think the immigration service are looking for hard evidence of his state of mind. But two of us seeing the same difficulties will help reinforce all the less clear-cut information we have.'

'Have you worked out how you are going to test him, then?'

I proudly displayed my efforts from the previous evening. She seemed unimpressed. I got out some of the tests I was going to use. Again, she looked at me as if I were mad.

'You are going to miss the point with those, Mike. How will you convince any court that he has undergone trauma of such magnitude that he lost his ability to speak?'

'As soon as we have a translator, I can use a trauma assessment. That's how they work, Anita, with results from formal assessments; we have to play their game.'

'But what happens if we can't persuade them that he mustn't go back?'

'Anita, we don't even know that. We know he had a terrible traumatic experience, but does that mean he was right to flee his country? We don't yet know which country that is and whether it was a local threat, or a national one.'

Anita looked at me. Her pupils were dilated. I felt under scrutiny from those large blue eyes.

'Don't let him down, Mike. Or I will never forgive you.'

'I will not let him down, Anita.' Even as I said this I remembered a scene from the hospital when Jamie was so ill. A promise I had made to Jamie.

'I'm here Jamie. Don't worry, I'll be with you. I will never let you down, I am your father.'

When Anita left the room, I put my head in my arms and cried. The tears were hot on my cheeks. My mind was fuzzy with emotions and images of Jamie superimposed on Musoke. I felt stupid and wretched all at once. A part of me despised myself; a grown man crying in his office when he was meant to help others find solutions for their difficulties. I tried to concentrate on where I was and regain control of myself, the adult.

I was still trying to pull myself together when Patricia rang from the secretaries' office to say she had a call to put through to me. It was only to do with my expenses, but it did the trick. I rearranged Musoke's file while I apologised for putting items in the wrong column on the expense form, and made sure I was ready to see him for his four o'clock appointment. By the time I had finished talking to finance, I had resolved I would do my best for this young man, but would not promise him or anyone again that I would not let him down.

34

Musoke opened the door and greeted me like an old friend. In fact, he carried on saying 'Hello, Mike' as he swung on his crutches through the house to the conservatory. I said a hasty 'Hello' to Jodie as I passed her, but carried on following Musoke with my bulging briefcase tucked under my arm.

The conservatory was covered with paintings and drawings. Musoke presented them to me, one by one, mostly talking in his own language, but with odd words in English. He sounded a little hoarse, as if he had been talking all day. I peered at the pictures, trying to make sense of them. The ones he had drawn with felt pen were the most clear, and I began to realise what they were all about.

'Musoke, you have drawn your story!'

Jodie was standing behind me. 'He's been working at it on his own for the past two days. Picture after picture. He has his own order for them, but hasn't numbered the pages. He's been trying to talk us through them.'

I remembered the Dictaphone in my briefcase.

'Wait a minute, Johnny, Musoke, I want you to tell me about the pictures in your own language.'

Musoke looked puzzled and started to speak, but I held up my hand and he waited. Then I said 'go on'. He carried on talking as before, with some English but mostly in his own language. He was pointing at particular objects in his pictures. I was getting the idea.

What I saw was a frightening account of how he came to flee and ended up in this country. It was all there – the reason for his flight, the loss of people important to him, the journey to a port somewhere and his final journey as a stowaway on the *Margarita*. For a moment I didn't know what to say or do. His eyes darted between Jodie and me, he looked scared.

I spoke in a soothing, calming voice, hoping that he would understand my meaning, if not my words.

'What happened to you was awful, Musoke. It should never happen to anyone, and certainly not to someone as young as you. I know now that you are lucky to be alive. I will help you all I can, to keep you safe.'

Jodie went round the table and put her arm around Musoke's shoulders. I realised that the tape was still running and switched the recorder off.

'You're a brave boy, Musoke,' she said. 'A brave boy. I am proud of you.'

Musoke seemed to relax at the tone of her voice. He looked at me and piled the papers up neatly. Then he passed the pile to me.

'Thank you, Musoke, I will use these to help you.'

I asked Jodie for a rubber band, then rolled them all together. Jodie found me some polythene to wrap round them and tied the whole lot with some string, fashioning a loop to hold it by.

I asked her to make Musoke a drink, to help him mentally move from his distressing past. They disappeared into the kitchen together and, after a while, there were sounds of laughter. I decided he would cope with some more formal testing.

When he came back in the room, I indicated to Musoke to sit opposite me on the cleared table. I produced the coloured cubes, showing him how some sides had triangles of two colours while other sides were red or white. Jodie brought him a hot chocolate and a black coffee for me, with a bowl of biscuits for us to share. I let Musoke play with the blocks and study them while we had our drinks, then I produced my stopwatch and the book of designs. Musoke understood straightaway and raced to make the pattern on the sample page.

Ten minutes later and I had the first measure of Musoke's intelligence. Without scoring the test against his age, I couldn't be sure of his exact level, but with only the most difficult pattern defeating him, I could see he had done very well. I knew I could use this to help back up the authenticity of some of my other information.

I then tried with some of the copying of shapes. Musoke understood this, too, and even seemed to understand when I left a time gap in between to see if he could remember with a delay. Again, the tests indicated that he had above average intelligence and an excellent memory. But didn't I know that already, from the way he could show me things through pictures and was learning a foreign language so fast?

Then Musoke went and fetched a game from the living room.

'Who's been teaching him snakes and ladders?' I asked over my shoulder.

Jodie replied, 'That will be Mark. Those two have been inseparable. He's working today, or they would be playing together now.'

'Where does he work?'

'At the day centre, he helps prepare and serve the lunches, and does the tea and coffee during the day.'

'What a role model for Musoke,' I thought. 'Mark is coping with his own handicap so well that he is able to do something positive for other people. And Jodie, just there and motherly, tuned in to his emotions. He is in an excellent foster home.'

Musoke beat me at snakes and ladders twice and I managed to concentrate enough to teach him noughts and crosses. He played with much thought, but I was not going to go easy on him so I beat him at it twice before he managed to outwit me. By then, it was nearly six o'clock and the smell of something delicious was creeping out of the oven. I thought I had better leave him to have his tea.

Before going, I went into the kitchen to quickly update Jodie about the immigration service and the report. I remembered to tell her that Musoke would be getting an interpreter and asked whether she'd be prepared to bring him in to my office to meet him or her and to have a session telling his story there. I wanted to keep this secure home as a safe place for him. He needed to continue to develop into an ordinary adolescent with a future before him. That basic right had been denied to him for a long time now.

I tied the string of the rolled-up pictures to my briefcase and left Musoke drawing large grids for noughts and crosses. Probably ready to play with Mark.

I wished I was going straight to Ella, but I knew better than to push in when I wasn't invited. Instead, I made my way to the centre of Bromley to see if the department store stayed open late, or at least to buy something to eat. Having walked from a warm, loving house and with time to kill before I saw Ella, I felt extraordinarily lonely.

35

I made my way to Bromley centre on the 119 bus. The shopping centre did have a late-night shopping evening, so I bought two shirts and a blue, thick jumper from the department store. I asked for a large carrier so that I could change in the gents and cram my dirty tweed jacket and not very fresh shirt into the bag. There was no disguising the fact that I had bought and changed into new clothes, but maybe Ella would appreciate that I had made an effort. I now had two bulky bags to carry, and I noticed that Musoke's pictures were becoming a little bent.

As I walked back through the shop, I saw sheets and pillowcases in the pre-Christmas sale. I thought about the fresh, clean bed when I stayed the night with Ella, and bought a set.

I found a café in the high street which served jacket potatoes with beans and cheese. Nowhere near as good as anything Ella would have served me, but filling anyway. It was nearly 7.00pm and it could take another half hour to reach Selsdon by bus. Glad to have filled in the time, I picked up the two bulky bags with the attached roll of pictures, and left.

It started to drizzle as I walked from the bus stop towards the house. I ran the last few yards and rang the doorbell. It was then that I realised I no longer had my trench coat. I was sure I had it when I arrived at Musoke's foster home, but couldn't remember if I had worn it since.

Ella answered the door and all thoughts of coats were forgotten. She greeted me with a peck on the cheek.

'Where's Shaun?' I asked.

'He's gone to David's for the evening. He'll be back about 9 or 9.30.'

'Don't you worry about him going out now?'

'He's an adult, Mike. I have to tread the fine line between ensuring he is safe and giving him an appropriate amount of freedom.' She saw I wasn't convinced, and laughed. 'Don't worry, I asked David's father to pretend he was going to the pub and stroll down the road with him!'

I laughed too. 'So you're going to be overprotective for a time, I should think.'

'Probably, yes. But as I said, it is a fine line to tread. I am trying to teach him not to go off with anyone without letting me know. He doesn't understand because he knows not to go to strangers and he knew Babs.'

'Is he capable of understanding the difference?'

'I don't know. But enough about Shaun. Let me find you something to drink and then you can tell me all about meeting Henry. If you want to, that is.'

'There's not much to tell, really.'

I followed her into the kitchen and sat on one of the high stools, watching her as she made our drinks. She was still a lovely woman. A little more round in the waist, perhaps, but the slight fullness of her face suited her. I remembered sliding my arm round her waist for the first time as I walked her home from the cinema.

'What are you thinking?' she said.

'Oh, just remembering things we did together. I can't stop myself these days.'

'I've been down memory lane a bit too. We had some good times, didn't we?'

We forgot all about my counselling session as we took our drinks into the sitting room still sharing memories. Ella found the photos of our wedding day. The photos were revealing. I looked awkward and uncomfortable, whereas she was confident and in control. Although I was older than her, I was the one who struggled with the day. I could remember how out-of-sorts I felt, wearing a morning suit and leather shoes. As now, I hated being the centre of attention. I detested all the speeches and the formality that Ella's parents had insisted were right for the occasion. By the evening I was exhausted. We had gone away for our first night to a hotel that cost us far more than we could afford, but were both so tired we slept until late the next morning in the large comfortable bed.

'Do you regret getting married?' I asked.

'No. I disliked the actual day, but I will always treasure our vows.'

'Even after everything I've done?'

'You leaving me, you mean? Yes. Even after that. Because we had each other and we had Jamie. Nothing can take that away, even though we no longer have either.'

'I am so sorry. I'm sorry I couldn't stop Jamie dying and I am sorry I left you. I should have been there for you, and I wasn't.'

'I know, Mike, I know you are sorry. You couldn't have stopped Jamie dying, but I needed you so badly after he did. I don't know how I can trust you any more, but...' she paused; I waited, sensing more to come. 'Did you really think Henry was a man?'

'Yes, I did.' I could remember the pain I felt when she was constantly quoting what Henry said, booking more appointments with Henry, telling me Henry was the only person she could talk to.

'You must have been very jealous.'

'I was. And helpless.'

Ella moved up on the sofa, close to me. She took my hands in hers.

'I have never been unfaithful to you Mike. Never, ever.'

I wanted to say the same to her. Legally and physically I had never been unfaithful to her, even after we had separated. But now between us was the fact that I got on so well with Anita. Had it only been as work colleagues?

'I love you, Ella.'

I don't know if Ella wanted to say the same to me. I don't know why I said it to her then. But I felt as if I was bursting with things I wanted to tell her. Things I hadn't said since Jamie had died. How I had felt about him, about her. My plans for our life together, and how they had been shattered. I had so much to say and it was nearly too late to say it all.

'Ella,' I opened my mouth to start telling her everything. She put her fingers to my lips.

'Shh, Mike. You've said enough for one day. I don't know if we will ever be back together again, but thank you for telling me you love me. That makes everything easier.'

We were sitting close on the sofa. I longed to put my arms around her. Instead I took one of her hands and gently stroked it. Then I kissed it gently. I must trust her. If this was right, we would be back together one day.

Ella carefully pulled her hand away. She carried the dirty mugs from our drinks out to the kitchen. I wondered if I had blown it and she would refuse to see me from now on. I stood up, ready to collect my things and leave.

'Mike,' she called from the kitchen, 'come and chat to me while I make some more drinks. I need an update on that client of yours. Did you see him this morning?'

I didn't realise how stressed I was until I felt the tension leave my shoulders.

I walked through to the kitchen.

'I saw him this afternoon. It's finally going very well. I managed some assessment, and he is talking so well he should be able to use a translator without too much problem.'

'Mike, if you saw him this afternoon, what did you do between seeing him and coming here? You didn't have to go back to the office, did you?'

'Oh no, I didn't finish until gone six. Didn't you notice what I did afterwards?'

I did a little twirl.

'Ah, you've only just bought the shirt and jumper. Did you get any tea?'

'I had a jacket potato.'

'Next time, give me a ring and I'll feed you. In fact, I think I'd better make you an omelette now. You need something nourishing, I can see you don't look after yourself.'

Despite my protests she made me a beautiful frothy omelette with tomatoes and mushrooms. As she finished cooking, Shaun arrived home, so while I sat on her high stool at the counter and ate mine, she cooked one for him too. All her attention was taken by him as he told her about being at his friend's house and how next time he would stay the night. Ella suggested he went in the other room to eat his omelette, but he sat on the second high stool next to me and continued talking all the time he was eating. Ella sent me apologetic glances over his head.

I didn't stay too late. I needed to get up in the morning to go to work. I gathered up my briefcase, Musoke's pictures and the carrier with my shabby tweed jacket in it, and began my journey back to the barren, soulless flat.

36

There was already a message waiting for me when I arrived in the office at 9am the next morning hoping to get working on Musoke's report before I started seeing any clients. It was immigration, asking how long it would take me to record Musoke speaking in his own language. I took the Dictaphone through to Patricia and asked her to find a courier to take the tape straightaway.

'I told you I would anyway!' she said, obviously slightly irritated that I had made it sound like my idea.

I rang and left a message with immigration that the recording would be with them some time during the morning.

This left me with enough time to score the assessments. I still didn't know his age, so I rated them against the highest age when looking up the averages for an age group. I was right; he was above average on both assessments. I was looking forward to doing the rest of the testing with a translator, which would be much easier. I knew I still had to find items that were not culturally sensitive, so I emptied out all the items in the WISC and studied them one by one, imagining how they would appear to a person from a less developed country. I had to automatically discount the tests with items missing from pictures. Musoke would be unlikely to notice a hole in a trellis fence, or even recognise what it was, and I judged the picture of the telephone would not represent an everyday object for him. By ten o'clock I had a list of four items on each of the two sub-scales, so could easily draw conclusions from any results.

My client had moved her chair to have a view of my door. She rose before I called her. She was a lady who was coming for a three-month review. Somehow she had managed to reduce her anxiety at a time when I knew I was being a very inefficient psychologist. Some people benefit from a very small amount of input, which I think she had. She was a small, fragile-looking woman, who still looked anxious but could now cope with her life quite well.

She walked swiftly across the waiting area and followed me into the room. As she was sitting down, she put her head on one side and surveyed me. 'I like your new look, Dr Lewis. Much better.'

I flicked a crumb off my jumper and smiled at her. 'And I am delighted you feel bold enough to say so!'

The session went very well, with my only task being to help her with preventing relapse. She didn't need any more appointments, so we ended the session with a little frivolity as she cheekily announced that she would miss me dreadfully but was delighted to be rid of me.

I opened the door for her to leave, saying my goodbyes and wishing her well. Anita was loitering in the corridor.

'Are you waiting to talk to me? Come in, Anita.'

'I will, thanks. But what was all that laughing I heard in here? It sounded like the old days.'

'What do you mean "the old days"?'

Anita made a quick movement with her hand as if to tell me not to go there.

'No, what do you mean?' I said again.

'Well, you used to be like this before you became so...' she stopped.

'Depressed? I think that's the word for it, Anita. I am coming out of a five-year, maybe even a six-year depression at last.'

'Everyone grieves in a different way.'

'I should have found some help, but I didn't. But that's not what you wanted to talk to me about, is it?'

Anita shook her head. 'No, I came to see how your appointment went and if there's anything I need to know before I go to see him this afternoon.'

I unrolled the slightly battered pictures that Musoke had done and spread them on the coffee table. She sat down and began to study them.

'Did you help him to do these?'

'No, he had drawn them before I came and Jodie said he had drawn them on his own. They're a bit battered because I wasn't going straight home.'

'They're fine. They are fascinating, a real cartoon strip.' Some of the pictures were a little difficult to make out, but Anita persevered and went through them all. When she looked up she had tears in his eyes. 'That poor boy,' was all she said. She reached for a tissue to dab her eyes, then sat quietly.

I wanted to make it all right for her. 'He is really good at the moment, Anita. The foster parents are superb with him. Did I tell you Mark is disabled? He shoots about in his wheelchair and goes off to the day centre to help the old people a couple of times a week. Johnny, I mean Musoke, and he have really hit it off.'

'What's happening about Musoke's leg?'

'The plaster cast should be off next week, I think. With all that's happening I forgot to ask Jodie about it.'

'I'll ask today. If he doesn't understand what's happening, maybe I can draw more pictures to show him.'

'Another thing you can do is see if you can find out what suddenly made him able to speak. Is it because he feels in a safe place? Or was it something Margaret helped him with in the secure unit? I'm left with the big question about it. If I can't give an answer, it will look odd in my report.'

'Especially if Shirley is still saying he's making everything up to stay in the country.'

'I can't imagine she still thinks that. Her attitude has definitely changed towards him. But that reminds me, I don't know whether she has to write a report too. I need to give her a ring, anyway; what's the time now?'

Anita glanced at her watch. 'I make it ten past eleven.'

'My next client will be waiting. I'll catch up with you later.'

Anita stood up and gathered together all the pictures. 'I'll copy these with the larger photocopier downstairs and return them to you before I go, if I may.'

'Certainly.'

Anita left the room and I looked out. Sure enough, next victim waiting. This was the gentleman who we thought was stalking Georgina. For once I felt ready to take up the challenge.

By lunchtime, my brain was zinging. This client needed psychiatry first, before I could work with him. He was a bundle of obsessive behaviours and high anxiety. I wasn't even sure he should be seen as an outpatient. He seemed very much focused on the idea of a girlfriend and told me that Georgina had told him on several occasions that she loved him, so he knew they would be together soon. I spent most of my lunch break talking on the phone to the psychiatrist, then the client's GP and the community psychiatric nurse. He was well-known to them all, and in active treatment. I suggested we were not the right service for him at present and my recommendation was that he should be sectioned.

'Been there, done that, no change,' said the chirpy psychiatric nurse.

'I think he's dangerous,' I persisted.

'We can't actually do anything until he's done something wrong.'

I explained about his persistence with Georgina, and how we now had to keep him out of the department when she was there.

'It won't stop the obsession, you know. His mother abandoned him when he was three. He is desperate for female company. He stalked one of our staff for three years.'

'What happened then?'

'He broke into her house. She was frightened but the police got there before anything happened.'

I resolved to walk in and out of the department with Georgina for the next few months until her placement ended. I couldn't really think of anything else to do. I wondered if she had any holiday time left. But then I could scarcely tell her to take a holiday. Compassionate leave, perhaps?

I was mulling over the problem when Anita knocked on the door. 'Here are the pictures, Mike. I can't stop, or I'll be late.'

I took the rolled-up drawings and put them on my desk. As I did so it struck me again that working with Musoke was incredibly important. He was a young man, and whatever I said in that report would affect him for the rest of his life. Somehow I had to get this one right.

Late in the afternoon I had a phone call from Dr Harding from immigration. A translator would be available for me whenever needed. Musoke's language had been identified as a fairly obscure Ugandan dialect, Rukonjo.

'Don't ask me how he ended up on the *Margarita*,' said Dr Harding. 'It's a long way from his home.'

'Maybe we can find out now he can talk,' I said, 'and he can give us more details about the trauma that happened to him.'

'More details? How has he told you anything without a translator?'

I told him about Musoke's latest pictures, but I kept it brief because I really felt I didn't want him thinking psychologists made decisions on a few drawings. Anyway, there was no proof that this was really something that had happened to him. It certainly looked as if it was to me, though.

As soon as I had finished speaking to Dr Harding, I phoned the carers and had a discussion with Mark about how to begin to prepare Musoke for a disclosure meeting. I had hoped Anita would still be there and I could get her to make a start, but she had just left. I arranged to go there myself on Monday evening. I wondered whether to contact Ella to suggest seeing her afterwards, but then pulled myself back to try to concentrate on organising this for Musoke.

I needed to prepare him, and then arrange a time with him and the translator. I would have to look up all the protocol first, to see who would be allowed in a disclosure meeting. Did I have to have anyone else from immigration there, apart from the translator? Could the carers attend? I had no idea. I went to look in the room bookings to find out when the family room would be free. It wouldn't be the best place, but it would be better in this department than the unknown Immigration Office. Time was short now, before the tribunal. I hoped I would get everything done quickly. I wrote a message for Patricia asking her to cancel all my non-urgent clients for the next two weeks.

There being nothing else to do, I finally went back to the flat.

The weekend started off as bleak and soulless as it always was. But something was a little different. I had a sense of purpose. And many thoughts of Ella. On Saturday I tidied the flat, in case Ella came. I even gave the inside of the fridge a bit of a wipe round and threw away a few things that smelled revolting. I did some shopping for fresh food and when I came back, I watered the slightly drooping plants. Then I found myself a quick lunch of cheese and biscuits.

I was feeling good. I noticed the glass on the front of Jamie's photo was dirty, so gave it a quick wipe over. It looked better and made me think of the album that Ella had given me. By the time I had looked at all the photos, I knew I wanted to put more on display, so I went out again and scoured the local shops to find some more frames. On my return I put my favourite one of the three of us in the largest frame and two of Jamie as a baby in two wooden ones. I used the last frame for one that Ella had done professionally. She looked stunning.

By mid-afternoon, I had run out of steam. I found an old anorak and went for a damp walk through the foggy park opposite. I even started to think about having a dog and which sort it would be. It would have to be something that Ella wanted too in case we ever lived together again. I was appalled that I couldn't remember if she liked dogs; perhaps it was cats she preferred? Maybe I had never known. Jamie had been our focus, our centre; we didn't really think about animals.

I finished my walk back at the gate near my flat. As I went up the stairs, my heart skipped a beat as I saw someone at my door. I thought it was Ella, but she turned round to greet me and I realised it was Anita.

'Hello Mike, I've brought your coat. You left it at Musoke's foster home.'

'Oh, that's very kind of you. You could have brought it to work on Monday.'

'I thought you would be cold! I didn't think about the possibility of you having more than one coat.'

'Thanks.' Anita stood there. I moved to one side in case she wanted to go down the stairs. No movement. So I offered her a cup of tea.

'Yes, thank you. But I don't have very long,' she glanced at her watch. 'No more than forty-five minutes.'

I wondered where she was going, but didn't ask. I showed her into the flat. If she thought it was a bit minimalist, she didn't say. She admired the bit of Spanish cloth and I found myself showing her that it hid a wooden storage box.

I had left the photo album open on the sofa when I went out. When I brought in tea, with biscuits, she was looking at it.

'You don't mind, do you? I love people's photos.'

I felt uncomfortable. Of course I minded. But I could scarcely say so. I sat on the furthest arm of the sofa, wishing I had more chairs in this room, and made grunty noises each time she made a comment about a photo.

'Sorry,' she said. 'I'll stop looking now.'

'Do you mind if we talk work for a minute or two?' I asked.

'Not if it's about Musoke.'

I filled her in with all that had happened and what I'd arranged so far. Then she told me about her appointment with him the day before. So we filled up the forty-five minutes and I stood up and said, 'You said forty-five minutes, you'll be late.'

With a rueful sigh she heaved herself out of my people-swallowing sofa and gathered up her bag and coat.

'See you Monday, then, Mike. Thanks for the tea.'

'Thanks for bringing the coat,' I responded. The peck she gave me on my cheek was not reciprocated.

37

All day on Monday I was thinking about Musoke. It had been easy to book the interpreter, who said it was an excellent idea to meet him and be sure they had the right language before having a disclosure meeting. He sounded quite young and had quite a strong accent which I couldn't place. He said his name was Simon, I got that, but I couldn't work out what he was saying for his surname. I would find an opportunity to ask him to write it down when we met. His easy manner made me think he would be ideal for Musoke.

I arrived at the foster home a little before 4pm. Mark opened the door. Simon was already there, talking to Jodie. He turned to me.

'Hello, I'm Simon, you must be Mike.'

'It's good to meet you. Have you seen Musoke yet?'

'No, I've only just arrived and I was asking how long he'd been here and how much English he understood.'

'Well, let's go through together and I'll introduce you.'

Musoke was in the conservatory, drawing. This seemed to be his favourite occupation when the adults were not with him.

'Hello, Musoke, this is Simon who will be your interpreter.'

Musoke said, 'Hello, Mike.' Then he looked puzzled. Simon took over, speaking to him in a fluid soft language. Musoke's face was quite something to see – his mouth dropped open and his eyes widened with excitement. He turned his full attention to Simon, speaking in his own language.

Simon held his hand up and turned to me. 'He says, "Mike is my friend, he has helped me a lot. He saw me in his office and at the hospital and now he has brought you here so that I can speak freely."'

'I am very pleased to have helped you, Musoke.' I paused and the translation happened. 'I have been asked to find out why you are here and what has happened to you. I know some of it from the pictures you have drawn.'

Simon finished translating, and then Musoke spoke again.

'Will they send me back?'

'I don't think so. But they will need to know why you are here. I have arranged a meeting when Shirley will be there, and maybe Anita, Simon and myself. I do not know who else has to come yet.'

Musoke obviously understood what I was saying; he nodded as the translation was given to him. I carried on, 'You do not need to tell me anything about what happened to you today. Tell me on the day of the meeting. You do not need to be afraid. The meeting is only part of what we are finding out about you.'

Musoke listened to Simon, then asked, 'When is this meeting? And where will it be? I am frightened already.'

'It will be on Wednesday morning in a room at the place I work. I will not let anything bad happen to you in the meeting, but you will have to tell your story.'

'It makes me afraid to tell about my brother.'

'I am sorry, Musoke, you will have to tell us.'

He nodded, and looked at the floor.

'What else will happen to me?'

'You will do some more assessments with me, and Simon will be there to help you understand. I will find out how badly you were upset by what happened to you. Then there will be some more puzzles to do, like the ones you have done already.'

'That does not frighten me,' he said, once he had heard the translation.

'For the rest of our time today, we are going to play games and practise speaking to each other through Simon. Is that good with you?'

Musoke nodded and went to the cupboard in the conservatory. It was chock-full of games. I was reminded of when Jamie was alive. He loved games like Connect 4 and even played Monopoly. Both were there in the cupboard, but I asked Musoke which ones he knew how to play. He selected a battered box with the title down the back 'Quadwrangle'. I was pleased I had no idea how to play; it gave Musoke an opportunity to teach me through interpreted rules and descriptions.

Musoke won the first game, while I floundered around trying not to keep asking him the rules, but we had time for the second game, which I won. I wasn't sure if he had let me win, but he had a definite twinkle in his eye as I got my third counter home.

It was time for his tea, so Simon and I left together, talking about how well Musoke had fallen into speaking at an easy pace to translate. Jodie ran after me as I went through her garden gate. I had almost left my coat there again.

But I did have the presence of mind to ask Simon to give me his surname and contact number. He laughed as he pulled out a business card.

'Everyone asks me to write it down,' he said. 'That's the problem with my dad being Ugandan!'

I had forgotten to call a taxi, so decided to take the bus to Beckenham Junction and go on the train to Sydenham Hill. It would be a longer walk the other end, but I was in no rush. It was when I was jammed into the crowded bus that I realised Simon hadn't told Musoke that his father came from Uganda. I wondered if translators found it easier to do their jobs if they faded into the background and didn't form a connection with the clients.

I began to look forward to Wednesday and even the following days of hard work as I put together a coherent report.

38

It was Wednesday. I arrived early at work, before nine, although the meeting wasn't until 10.30. I wanted everything ready.

I was really pleased that Dr Harding was not going to be there. He had taken some persuasion. I told him that Musoke was frightened about the meeting and that he had told us he was only fourteen years old. I suggested that we treat him very carefully as I was not sure where a more interrogative style of interview left us legally. He had agreed that children seeking asylum was a completely different matter and that my report was now the most relevant, especially if I could determine whether or not Musoke was telling the truth about his age.

So the only people from the immigration service were Simon the interpreter and an older, gentle lady, Mrs Shepherd, who described herself as 'the observer'. She had phoned to request a chair in the corner of the room, out of Musoke's sight. I had been given strict instructions to be careful not to lead or prompt Musoke, nor reinforce or comment on anything he said. The session was to be recorded.

I asked Shirley to be there, and Anita. I decided not to ask the carers to come because Shirley would be there *in loco parentis.*

Musoke and Shirley arrived first. I took them through to the family room. I was pleased to see the secretaries had sorted it out a bit, so the correct number of chairs was already neatly arranged and there was a table for the recorder and my notes, with a box of tissues on it. The room looked very clean and the hedgehog playhouse had disappeared. Musoke and I were to sit opposite each other with Simon on the furthest side of the table. Anita and Shirley would sit on the same height chairs, but behind Musoke, so that he didn't feel overpowered with people.

The secretaries let me know that the others had arrived and they were waiting in the small reception area. I took Musoke with me to fetch them and introduced him to Mrs Shepherd. He shook hands in a very formal way, saying, 'Hello, Mrs Shepherd. Hello, Anita. Hello, Simon.' He then dropped the formality and started to talk in his own language with Simon, who speedily summarised what he was saying.

'Musoke will be glad when this is over and he is afraid he may be sent on another big ship. He has no money to get home and is very scared of what will happen.'

'Please tell him that we can talk about that later, not here in the corridor,' I said.

'He says he is sorry and he will talk when you ask.'

Simon seemed pleased with the arrangement in the family room. He took a series of dictionaries out of his bag. I was surprised he thought he needed them. We all settled quickly into our positions. I asked Musoke if he was comfortable and ready. He waited for the translation and then replied that yes, he was ready. I pressed the 'record' button.

I began, 'Musoke, please will you tell us about the events that led up to your decision to come to England?'

'I will start with the day the troubles came to our village.' Musoke took a deep breath while Simon translated. Then he continued, 'It was an ordinary day and we had no need to think we would be under attack, so we were all doing our usual things. I was practising shooting arrows. I was angry because my mother did not let me go on the hunt because I had a thorn in my toe.'

He realised the interpreter was not keeping up and slowed down.

'It was peaceful. I could hear the noises of the village and they sounded ordinary. Then, as if from nowhere, there was a huge war cry and the women began to scream. I ran back to my hut. My mother was being dragged out of the hut by one of the rebels who had come to attack her. I shot my arrow at him. It did not kill him but he let go of my mother. She snatched my baby sister and shouted at me, "Run with Mwanje, run."

'My brother was behind me, so I grabbed his hand and we fled into the forest. There were shouts behind us and crashing branches, but I do not think they were interested in the children. Mwanje was only small, five years. I scooped him up under my arm when he could run no further and we hid in a hollow with me keeping him quiet. We stayed there until dark.

'Once it was dark, my brother started to cry for our mother. I did not know where she was. We had passed several women with babies when we were running, but I did not see her. I told him to be brave and that I knew the way to our uncle's house. It was a long way and I had only been there during the day before. We walked.'

Musoke stopped and had a drink of water. He then resumed his tale, telling us how he had carried his brother. His own feet were sore and blistered and very painful, especially the one which had the thorn in it. Eventually they arrived before daybreak at his uncle's village.

'I put my brother down. He had been sleeping and he stumbled, but I helped him up. My back was aching and I was very thirsty. We went and woke my uncle up. He looked after us. All the men in the village got ready in case the rebels came. But they did not. Every day I hoped my mother would come, but she did not.'

He continued in a stumbling voice. He told us how news filtered to the village that the rebels had waited for the men to return and had ambushed them. It was feared that Musoke's father had been killed. Then the rebels left. The next day some of the women came back to the village to bury the dead.

'We heard it was a trick. Some women were taken, we do not know who. Others were killed. Maybe my mother.' Musoke bowed his head. He was mumbling, so Simon had to ask him to repeat what he said. 'I do not know if my mother and sister are dead or alive. I have never seen them again.'

Musoke went quiet. I asked if he wanted to have a break. He understood me without the translation and nodded.

'Only to move a bit. My leg is hurting.' He took his crutches and moved around the room a few times. He stood in the corner. Anita picked up his glass of water and went over to him. She spoke softly to him and he followed her back to the table. Someone had put a cushion on his chair. He sat down and started to talk.

'My brother was crying night and day for my mother and for our village. So after many days we took food and water and made our way back. I was still scared there may be rebels about, so we hid at every noise. But eventually we arrived.'

Musoke took several sips of water. He was perspiring. We sat there waiting to know what happened next.

'Many of the huts had been burned down. The ashes were there. People were living in the other huts, some men but mostly women. We knew them from nearby villages. I ran from hut to hut searching for my mother and for my father. But they were not there. No one from our village was there except for our chief. Other people had to look after us.

'They treated us well at first. We had a hut to ourselves. It was a traditional hut with mud walls and the usual high twigged roof. It was very cosy but dark because they had not cut out window gaps. My little brother was scared in the village and scared of the village people. I thought that he remembered the night of terror so I kept telling him, "We are safe now, the chief will protect us," but Mwanje, he did not believe me.'

Musoke paused. His breaths were coming fast and he was gripping the edge of the table. The tone of his voice changed as he described how he felt back in the village.

'I was so sure of myself, so proud I had rescued him and brought him to safety. Why did I not listen, why did I not follow his instinct?'

Simon had paused before saying 'instinct' and now he held up his hand as he fished around in his mind for a more precise translation. As his hand hovered over the dictionaries, he tried out other words, 'foretelling, fear of the coming'.

I nodded to show I understood and he let Musoke continue. Musoke's eyes were staring now as he looked far ahead, as if trying to recall every detail.

'The first two nights, yes, they were good times and we were fed well and treated like sons of the chief. During the day we walked around the remains of our village. There were some distant relatives there and some friends, but they were all people from the villages around. They spent time with us and were interested in us. They spoilt Mwanje, offering him gifts and presents. Sometimes we were with the chief, who wailed to the gods at each charred remains of a hut and laid himself prostrate on the ground.' Musoke's thin hands showed us the ground. He paused, remembering.

'Always there was a guard with us, to protect us, they said, but now I know it was to stop us leaving. But we had no intention of going – I had the safety of my little brother in mind and I thought we were safer than we had been since the night of terror had come.'

Musoke paused again. I noticed he was shaking. I nearly crossed professional boundaries as I thought about putting my arm round him, but there was no need. Shirley moved quietly across from her chair behind him and cupped both his long bony hands in her broad stubby ones. He seemed to draw courage from this and, looking up at her, he haltingly continued.

'The third night I woke to a scuffling sound – the guards were in the hut and they were taking my brother. He was trying to shout out but they covered his mouth. I threw myself across the room but was held back by Bwanbale, the strongest of the guards. Until now he had been my friend, joking with me in the mornings and letting Mwanje ride high on his shoulders. Now he was different – huge, frightening, menacing. One of the others put something over my brother's mouth and I saw Mwanje go limp like the captured deer they brought back to slaughter, and I feared then what would happen to my brother.'

Musoke's eyes were huge with the horror of the memories.

'I was pushed back on my sleeping mat and Mwanje was taken from me. Now they were blocking the door hole of the hut with large boulders – Bwanbale threw me across the hut and while I picked myself up, he scrambled out over the barricade they were making. They blocked the door completely, even while I tried to pull myself out. They kept pulling my hands off the top boulders and pushing me back. Then I had no light at all apart from small chinks between the rocks which I could only see when the villagers passed with their flare torches. Then I heard the chanting begin and I recognised that this was to be a voodoo ritual with my little brother the sacrifice.'

Simon's voice was shaking with emotion as he tried to translate. I switched off the tape recorder and told everyone we would have fifteen minutes rest. Maybe the gap in the tape would look suspicious to immigration, but I was the psychologist here and I could see that everyone, including me, needed a break. I could hardly cope with this, and I was only listening. The emotional load for Musoke was all too easy to see as he heaved and shook, desperately trying to hold back his tears.

With Shirley comforting him, I excused myself and, only stopping to ask the secretaries to take in drinks and more tissues, I made for the gents. I sat in a cubicle and howled. I knew from Musoke's pictures what was coming next but to hear it from his own lips felt like too big a burden to bear. I found myself praying like a small kid, 'Please God, make it OK.'

But it was not OK already and I knew that, so with a calmer prayer, asking for the strength to cope, I gathered myself together to sort out the room of traumatised people.

Shirley had stood in for me well. There was an almost cheery atmosphere as she poured tea – warm water with sugar for Musoke – and made everyone pass round the biscuits. The atmosphere was quite different from a few minutes earlier, a little time capsule of cosiness among the terrors of war and fear. But even the more positive Shirley needed a break. After a quick questioning glance at me, she hurried out of the room. Anita stood forward and took over as hostess. The previously silent Mrs Shepherd had left her observer's chair and started gathering up cups and taking them to the kitchen. When she came back she smiled at Musoke, briefly touching his shoulder as she passed him to return to her seat in the corner.

With drinks over, cups away and everyone back in position, almost as before, we were ready to start again. But

Shirley, steady now, but with red-rimmed eyes, moved her chair up closer to Musoke. Blow the immigration protocol for disclosures; he needed support while we went through this ordeal.

The interpreter had resumed his 'nothing-fazes-me' look and Johnny picked up his story.

'I was too shocked and scared at first to do anything, but I gathered my spirit after a while. I realised I had to get out of that hut. I wasn't sure how much they could see when they turned their flares to the gaps between the rocks, so I gathered up bedding to make it look like I was under my cover. I then went over to Mwanje's side and, using the small table, I managed to reach the roof. I needed to pull the twigs out one by one to make a hole to get out.'

With his long fingers he showed us one by one as he said it, the interpretation lagging behind.

'By now I could hear a lot of noise further up the hill with dancing, drums beating, shouting and clapping, so I took some risks, pulling quickly at the twigs. My arms were aching from reaching up and my hands were bleeding from the thorns. As the hole became larger I could see the stars and the full moon. It was lighting up the inside of the hut. I needed to get out quickly before they next peered in and noticed. I pulled myself up onto the wall of the hut and crouched, waiting for the moment to jump down.'

Musoke had been talking fast and paused for breath and to let the interpreter catch up. When the interpreter had finished talking he continued, 'I tried to cover the hole a little, but not well. I was trembling – fearful of being spotted. I heard a cheer going up from the group on the hill and I was down on the ground darting between huts then through the bush, up the slope towards the noise. Suddenly all was quiet, expectant, nothing happened for at least two minutes as I stood completely still, not daring to move. There was a collective intake of breath from the crowd and I heard the dreadful thwack of an axe crunching, and then hitting stone. There was a pause and someone cheered – these neighbours, these kind people started cheering too, and stamping and shouting. I knew what I would see when I looked again. I forced myself to look, hoping I was wrong.'

Musoke took a deep breath and gripped the table before whispering, 'But I was not wrong. It was my little brother, dead on the altar.'

No one spoke for a moment. Then Musoke screamed out, 'I was too late to save him.'

Racked with sobs, he laid his head on the table. I leaned forward and touched him.

'What happened next, Musoke?'

He mumbled something. There was a pause before the interpretation followed in a barely audible voice, 'I ran.'

As one, we silently wept.

39

I thought we had plenty to be going on with, and all of us seemed exhausted. I finished the meeting and took Musoke and Simon back into my room, where we spent time catching up on all the ordinary things I could usually have found out from a client on their first attendance.

'Well, Musoke, now we can talk about you and the things that are important to you.'

While Simon translated, I realised I knew the answer.

'Most important are my people. My family and my friends. But I do not know who is still alive.'

His head drooped down and one bony hand stretched out for a tissue. I waited.

'When you were living at home, what activities did you like doing most?'

He lifted his head a little as he replied. 'I liked things I cannot do. I liked the hunt and using my weapons. I enjoyed walking in the forest and seeing the creatures scurry away. I knew about the animals.'

'Do you still like animals?'

'Oh yes, when I was in the first place with other boys, I went often to see the animals in the pet shops.'

Simon had shrugged as he translated the sentence about the 'other place' and had a little conversation with Musoke before he said 'pet shop'. He now explained, 'I think he meant when he stayed in a hostel. And he didn't know what to call a pet shop so he called it an animal sanctuary with cages.'

'My friend from the ship showed me. It was a ride on a bus.'

I asked Simon if Musoke could explain where that might be. All Simon managed to determine was that the bus was a number 25. It wasn't important.

Musoke was looking very tired and kept lifting his plaster-covered leg as if it was uncomfortable. I thought we had kept Shirley waiting long enough and it might be better if he went back to his foster home now. First I wanted to help him remember that he was in a safe place.

'What do you like doing in Jodie and Mark's house, Musoke?'

'They have a cat, I do not remember its name, I call it "Gentle" in my own language. I like sitting with the cat and stroking it and feeling calm. But I like it too when Mark plays tabletop football with me. I like shooting the ball all the way down. Drawing has helped me a lot since I have been here in this country, and I want to carry on doing that. I did not draw at my home. The bright pens are very good.'

'What do you like to eat here, Musoke?'

'I like especially when Jodie makes a burger and we have chips. It is very good to eat.' It was no surprise that 'burger' and 'chips' were used in English.

One more question, for the court: 'Musoke, do you want to stay here or go back to your country, to Uganda?'

'I do not think I am safe in Uganda. I like the football here and I know I am safe. My spirit is frightened whenever I think of Uganda. But one day I would like to find my family or know what has happened to them. Maybe I will no longer be frightened one day and I will be strong enough to go.'

'Thank you for answering that, Musoke. That is very helpful. I think it is time that you went back to Jodie and Mark, now. Shirley will take you.'

'Thank you very much, Mike. When will we be talking again?'

'I'm not sure, but I will arrange it when Simon can be there and we can talk properly like this.'

'One day I will have good English and we will not need Simon.'

'Yes, Musoke, I expect you will – you are learning fast!'

I took him out to Shirley, who was sighing slightly and looking at her watch. I suspected she had more clients this afternoon and was running behind. I was right.

'I wonder if you could ask your secretaries to call us a cab, Mike? I am going to be very late for a case conference this afternoon.'

She had been overheard by Patricia. 'Where would you like to go, Ms Hills? Would you like it straightaway?'

I left them sorting it out together and went back to arrange dates with Simon.

That afternoon I started on the report. The words flowed easily as I described the two traumas that had happened to Musoke. I was able to relate these to the DSM IV criteria which were used to define mental health problems, in this case, post-traumatic stress. I would do a stress inventory with him, probably, but the way he had described his emotions gave me a very clear-cut picture. And how long was it since he had been discovered on the *SS Margarita* before he had been referred to me? I hunted for the original referral letter in the file. Ten months, and that was back in July. So he had been only thirteen or even younger when his brother was killed. I could certainly define his condition as chronic post-traumatic stress disorder because, even now, talking about it revived the fear reactions.

More problematic than the definition of stress was his wish to stay, yet his longing to go back. I could understand that completely from the point of view of a child whose mother may still be alive somewhere, but would it muddy the waters as to whether he was seeking asylum or not? I wished I knew someone who might be able to give me the information who was not involved in the decision-making.

I finished the first draft of all the information I had already gathered, and compiled a list of all the rest to be collected. The largest part was his journey here. This was still a mystery and would be difficult to sort out unless he knew which countries he went through. His journey must have taken many months to complete.

I realised that the child who could not save his brother was probably not even thirteen when he saw him being murdered. Would I be able to stop Musoke feeling guilty and help him with his grief?

It was Thursday afternoon when Simon and I turned up together at Musoke's foster home. We had agreed with the immigration service that the interviews about his journey could take place in his home as they were less relevant to his request for asylum.

Musoke opened the door. His plaster cast was off and although he was using a stick to walk, I could see from the way he was walking that his leg had healed well. In very good English, he slowly said, 'Hello, Mike and hello, Simon, how are you?' We both replied that we were very well.

The conservatory looked less cluttered than usual. Jodie had cleared the table of all the drawing materials. The only thing on it was a box of tissues. She was obviously expecting Musoke to be upset. I left the ones in my briefcase where they were.

I made everything ready for recording. Musoke sat and watched me, rubbing his hands together and fidgeting on his chair. When I turned my attention to him, he crossed his arms in front of him.

'Musoke, today all I am going to ask you about is your journey to come to Britain. It doesn't matter if you did anything wrong on the way, to survive, or that you were a stowaway. All I need to know is how you got here.' Simon's fluid translation followed close on my words. Musoke nodded, but did not unfold his arms.

'You said yesterday that you ran. We stopped the recording then. Can you tell me what happened next?'

'I ran all through the night. I did not know where I was going. I came to a big track and I knew from where the stars were which way to turn to keep away from my village. It was very lonely. There was nothing on the road. I was getting thirsty.' He paused in his tale and Simon's translation caught up.

'I do not remember how long I had been running, but it was getting light. I heard something on the road. It was an elephant, on his own, like me. I thought he must be a rogue male and maybe dangerous. I stopped still so that he did not hear me. I was feeling faint. When the elephant was gone, I crawled into some thick bushes to find a place to rest. I wanted to sleep, I was so weary I did not care if I did not wake up.'

'So far this makes sense,' I thought. 'But that's a long way from any port. And did he really stop by the side of the road after seeing the lone male elephant?' But that wasn't for me to decide, all I had to do was collect the information for my report.

'I had no energy left. I woke and again it was animals. I heard them moving around me, but I kept very still in the bushes. I do not know what they were, but I did not want them to see me. I wished I had my bow and arrow or a spear to shoot an animal for food.

'It was dawn when I came out of the bushes and began to walk along the road. My feet were blistered and torn. It was very painful. I heard a truck come along. I thought it was the rebels, so I tried to hide but there was nowhere to go. I could not run.'

Musoke fell silent. We waited.

I imagined the child with feet pouring blood, hungry and thirsty, with no idea where he was going. I tried to think how he must have felt. To be so alone in such a place would be terrifying.

'Who was in the truck, Musoke?' I prompted.

'The men had guns. There were elephant tusks in the back of the truck and the smell of blood. So I think they were after the ivory. It is important in some countries, isn't it?'

'Yes, Musoke, some people take the ivory and sell it for a lot of money. That's why elephants are killed for them.' I wanted to say what a brutal trade this was, how cruel it was that baby elephants were left as orphans. Instead I let it go so that Musoke could continue relating his experiences.

'The men were not so bad. They carried me into the front of the truck and gave me water. They had some maize bread which they shared. It made me feel sick at first, but as we travelled along I was able to eat more. They asked me where I wanted to go and I told them I was running from the witch doctor. I told them what had happened to my brother.'

'So these people helped you?'

'Yes, they were my friends. They wanted to make money from the elephants to feed their families. They took me back to their homes. I do not know where that place was. I was looked after there for many days. I was frightened at first in case it was a trick and they would kill me.'

'Where did you go to next, Musoke?'

'One of the men was sick and had to go to the mission hospital. They thought I should go too because one of my feet was not healing. It was the one that had the thorn in it on the night of terror.'

He was remembering the night of terror again. His body started to shake.

'You are safe now, Musoke. You are safe here. Did you go to the hospital?'

Musoke nodded. He took a tissue and blew his nose. He got up to put the dirty tissue in the wastepaper basket. His scar was showing down his arm, a white ugly streak denting his smooth black skin. He came and sat down again.

'I went to the hospital and they looked after my foot. My friends went back to their homes but I stayed there until the foot was better. At night I slept in one of the houses, not in the hospital. The doctor said he would take me to the big city and I would find some help there.

'I did not feel brave on the day we went to the city. I was worried about the doctor because he had asked me many questions. During the ride in his jeep this did not stop. He told me on the way that we were going to an orphanage where they would look after me and I would be happy. I did not want to go there. I thought the rebels would find me, or the people who had killed my brother.

'On our way, we were ambushed. I was asleep in the back of the jeep, which was covered, but I heard the noise and the shouting and a shot. I do not know if they killed the doctor. One of the men jumped into the jeep and tried to make it go. I could hear him revving it up and then he crashed through the gears. The men were laughing. They did not know I was there.'

Musoke paused. I wondered if we should have a break, but then he continued, 'The man made the jeep jerk. I was thrown about as he stopped and started and then he was driving properly but very fast. He left his friends behind. He was shouting and cheering. He still did not know I was there.'

I forgot I was meant to be taking his statement and went into therapist mode.

'That was terrible for you, Musoke. What were you thinking?'

'I thought I would be dead because he could not drive the jeep well. We bumped off the road many times, and now we were going up a hill and through a tear in the tarpaulin I could see there was a place to fall on one side of the road. This was most frightening. He nearly drove over the edge, but he stopped in time with the gears and brakes screeching. He jumped out.'

'When I looked out I realised the back of the jeep was hanging over the edge of the cliff. I shouted, "Help!" The man was watching and he saw me. 'Musoke carried on talking. I could see it was frightening because Simon forgot to translate, his jaw had fallen open and he was just watching Musoke.

'Simon, what did he say?'

'Oh, sorry.' A hurried translation followed. 'He did not leave me, he shouted to me to climb in the front of the jeep.'

Now I was sitting on the edge of my chair, waiting for the rest of the story. Musoke looked at us. Maybe he realised we were caught up in his tale. 'The jeep was rocking as I climbed forward. The man was trying to encourage me, but I was very scared. Each time it rocked I thought it would go falling down the hill and I would be killed. Many days I had not wanted to live, but now I did.

'The man saw I was frightened. He came to the front of the jeep and reached through to me. I took his hand and he pulled me. I fell through the open door and the jeep wobbled again then went down over the cliff.'

'Did the man hurt you?'

'No. I did not understand his dialect well, but he looked me all over to check I was not hurt. He put his arm round my shoulders and said, "Come with me." He was warm and friendly to me, but I did not want to go. When I kept pulling away he asked me if I wanted to go back to his friends. I shook my head and walked away. He did not come after me.'

'Why did you decide to walk away?'

'I didn't trust anyone. I wanted in my spirit to be free. I wanted to find a place where I chose to be safe. I did not feel safe with people who killed elephants or with the man who took the doctor's jeep.'

'I can understand that.'

'I walked away but I wanted to find the jeep. I knew there was food and water in it. When the man was a long way away, I turned back and started to climb down the cliff. I had to hurry because I thought he would bring his friends to get the jeep, if it still would go.'

He paused, as if remembering.

'I got to the jeep, it was on its side. I made sure it would not fall if I crawled in and got the food. It was in boxes, so I took some clothes of the doctor's out of his bag and filled it with the cheese and some bread and fruit and took some water in two bottles. I was sorry to steal from the doctor but even if he was still alive, I did not think he would get it back if the men came for the jeep.'

'Anyone would have done that, Musoke. I don't think you need worry about stealing.' As soon as I said it I realised I shouldn't condone a criminal act, even as far away as Uganda and when he was in survival mode. I added, 'Anyway, the doctor had been kind to you. He would have wanted you to have those things to keep alive. Did you take them all, or did you leave some?'

'I left him some clothes and food. I took bandages and medicine he had used on my feet. I went quickly and I did not go the way the man saw me leave. I did not want them to find me. I dropped down the valley and found a stream. I followed the stream which was going nearly in the same direction as the truck had been travelling. There were trees growing by the water and it made me feel safer.'

Musoke then went on to tell us about how he stopped staying by the stream when it turned into waterfalls and instead started to climb back to the road. He followed the road through the mountains. He rationed the food and the water, but had to find the stream again after two days to refill the water bottles.

'When I had filled the bottles, I climbed back up to the road. I saw a square building in the distance. I had been on my own for some time so I thought it was not real. But then I made myself walk towards it. There were chickens by the building and smoke from the roof. I thought it must be a house, but it was not like one I had seen before. A lady came out and I did not understand what she said.'

I had become completely lost as to where he might be. I don't think he knew either.

'She gave me food and found a bed for me. It was a very different kind of bed, strange to me. It was like the beds you have in this country. She fed me and looked after me for many days. I woke screaming in the night and she came to me to talk softly until my spirit went quiet and I was ready to sleep. I did not understand her words but it was gentle to me.'

I was not surprised to hear that this safe place had allowed the surge of trauma symptoms. The fear as he was escaping had probably caused a rise in adrenalin which would keep him on alert. Now this was not needed. I was finding it difficult to keep a professional distance from this lad. I wanted to nurture him, rescue him. As if he understood, he moved his chair a fraction closer to me. He was leaning forwards across the table, sharing his story in an almost conspiratorial way.

'She took me to the market about a week after I arrived. This was in a big place with lots of trucks, cars and carts and many, many people and animals. It was noisy. I covered my ears.

'She took me to a man who was selling fruit. He could understand me, but I was finding it difficult to talk to him. My head was full of the frightening things that had happened. I was shaking and my voice was jerky. I could only tell him I needed to go a long way away. The man took me to where lots of people were who wanted to leave my country. He told me to go and find the tall lady with lots of children, so that she would keep me safe.

'I saw the lady quickly. She had a white face and it was very different to me then. She said she would help me get away. She asked me if I wanted to go, even if it was a difficult journey. I was too frightened of my thoughts to reply. I could not say, although I nodded my head. Lots of us travelled in the back of a lorry. It was very smelly and hot and we did not have much water. I did not know where we were going or who we were going to. I thought I would be the white woman's slave.

'When we stopped we were by the sea. I had never seen the sea before and lots of the children were frightened, like me. We were told to hide. People were taken in groups to go into hiding places. I saw some white people in smart clothes going onto a big ship. Then I saw two black people who were wearing clothes the same as the white men. They also went on the ship. I did not like the other ships but this one looked very big.'

Musoke's expressive hands drew the outline of a ship. I imagined how strange this must have been to a child who had never even seen the sea, and had certainly never seen a huge container ship, if that's what it was. He was talking again.

'I left all the other children and went to look at the ship. Some men and boys like me were carrying big sacks onto the ship. A man with a sack stopped near me and put down the sack to light a cigarette. He walked away to talk to a girl who was carrying things to sell. I picked up the sack and walked onto the ship, hiding my face. The smart white man let me past and pointed to where the sack should go. Then I put the sack down and hid out of sight from him. Lots of people were coming and going. He did not know I stayed.'

He took a drink from the glass of water then cleared his throat.

'People were going down some steps. When no one was looking, I went down too. Then I saw a door with more steps. I thought it would lead to the sea, but there were some rooms with pipes. I heard someone clanking down the steps after me, so I squeezed into a very small space. While I was hiding in there the door was shut on me. I thought I would die.'

That's how Musoke got on the *Margarita* then. Immigration could find out where it had been and see where he must have boarded.

'Musoke, could you talk when you got on the big ship?'

'I had not talked any more when we got into the lorry. I opened my mouth but I could not get the words out. It felt like my voice was swallowed.'

'I think we had better stop there, Musoke. We know about how you were found when you had been in the hold for many days and how the sailors looked after you and tried to help you to speak.'

'Yes. They spent time with me and I learned to understand them. They were my friends. They brought me food and drink at first, but then I cut my arm when the ship was rolling. They said I could not hide any more and they took me to the captain. He gave me a bed and the doctor looked after my arm. I did not care what happened to me any more.'

I knew that the immigration service were aware of most of this, although there had been nothing in the letter to explain the cause of the long scar on his arm. I called a halt and then spent time with Musoke playing various games. Simon joined in and then we both spoke to Jodie and Mark before we left together.

We reached the pavement and I asked about Musoke's future.

'Do you think he'll be granted asylum?'

'It is very likely he will. He is an unaccompanied minor and many young people say they want to find their mothers one day. Anyway, Shirley is on the case. She has started badgering the immigration officer to make sure he not only stays but is left in the same foster home.'

I felt relieved. I laughed. I was about to turn away to leave when Simon stopped me.

'Wait,' he said. 'I wanted to tell you something I find interesting.'

'What was that then, Simon?'

'I thought you might like to know that the name "Musoke" means "born while a rainbow is in the sky". I gather he draws a lot of rainbows.'

'He does. It was the first drawing he did in my office. I took it as a symbol of hope.'

'Well maybe it is a "foretelling" and there is more hope for him in the future. I'd better get off home, or I'll be late for tea!'

Simon turned away and walked quickly down the road.

But the word 'home' richocheted around my head. A longing to see Ella and my house churned up in me. It was so powerful that I changed direction, determined to drop in on Ella.

40

I stood on the doorstep of my old house and my hand hovered over the bell. I wasn't sure I would be welcome, arriving unannounced. I tried to think of a reason why I was there, or any excuse for my presence. I had none. Maybe I should have got copies of the pictures in the album for myself, so that I could have returned the album to her, but it hadn't occurred to me before and now I was shuffling like a naughty boy outside our home, Ella's home. I pulled myself up straight and pressed the bell.

A floury Ella appeared.

'Oh, hello, Mike, come in, I'm baking a pie for tea. Are you hungry?'

I wanted to hug her.

'I don't want to impose. It's bad enough barging in like this. I don't want to get in your way.'

'Don't be silly. You look awful. Tired and rather thin. Go and sit in the living room and I'll bring you a coffee when I've washed the flour off my hands.'

'It's on your face, too.'

'Is it? I must look a real fright.' She automatically tried to smooth her hair, getting flour in that too.

'No, no, you don't.' We stood there in the hallway and I felt tongue-tied. We both started to speak.

'Mike...'

'Ella...'

'You first,' I said.

'I'm going to say this really quickly before I lose my nerve,' she said. 'I miss you very much and I was wondering if we should try to get back together.'

I couldn't say anything. My mind was reeling. It must have been harrowing for her as I let those incredible words sink in. She was looking at me directly, almost defiantly, as if she had done wrong in saying it.

I was filled with a surge of happiness that powered through my body and into my arms as I gathered Ella up to me. I hugged her gently and kissed the top of her head, then her beautiful smooth forehead. Gently, I turned her face up to mine and kissed her tentatively on the lips. We rocked together. She reached out and wrapped her arms round my neck. I wanted to carry her up to the bedroom, but I felt something in me say 'too soon'. The feelings were racing through me. We kissed again, still gently, exploring each other's lips. It felt so right, it was where we belonged.

Ella pulled away, keeping hold of my hand. I realised I was covered with flour. I didn't care. She pulled me with her into the kitchen, only letting go of my hand to put the pie into the already warm oven. I put my arm round her waist while she bent over and she stood up, kicked the oven door closed and we started kissing again.

'Where's Shaun?' I whispered into her ear.

'At David's.' She kissed my ear as she said it.

'Why have you cooked a pie?' I nuzzled my nose into her hair, it felt wonderful.

'For us, I prayed you would come.'

She pulled back from me and looked at me directly, maybe wondering if she shouldn't have said she had prayed.

'You don't mind, do you? I've prayed for you every day since we parted.'

'Thank you. I needed your prayers.'

Practical Ella seemed to come from somewhere. 'I'll get the veg on, then we can talk.'

'We don't need vegetables.' I tried to pull her close to me again.

'Yes, we do, I want our meal to be perfect.'

She pulled me into the living room and made me sit on the sofa. There were peanuts on the coffee table and she brought me a glass of red wine. Through the arch, I could see the table was laid with candles and our most expensive glasses.

'I don't think we need the romantic dinner,' I said.

'We can have a fresh start. I want to cook you a special meal.'

'I'll come and help you with the vegetables.'

'No, you won't, you'll distract me. Your turn to cook tomorrow.'

'Tomorrow?'

'Or whenever you move back in, if that's too soon.'

'Tomorrow will be fine, but only if you're really sure you want me back.'

'We'll speak when we've eaten.'

I sat in my own home, marvelling at the wonder of it all. I kept muttering, 'Thank you God, thank you.' I didn't deserve to be back here; I had walked out on Ella when she needed me and yet she was willing to give it another go.

No, not another go, this was not something we would try out, this time it would be for the rest of our lives. I sat there and imagined us as really old people. I used to do this when we were first married, but I would always imagine the grandchildren. There probably wouldn't be any, of course, but I would have my Ella back. My soulmate.

I put down my drink and started to wander round the room, just touching things. There were my books in the bookcase along with Ella's. On the mantelpiece, there was a photo of us laughing together, and another one of us with a very small baby Jamie. We looked so scared, as new parents. I could remember feeling weighed down with the responsibility of having something so fragile and beautiful. I wanted to keep him safe and protected from the world. Why couldn't I?

I didn't want to think about this tonight. I wanted to concentrate on Ella. I went into the kitchen. The vegetables were boiling away and she was wiping down the surfaces. There was the beautiful smell of a steak and kidney pie. Only there was something missing.

'Ella, I wish Jamie were here.'

She turned and came and leaned against me. I put my arms around her.

'I miss him every day,' she said, 'but we had him for six years. Nothing can take that away.'

'No.'

We stood there together. I missed Jamie, it still felt like a gap between us, but somehow we were also more together than we had ever been.

Later, when we had finished eating my favourite pie and mash with three different types of vegetables we carried on talking in the candlelight. I had spotted Ella's rings above the sink and smuggled them into my pocket. She probably knew, but she didn't say anything. The whole meal had been a catching-up time – I had very little to report, having spent most of the five years spiralling down, as Mrs Bayton would say, although I did tell her about the card from the little girl in the park and how I had thought it was from Jamie for a brief confused moment.

Ella had been abroad twice as a volunteer in children's homes. She had carried on teaching at the local primary school after I left, but working with the children made her loss feel even greater. She had undertaken training as a foster carer, then taken on the care of Shaun.

'Basically, I tried to rebuild my life,' she said, softly.

'Now we can do that together.' I walked round to her side of the table, and knelt down. 'My darling Ella, would you do me the honour of being my wife again? I promise to love and cherish you even better than the first time round. I will be there for you, always.'

'And I will be there for you. Get up, you fool, you're making me laugh with your sheepdog eyes, exactly like you did the first time!'

I remembered her laughing and blushing. But that was in a restaurant and we were both all dressed up and knew exactly why we were there. But the glorious thing now was that when I had stood on the doorstep a mere two hours earlier, I had not even known that I would be welcomed.

'What made you change your mind about me?' I asked her, as we snuggled together on the sofa with our coffees.

'Lots of things, really. The way you were so concerned over your client. The memories that rose up when we looked at the photos. How you were with Shaun.'

'That doesn't sound enough to make you think we could make a go of it again.'

'I always loved you, Mike, but I hadn't understood why you became so odd towards me. It was a revelation to me when you told me you thought Henry was a man. It suddenly all made sense as I realised how awful it must have been for you when I kept going off to see her.'

'I am so sorry I was so jealous. I thought you were in love with him.'

'That's just it. You kept going on about me seeing her, only of course you thought I was seeing a man. Which must have made you feel totally inadequate and completely rejected.'

'I wonder if you said "her" and for some reason I didn't hear it.'

'I don't know. I would have thought I did.'

'I said awful things about you preferring Henry to me; that can't have made sense at all.'

'You said I loved Henry more than you. I was furious. I can remember shrieking at you that Henry was only my counsellor.' Ella shuddered.

I didn't want her remembering that awful time. 'I'm so sorry, my darling. Will we be able to move on from that? I really regret my anger. I've wasted so much time.'

'No, Mike, *we've* wasted a lot of time. I should have come round to your workplace and pleaded with you to come back. I should have convinced you that I loved you and even if you were depressed I would help you. But I couldn't bring myself to do it.'

'No, it's my fault, I should never have gone.'

Our claim to guilt became silly as we began to laugh and trump each other with things we should have done. I pulled her towards me.

'Shh, it doesn't matter. We've time to make up.'

I didn't stay the night. We discussed it like sensible adults although we both felt like giddy teenagers. We decided it would be bad for Shaun. Although he kept asking when I was 'coming for a sleepover' it was best to prepare him, especially when we would be back in our bedroom together. Ella called a cab for me, because I was being so frivolous when it was time to go that she thought I would be totally incapable of getting back to the flat

I couldn't wait to move back.

As I travelled through the streets in the cab, I worried about what I would tell Anita. She had told me to try again with Ella, but did she really mean it? I wasn't sure how she would take it. She was such a great colleague, I really didn't want to hurt her.

41

I was in my office before 9am the next morning. I now had an urgent report to complete, Musoke's therapy to arrange, my wife expecting me to move back in with her, and I was receiving therapy for the first time. Yet somehow I felt on top of things.

I sorted out my desk, clearing a space to get on with some notes for the report. Simon had taken the recordings of both sessions back to the immigration service and I already had the transcript for the first disclosure session. I had written an introduction for the report and the hypothesis that Musoke was suffering chronic post-traumatic stress disorder with delayed onset. Now I was drafting the causes of the traumatic stress. I had to start thinking in a very professional, detached manner to stop myself from sitting back and wallowing in the misery of it all.

As I wrote the next section of the report, I realised what a tortuous path I had taken to get to the point where I could write anything at all. I still didn't know how Musoke had become unlocked. Was it partly the art? After all, the Tate Modern was where he made his first noises. Was it Anita's empathy and understanding? Maybe. I thought about their heads nearly touching as they painted, trying out various colours. Or perhaps it was Shirley's constancy? Because she had stayed on the case whatever she thought about him. She hadn't given up and she did find him a good foster placement. I didn't know, but what I did know was that Musoke had helped me enormously.

I was considering how he had affected me and turned me round from my grief when Rachel knocked and said Anita had asked to see me urgently.

'Tell her to come in,' I said, somewhat surprised that she hadn't knocked herself.

'No, she's downstairs, in the art room.'

I stood up and stretched my arms. I hadn't realised how long I had been scribbling away, and I was feeling stiff. It was nearly time for my meeting with Georgina, anyway.

I went down the stairs two at a time. Then slowed my pace as it occurred to me that this was the ideal opportunity to speak to her about myself and Ella. Whatever was I going to say?

I walked into the art room. Anita was sat huddled at her desk, her head in her arms. She looked very small in this large room. I went over to her, she didn't move.

'Anita?'

She turned round. Her face was swollen and puffy; there was blood in the corner of her mouth.

'Anita, what on earth's happened?'

I wanted to hold her and comfort her. Yet I didn't, couldn't.

'Come over here where we can both sit down and tell me who did this to you.'

I gently touched her shoulder and she winced. She walked over to the table and slowly lowered herself onto the chair. I sat opposite and took her hands.

'Who did this, Anita?'

'Your client.'

Flashes of Shirley's conversation at Musoke's first appointment with me burst into my brain. She had accused Musoke of molesting her on the Tube. Was she right? I shook my head.

'It can't have been Musoke?'

Her eyes were glazed as she looked at me. 'No. Not him. Gerald.'

Gerald, the nearly stalker of Georgina, the client who was not appropriate for me, the chap I had thought was mad and wanted to refer to psychiatry. 'Why?'

'He said you took Georgina from him so he was going to take me from you.'

'But why did he think we were together? No, that's not important. Where did this happen?'

'Here.'

I was looking around us when I asked, 'Where is he now?'

'He left through the fire exit. I closed it after him.'

'Have you called the police?'

'Yes, but I couldn't tell them, I didn't tell them, I didn't know what to say.' She was struggling to push the words out as her body heaved. 'They want me to go in to the station to make a complaint. I can't go on my own.' Anita was no longer able to stop her sobbing.

'Don't worry. Of course you can't. You shouldn't have to. I'll take you. I'll have to cancel my appointment with – oh no, Georgina. Anita, I'll be back really soon.'

I raced up to the secretaries' office.

'Where's Georgina? Check on her. Get her in here with you and tell her to stay. Don't let her go anywhere. And call the police, tell them we have an incident and need them now. And an ambulance. Gerald has beaten up Anita. Blankets?'

Both the secretaries looked at me blankly for a moment then Patricia threw her coat at me, Rachel was on the phone commanding Georgina to come straight here from her room immediately and then Patricia was dialling 999.

I rushed downstairs with Patricia's coat. Anita was sitting staring forward, gently rocking. I wrapped her up in the coat and flicked her kettle on.

'Anita, the police are on their way, and an ambulance, you need checking out. Georgina will be kept here until we know it's safe for her to go.'

Anita clutched my hand. 'I couldn't talk him down. I tried.'

'It's all right Anita, you did well to shut him out. We must look after you now.'

'He did awful things to me.'

I didn't know what to say. I daren't ask what the awful things were. And I felt to blame. I should never have let Georgina take him on without knowing who he was. This was all my fault.

'Anita, I am so sorry. I am so, so sorry. They'll get him, Anita.'

Anita clutched my hand more tightly. 'Don't leave me, Mike.'

Rachel came into the room piled up with blankets and two pillows. I took Patricia's coat away and wrapped Anita up while Rachel made her sweet tea. Anita reached for one of the pillows and pulled it across the table to rest her face on it.

'She needs her feet up, really,' said Rachel.

I looked around the studio. Just right for painting, hopeless for comfort. No easy chairs or sofa.

'I'm all right here,' Anita's voice was muffled by the pillow.

Rachel and I looked at each other and Rachel shrugged and fetched the mug of tea. I noticed her sip a little to test the temperature, before saying, 'Anita, try drinking this. It's tea with some sugar in.'

Anita clasped the mug with both hands and Rachel kept by her, ready to take it.

'I'll leave you with Rachel, Anita, while I go and check on Georgina, I'll be right down.'

Anita looked up at me, gave the smallest of nods and sipped her tea.

Upstairs, before I even reached the room I could hear Georgina's voice, much higher than usual, 'I need to see her, I need to see what he's done to her!' Patricia was mothering her, trying to calm her down.

Georgina turned to me. 'Mike, let me go and see her. Is she all right? Where is Gerald now? What's happening?'

'She's very shaken. She needs space. Speak to her later when she's feeling a bit better. Rachel's with her now. She shut the fire door behind Gerald, but we don't know if he might have come in via the door up here, so that's why you're to stay with us.'

Georgina was stunned into silence. She recovered with a shake of her head.

'So you think he may come back for me?'

'I have no idea, Georgina, but as a precaution we have called the police.'

As if on cue, we heard the sirens coming up the road.

'I'll go and unlock the door,' said Patricia.

'No, you stay with Georgina and I'll go.'

Fear was making the hairs on the back of my head stand up. There was something very strange about the empty department – I realised the waiting clients had gone, probably sent home by Rachel.

Glancing behind me, I undid the bolts on the door and went into professional mode with the police, explaining what had happened and why this man still posed a threat to our trainee and in fact anyone in the department. I took two policewomen down to the art room. I was aware of more police, spreading through the building.

I asked the police to hold back while I talked to Anita. I wanted to prepare her for their presence. I walked in and Rachel jumped. She always looked so competent; it hadn't occurred to me that she might be frightened, left down here with Anita. I gently said to them both, 'The police are here now. The ambulance will be here at any moment. The police need to talk to you. Is that all right, Anita?'

In response, she stretched out a hand to me. I beckoned the policewomen in and went to sit next to her.

'Perhaps you'd leave us for a while, Dr Lewis. The young lady can stay.'

'Yes, sure.'

With mixed feelings of relief and reluctance, I walked away.

Upstairs, Georgina was talking to a policewoman. When she saw me, she called me over.

'Mike, they need to know all about Gerald. Am I at liberty to say?'

I turned to the policewoman. 'Am I right in thinking that all patient rights to confidentiality are not applicable when there is a crime committed?'

'This man is dangerous, we will need to know about him to try to find him and arrest him.'

This didn't quite answer my question, but at least I had asked it and been told by a representative of the law that they needed to know. I went and fetched his file.

Between us, Georgina and I outlined the risks he now seemed to present. The more we talked about him, the more foolish we felt that we had not recognised the risk more fully before. I was feeling very guilty about what had happened to Anita. But why did he think that Anita and I were an item? Is that what she thought?

It was uncanny that while I was musing over this enigma, one of the policewomen who had been talking to Anita came to fetch me.

'The ambulance is here and Ms Goodwin asked me to fetch you to go with her.'

'Me? Wouldn't she prefer one of the ladies?'

'She asked for you, Dr Lewis.'

'Go on,' said Georgina. 'We'll be all right here. The police are going to take me home to pack a bag and then they'll take me to my sister's. I'll be fine.'

'They are taking Rachel and me home, too,' said Patricia, 'just in case he is still hiding in the building somewhere. Anyway, Anita needs you, not us.'

Hounded by all these women, I went downstairs. Anita was lying on a stretcher with a neck brace on. She reached out to me. She was about to be carried out by two paramedics.

'Thank you for being here for me, Mike.'

I smiled and nodded. I would have rather been anywhere else.

'This way, sir.'

I followed the paramedics out into the cold afternoon and into the ambulance. I felt trapped. I wanted to be with my wife. I realised I should have contacted Ella, who thought I was moving in this evening. Or perhaps I would be able to arrive straight from the hospital as soon as I could and tell her all about it.

Would she understand? I hoped so.

There was a natural assumption at the hospital that I was Anita's other half. No one asked if they could undress her in front of me, it just happened. I accompanied her to X-rays and doctors and I was asked many questions I didn't know, like her date of birth and whether she was allergic to anything. I was rapidly learning about her as she answered the same questions again and again. But all the time I wanted to confess I was nothing to do with her, and disappear out of the hospital. How could I? She was my friend and colleague. I couldn't let her down.

I was asked yet another question by a doctor. I couldn't cope any longer. 'I'm sorry, I don't know. I am a work colleague who happened to be around. I really can't answer all your questions.' The doctor looked unconcerned. He glanced at my ring finger.

'I see, sir. Can you tell me her date of birth?'

Of course I could now; she had recited it about eight times since we had been in the building.

'Thank you, sir.' The doctor gave me a sideways look. I felt so angry, but Anita was stretching out her hand again.

'Mike, thank you for being here for me, you are such a love.'

'That's OK. But I really need to get going now. You're in safe hands.'

I took her hand gently out of mine and placed it by her on the bed.

'I'll ring later.'

As I left her in Accident and Emergency, I glanced at my watch. It was nearly 9pm. I searched through my pockets for my phone. I couldn't find it. I found a pay phone and phoned Ella.

'Where are you, Mike?'

'I'm at the hospital. Anita was attacked.'

'I saw it on the local news. Why did you go with her?'

'She called me soon after she was attacked; I was the person who happened to be there.' This wasn't going well. I tried again, 'Look, Ella, I can't move any stuff in tonight, but can I come back and stay, at least?'

'I don't know, I really don't know.'

'I'm coming round to talk to you now.'

I put the phone down, then worried that I had been too dominant. But the stakes were high. More than anything I wanted to be with Ella. I called a cab.

It took nearly as long to go by cab as it did to take buses, but eventually I was outside our home. The lights were off; it looked as if she had gone to bed. I rang the bell.

Ella opened the door on the safety chain. 'I don't know why you've come, Mike. It's far too late to talk.'

'Please can I come in?'

She opened the door for me. I realised she was wearing her pyjamas and a blue spotty dressing gown. Her feet were bare.

'Had you gone to bed?'

'Yes Mike, Shaun wakes me early, remember?'

'I'm sorry.' I tried to take her in my arms. She hardly let me give her a hug, before pulling away. 'I'll need to think about things, Mike. We may have been too hasty.'

'No, we weren't. I love you. I want to be back with you.'

'We'll talk in the morning. Go into the small bedroom. There's a towel and what you need on the bed. Goodnight.'

I took her hand and kissed it gently.

'If you think that there's anything going on with me and Anita, you are wrong,' I said.

'That's not what it said on the news. You should have told me about her.'

'There was nothing to tell, Ella, really.'

'That's not what it looked like. I'll talk to you in the morning.'

I hardly slept. Ella was receding into the distance in my dreams and Anita was looming large. I woke up once with a start and it took me hours to settle down again. Each time

I began to get drowsy, phrases from the day burst into my mind: 'thank you for being here with me', 'her date of birth', 'It was Gerald', 'I'm a work colleague', 'you should have told me'.

I went downstairs soon after 5am and put the kettle on to make a cup of coffee. Everything was still in the same place it used to be. I automatically put out two mugs, but it was too early to take Ella a drink. Probably not appropriate anyway. I felt totally miserable. I was so near, yet I had mucked it up. I sat on one of her tall kitchen stools and prayed for wisdom.

I felt a hand on my shoulder. Ella had crept downstairs. I smiled at her and moved over to the kettle to make her a mug of tea. Together, quietly, with Shaun's bedroom above us, we carried our drinks into the living room.

'I'm sorry,' I said. 'I didn't know what else to do.'

'Talk me through what happened.'

I included everything, the report which was now even further behind, the message from Rachel, the going downstairs ready to tell Anita that Ella and I were back together, the horror of seeing what she looked like. Her fear. What I did. My feelings while I did it, right through to the three women telling me to go with her. Then the embarrassment at the hospital and my statement that I was just a colleague and the doctor who plainly didn't believe me.

'OK,' she said, 'let me tell you what they said on the news. First, they said you and Anita were in a relationship and the attack was on her because you took over Gerald's case. Although they didn't name him.'

'Anita and I went for a meal once; we were never in a relationship. We were celebrating progress with Johnny, you know, my client.' Ella nodded. 'I rang you from the restaurant. Anita did seem keen on me, but I kept thinking of you and she told me to talk to you and tell you how I felt.'

'So you didn't come of your own accord?'

This was not going well.

'I did, I had already been. But I suppose I hadn't really told you quite how strongly I felt.'

Ella took my hands – hers felt slim and smooth.

'What do we do now, Mike? Anita is in hospital because of being beaten up for being associated with you, everyone thinks you have a relationship, you have further endorsed that by being around her while all sorts of things have happened in hospital…'

'I didn't look!'

'That doesn't matter, in the eyes of the world you two are an item.' Her voice was shaking, she was avoiding my eyes. She shook her head.

I tried to convince her. 'It doesn't matter what people think.'

'Look, let's take a step back. You help Anita to recover and when she is strong enough you can tell her, that's if we're both sure, that you want to come back to me.'

Ella had tears running down her face. Her breath was coming in gasps. I put my arm round her.

'I am so sorry I have mucked this up, Ella, I am sorry for both of us.'

42

We ate a solemn breakfast, Ella, Shaun and I. I thought Shaun probably picked up on the atmosphere, because I hadn't known him so quiet. I took the plates and washed them, then dried them and put them away. I really didn't want to leave.

'You'd best go now, Mike. We'll keep in touch; let me know what happens with Anita.'

I turned towards her and looked her straight in the eye. 'You do know I'm in love with you, don't you? I will sort out this mess.'

Ella gave the briefest of nods before she turned and walked down the hall. She opened the door for me.

'Bye, Mike,' called Shaun from the stairs. 'Come for another sleepover.'

'I will, Shaun, I promise,' I said, stepping outside. Ella reached forward and gave me a peck on the cheek and then started to close the door.

'I'll ring you, Ella,' I said.

'OK.' Her voice sounded sad and quiet.

I couldn't think of the right thing to do. Anita was in hospital with no one to see she was all right. It was probably expected, at least by her, that I would pop in to see her. I walked down the road to the bus stop, still unsure what to do. The bus towards Farnborough Hospital came first. As if on automatic I just got on it.

My mind was in tumult. Could I tell Anita that I was back with Ella? For that matter, was I back with Ella? Was it fair on Anita that I would let her down now?

The bus reached the hospital. I sat there as everyone else left their seats and moved forward. The bus emptied and the driver called to me, 'Final stop, mate. Farnborough Hospital.' I disembarked and slowly went towards the hospital. I wasn't sure I wanted to see Anita at all, so I wasted time in the shop choosing a cartoon get-well card and a large slab of chocolate. I thought that looked unromantic enough.

I realised I didn't know what ward she would be on, so I spent some time talking to the receptionist who herself took three phone calls to track down Anita. I was vaguely directed to a ward on the first floor. I found it difficult to walk along the corridors; the memories of Jamie were everywhere. It may have been a different hospital, but the smells and feel and even the layout seemed very familiar.

Eventually I found the right ward and rang the buzzer to be let in. A disembodied voice asked me who I was.

'Mike Lewis, to see Anita Goodwin.'

'Are you her partner?'

'No, a colleague.'

'Friends' visiting isn't until 3pm.' I glanced at my watch, 10.30am. I was going to explain that I was the one who came in with her and that she would want me to be there, when I stopped myself.

Instead, I said, 'Sorry, I didn't realise. Would it be possible to leave a card for her?'

'I'll come and take it from you.'

I quickly opened the card and was writing it when the nurse buzzed open the door from her side.

'To Anita, hoping you make a speedy recovery, Mike and Ella.'

Too late, I realised what I had done. The nurse was waiting, tutting. I hastily put brackets around 'and Ella' before passing her the card and the block of chocolate. The nurse tutted again and the door swung closed as she walked back.

All the way back in the bus to my flat, I was wondering whether Anita would be upset by the card, or relieved, or puzzled. I couldn't change it now. The flat was cold and unwelcoming. I put the fan heater on in the living room. I took cheese and bread to make a sandwich then slumped down in front of the television. It was football. I felt too exhausted to find anything else.

The phone woke me. I stumbled across the room and grabbed it before it went to answer phone. It was Anita.

'Mike, is there any chance you could get some things from my flat for me? The neighbour's got a key. I need clean stuff to go home in.'

'You're going home?'

'Yes, thank goodness. I have a broken collarbone. My arm is in a sling to hold its weight while the bone heals. Apart from that everything's OK.' Her voice dropped. 'Well, physically, at least.'

I didn't dare ask her how she was emotionally.

'So when are they releasing you?'

'Well, now. But my clothes are, well, you know, not suitable for wearing.'

I felt suddenly extremely angry towards Gerald. How could he do something like this?

'Um. I don't have a car or your address to fetch your things.'

She gave me an address less than three miles from my flat. Then followed a list of clothes and where to find them and which neighbour to talk to. I hastily scribbled it down, wondering how I was going to get out of this.

Anita's voice broke into my thoughts. 'Mike, are you still there? You'll have to get a taxi. Then we can get one back to my flat and you can go home from there.'

'OK.' She must have heard the uncertainty in my voice.

'For goodness' sake, Mike, that's the least you can do.' The phone went dead, but I had heard the fear in her voice.

I rang Ella.

'Ella, I'm in a bit of a fix. Anita's just rung and asked me to take a great list of things in. Then she wants me to go back home with her in the taxi. I think she may be frightened.'

There was a pause. I desperately tried to work out what the pause meant.

'Are you doing it?'

'I don't want to. But there wasn't an opportunity to say no. I suppose I could leave a message on the ward to say I won't be coming.'

'Do you know anyone else who would go instead?' Ella was being very practical. I couldn't tell what she thought from her tone of voice.

'No. No one. I just don't have other people's phone numbers.'

359

There was a pause on the line. I waited while my wife made a decision.

'Then we'd better do it together. I'll be over as soon as I can. I may have Shaun.'

By the time she arrived, I was ready with Anita's address, the name of the neighbour and a bag for her belongings. Ella didn't come into the flat. She just rang the doorbell downstairs then turned to go back towards the car as soon as she saw me open it. I followed her. With some relief, I saw she hadn't got Shaun in the car. Life was complicated enough as it was.

'He's at David's,' she replied tersely when I asked. She hardly spoke on the journey and I felt terrible; an encumbrance to her.

Anita's flat was fairly easy to find. We both got out of the car and I went up to the second floor ahead of Ella. I knocked on the adjacent door and a rather splendid elderly lady greeted me like an old friend. She had asked Anita what she needed and had it all ready in a carrier bag. So I didn't need Ella to go rummaging through Anita's bedroom for the items. I was relieved. I certainly didn't want to go in there.

I had the uncomfortable feeling of being watched as I got back into Ella's car. Someone drew away from the pavement in a small black car just behind us. I squirmed round in my seat, trying to see if it was Gerald driving.

'What are you doing?' asked Ella.

'I'm a bit worried that might be Gerald in the car behind us.'

'Haven't the police got him in custody yet?'

'I don't know.'

Ella turned into a road on the left. The car followed and parked to the left. Ella took the car down to the end of the cul-de-sac, turned it round and came past the car. The driver dodged down. I watched over my shoulder as he sat up again. He was wearing sunglasses and a raincoat. It looked as if it could be Gerald.

'Now what?' asked Ella. Her voice had an edge of anxiety. It took me a while to come up with anything approaching a plan of action.

'OK, this is what we will do. If he follows us, we turn into the hospital and park in one of those twenty-minute spaces. Then we walk together straight through A&E and alert the security people. What we do next depends on whether or not the hospital security men apprehend him.'

Ella's face took on an expression of determined courage. Her jaw was set and she was driving carefully and immaculately. I kept turning round to see if the car was still behind us. It was. I was feeling really jittery.

'Calm down, Mike. It will be fine.'

The car carried on tailing us as we came near to the hospital. There was a parking space. I jumped out quickly and ran to the other side. I put my arm around Ella as she got out and we ran towards the hospital. The man raised something. I pushed Ella behind an ambulance, yelling for security and shielding her body.

There was a flurry of activity and the man was held by two burly men in fluorescent jackets. His glasses had fallen off in the scuffle. It wasn't Gerald. The security men had 'disarmed' him, but all they had was a camera. He was talking to the security men, showing them a badge. A photographer, then. I hurried Ella into the building.

Anita didn't seem a bit surprised to see Ella. She looked even worse than the day before as the bruises had started to appear, giving her two panda eyes. I found it difficult to look at her, but I steeled myself to tell her how helpful her neighbour had been.

'Thank goodness you didn't see the state of my flat,' she said to Ella in a quiet voice that didn't seem to belong to her.

'You should see mine – I'm hopeless at housework.'

There was an effort at a smile from Anita. Ella must have realised that this wasn't the same vibrant Anita who had so inspired Musoke.

'You've been through a terrible ordeal,' said Ella. 'It will take a while to feel better. Can I help you get dressed so that at least we can get you back home?'

A slow nod from Anita encouraged Ella to draw the curtains round the bed to help Anita get her clothes round her broken collarbone. As I turned away to go to wait by the desk, I could hear them chatting quietly together. I felt very proud of Ella. This must have been difficult for her, yet she had definitely risen to the occasion.

We had a totally uneventful ride back to Anita's flat. As soon as we arrived, Anita started phoning a few people to see if they could come and stay the night. Ella put the kettle on and made us all some tea. The phone calls weren't going well.

'No one can come and stay,' she sighed. 'It's not that I'm frightened, just a precaution.' Ella and I exchanged glances over the top of her head.

My heart leapt as I heard her say, 'Anita, why don't you come and spend a few nights with Mike and myself? You'll have to cope with our lodger, but we'll make sure he doesn't hug you too tight.'

Anita looked at me. 'Are you two back together then?' Her battered face attempted to smile.

I was unsure what to do with her question. I shrugged a little and looked at Ella's large eyes, watching me. We held the gaze as I answered Anita.

'Apparently we are, yes, we are back together.'

'Well, thank goodness for that,' she said. While Anita went back in her bedroom to find some things to bring, I took Ella's hand.

'I'm going to need pyjamas and clean clothes, that sort of stuff.'

'Stop being such a worrier, Mike. We'll get them on the way, and a few of your other things. There'll be a fair amount of stuff to move, I should think.'

'Most of it's still in packing cases, remember?'

'Yes, I remember what you said.'

She squeezed my hand so tight it hurt.

43

I had thought that moving back with Ella would be difficult. I had expected that we would be very careful with each other, avoiding saying things, careful not to get too close. But it was beautiful. The next morning we woke early. I stole quietly downstairs to make us a drink, then we lay close in bed sipping our warm tea, talking. We talked a little about Gerald, who had been taken into custody the night before. Ella had insisted Anita still stayed the night, rather than return to an empty flat.

We had changed the subject to talking about holidays when we heard Anita go downstairs, closely followed by Shaun. There was noisy chatter and laughter from the kitchen.

'I'd better get up to look after them,' said Ella.

'No, they'll be fine looking after each other for a while. Anita's probably got him drawing. She can't help herself.'

We leaned against each other in the soft, clean linen. There was a comfortable silence. For a while we shared the moment of peace. When Ella started talking, it was about Jamie.

'Supposing he'd been here now.'

'He'd be twelve, tall and lanky with a slight down on his upper lip.'

She considered this, her head on one side, looking at me with screwed up eyes.

'He'd look even more like you. Only without the scruffy, messy beard.'

'It's a very fine beard.'

'It definitely needs a very good trim and sort out. I'll do it after breakfast.' She was pulling at long stray strands of my beard as she spoke. She was in danger of spilling her tea.

'Ouch. Leave me alone, you bully.'

'Sorry.' She was laughing.

I changed the subject.

'Let's get back to what Jamie would have been doing today.'

'You'd have been taking him to football.'

'No, he'd have been just like me, he would have hated football.'

'Or he might have been football mad and you would have become his greatest fan. You'd be like one of those dads you see in the park, yelling for their child to run with the ball.'

'And Jamie would have been really embarrassed by me.'

It was half an hour later when I realised we had talked solidly about Jamie. It felt comfortable and very right.

'It's time we shared all this,' said Ella. 'It's been lonely on my own.'

'I'm here now. Really here. With you, where I belong.'

'You old softie,' she mumbled, as I drew her close to me.